C. E. Ayr

Beginning of After

Copyright © 2023

C. E. Ayr

The right of C. E. Ayr to be identified as author of this work has been asserted by him in accordance with the Copyright, Designs and Patents Act 1988.

All rights reserved

No part of this book may be reproduced, or stored in a retrieval system, or transmitted in any form or by any means, electronic, mechanical, photocopying, recording, or otherwise, without express written permission of the publisher.

The characters and events portrayed in this book are fictitious. Any similarity to real persons, living or dead, is coincidental and not intended by the author.

First Published in 2023

Cover design by C. E. Ayr and Jenne Gray

My thanks to Jenne Gray, my editor, proof reader and, most importantly, friend.

And a very special thank you to Helen Burns.

For Jack

"I'll let you be in my dream if I can be in yours"

Bob Dylan - Talkin' World War III Blues

Beginning of After

Map of Scotland – North of Glasgow

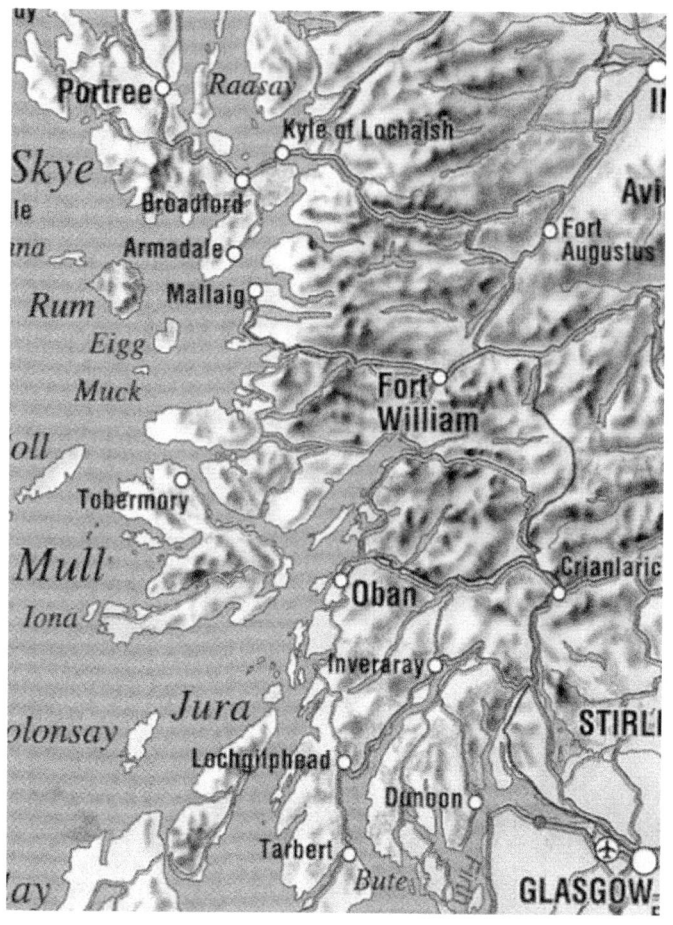

Prologue

We had some good days and some bad days.
Chester could be a lot of fun back then.
He was a good friend and a good partner.
The first job we ever did was nearly my last.
I laugh now, but if it wasn't for him I'd be dead.
As I walk, I remember…

We were Special Forces, then we were the darker, deniable, extension.
We were trained by the best, to do the bidding of our government, but unofficially, always.
So we know about black ops.
And we know about wet work.
Now we are hired killers, just the two of us, no great organisation, and no authority, behind us.
We have a contract to eliminate a gangster who lives in the hills behind the port.
He imports vast quantities of drugs and peddles the poison throughout the region.
He has a network of youths who feed it to school kids, get them hooked.
Our client is a local philanthropist who despises the drug baron.
We check him out, decide to nail him at his home when he returns from his nightly revelries.
The house is empty apart from a couple of hopeless sentries.
We leave them tied up in a garden shed; we don't kill indiscriminately.
We have a drink and a laugh, throw some stuff around to fake a

burglary.

As I exit the library, where I have rummaged about in a desk and some bookshelves, Chester hurls himself at me.

I crash back into the room, the shot ringing in my ears.

Chester is laughing fit to bust.

We're in a heap on the floor and he finds it hilarious.

You nearly got your fat head blown off by a kid, he hoots.

It's the son, Kris, he explains.

He's not due home until the weekend, but has apparently slunk in the side entrance to avoid a confrontation with his father.

Whose aggressive nature he has clearly inherited.

I shout to Kris, tell him we don't want to kill him.

Yes we do, says Chester, still laughing.

I shush him, tell Kris we'll leave quietly, that we won't shoot his father tonight.

What about tomorrow, he yells back.

I say he'll have a chance to make a deal, or to take precautions.

Or we can shoot father and son, and maybe mother, tonight.

Silence.

I tell Kris to go into the next room and hammer on the wall, and we'll walk out the door.

He does.

We do, Chester grumbling and reluctant.

As we drive off he regains his good humour.

We still have to kill this piece of garbage, you know, he mocks me.

Yes, I agree, but not the boy.

I see the headlights sweeping up the mountain towards us.

My lights are off.

Right on time, I say.

As our target hurtles up the narrow road I flick on my beams and twist the wheel.
He is momentarily blinded, instinctively takes evasive action.
We watch his huge SUV tumble down the gorge.
Chester stares at me, a massive grin on his face.
You lied to the boy, he says, delighted.
No, I remind him, I just said we wouldn't shoot his dad tonight.

Part 1 – Heading North

1

It is a dreich day in early October, as he strides along the A82 on Loch Lomond-side, rucksack on his back and dog out in front, wondering if the fat yellow clouds are getting closer or lower.

When he hears the sound of a heavy vehicle approaching from behind, he moves quickly to conceal himself behind some bushes.

He is surprised because, since the Dumbarton turn-off more than two hours ago, all he has seen are a couple of fast cars heading south, but nothing going in his direction.

Given the circumstances, an old bus from West of Scotland Motors is not at all what he expects, so he steps out, hands raised with fingers wide.

It shudders to a halt and the doors hiss.

He looks past a gun barrel at the driver.

'Ex-military?' asks the man in the bus.

Given his appearance, the other is impressed.

He gives no name, just a ten-word summary that stops a long way short of the whole truth.

The driver sticks the pistol into his jacket, gestures for him to get on.

'Steve,' he says, meaning himself.

He pauses when Vidock clambers on too.

'He with you?'

'Always.'

'Cracker, what is he?'

'German Shepherd/Husky cross.'

'Cool. So where you going?'

'North. And you?'

Steve grins and shrugs.

'Same,' he says, crunching the gears and shoving his foot down.

The newcomer grabs a pole and surveys the passengers.

An elderly couple, white-faced.

Two girls, one pretty, blonde, one plump, brunette, probably late teens, sitting close.

A woman, dirty and dishevelled, mid-late thirties.

Two boys, one lanky, shaved head, wide-eyed, maybe 14, the other a few years older, heavy, sullen.

They are not together.

'Where've you come from?' asks Steve.

'Troon, left yesterday, walked up the Stewarton road.'

'Walked?'

'Well, I had no idea what was happening, figured there'd be some sort of clamp-down. I'm not in a hurry, and I'm less of a target on foot.'

'You go through Glasgow?'

'I didn't fancy the Erskine Bridge, figured it'd be locked down tight, so not much choice.'

'What about the bridges in town, you still had to cross the Clyde?'

'We just strolled along the railway lines, over the Hielanman's Umbrella, down the stairs to Hope Street, wandered out Argyle Street and Dumbarton Road.'

'Very creative,' Steve laughs. 'No trouble with the authorities?'

A shrug.

'I'm not sure there are any, and anyway I have skills.'

'I know,' Steve grins again. 'That's why you're on board.'

'So where'd you get this,' the other asks, indicating the bus with a thumb. 'I guess it's not yours.'

'Borrowed it,' Steve says, still laughing. 'They've got loads of them at Buchanan Street! Surprising lack of security there, probably didn't expect anybody to be daft enough to nick a bus. And not only that,' – he pats his pocket – 'I was quite determined!'

'You couldn't have picked a newer one?'

'This one had keys in it, and I wasn't for hanging about.' Steve lifts his shoulders, then shakes his head. 'I don't know any more than you do about what's going on.'

'And after that?'

'Out the Cowcaddens onto Great Western Road. Didn't fancy the city centre, too many headbangers there, liable to be trouble. I turned down Byres Road heading for Partick, did what I had to do there then went up the Crow Road and crashed a barrier at Anniesland Cross. They didn't seem that fussed. I think there was just a guy and a dog there,' he snorts. 'No offence,' he grins at Vidock, who scowls back at him. 'Pretty sure they're more concerned about stopping folk going into the city, rather than out, and heading south, not north. Bloody lemmings, eh?'

'What's the story with this lot?' the stranger gestures at the passengers. 'Bit of a motley crew, aren't they? I mean, I get the woman and the girls, obviously, but the oldies?'

'A debt.'

'And the kids?'

'Another debt, the young one, the other was just there.'

'You've got a lot of debts,' he frowns.

'Not any more,' Steve grimaces, with an abrupt head shake.

The man studies him, and reckons he could be a useful guy in a tight spot, even without the weapon.
He's sitting, so his estimates might be slightly off, but he reckons the driver to be a couple of inches shorter than himself, maybe just under six foot, but a solid lad, so probably two, maybe three stones heavier.
In rugby terms he'd be a prop forward, whereas he himself played in the backs, usually at centre.
He puts him at early thirties, which makes him only a few years younger, but he's pretty sure he won't have the same background.
Not many do.
But he sussed him quickly on the roadside, which suggests he's no fool.

2

'There might be a roadblock at Crianlarich,' says Steve. 'Or maybe Tyndrum, and almost certainly at Ballachulish. Other than that I can't see a problem before Fort William.'
'You think there's anybody left with the authority, or the will, to enforce checkpoints? What was the last you heard?'
'I think everything went off at the same time. One minute we had television, internet, mobile phones, whatever, next thing nothing.'
'Pretty much same with me, except I was still asleep. Just wakened and found no electricity, and the rest, as you say.'
Then Steve curses, and points.
There is a patch of yellow fog drifting across the road ahead.
'Must be blowing in from Loch Long,' he barks. 'Make sure all the windows are tight shut!'
'You do that, I'll drive, trust me now!'
Steve looks at him, astonished, but when he sees the face, like the smart soldier he was, he obeys immediately.
Still steering, he stands, leaning forward to let the other slide behind him.
Then he lifts an old free newspaper and moves quickly down the bus, jamming pages into the windows with the loudest rattles.
From the front of the bus he hears 'Vidock, sleep!'
'Down low and cover your faces,' he snaps at his passengers. 'Now! Move!'
He is flat on the floor, nose to nose with Vidock, who is peering at him from under his tail, by the time they hurtle into the fog...

'Clear,' the driver calls, and Steve is on his feet, opening every window.
The bus grinds to a halt, and the doors shudder open.
'Everybody off,' Steve shouts, throwing open the emergency door and jumping out.
He turns and helps down the older woman and her husband.
The others have all piled out the front.
Not too smart, but at least they moved quickly.
He checks with the stranger who took control of the situation, and who was clearly in the most exposed position, up front and up high, but although he is breathing deeply, he seems calm.
'Have you seen what it does?' Steve asks, a hint of embarrassment in his voice, and when he gets a nod in return, he asks the obvious question.
'Why did you do that?'
'I have techniques to control my breathing.'
'Far Eastern techniques?'
'In the main, yeah, but just training and practice.'
'Thank you, Sensei, I'm in your debt.' Steve puts his palms together below his chin, and bows his head formally.
The other returns the gesture, then grins.
'Sensei, I like it!' and smacks his arm.
'You did well,' he says. 'And you gave me a lift, so we're even!'
'I'll see to the bus,' Steve says. 'You want to check the others?'
He nods, and saunters down to the water's edge to fill his canteen.
He sees Vidock watching him.
'You okay?' he asks.

His tail moves left, then right.

'Drink,' he says, gesturing towards the loch.

Then he goes to the elderly couple, who introduce themselves as Mr and Mrs Fraser.

He takes their water bottles and fills them.

All the youngsters are also topping up their water, but the woman is standing beside the bus, looking lost.

As he approaches her she flinches.

He stops three metres away, hands raised in the standing back position.

She stares at him, her eyes showing uncertainty, perhaps even fear, which is probably not too surprising given his appearance.

He is wearing Scarpa R-Evo hiking boots, Levi's, a black tee-shirt and a brown leather jacket.

He hasn't shaved for several days and his once blonde shoulder-length hair, darkened by the years and now flecked with grey, somewhat prematurely, in his opinion, has a decidedly bedraggled look after two days of intermittent rain.

He realises that she is not a down-and-out, as he first thought; her clothes are good quality, but filthy, as though she has been rolling in mud.

Her face, hands and hair are also caked in dirt.

'Somebody hurt you?' he asks.

She wraps her arms more tightly around herself.

'No one else will,' he says. 'I promise you that. We have enough problems, we need to trust each other, be on the same side, okay?'

By his standards this is almost a speech, so he pauses, reaches into his backpack, and hands her an unopened bottle of water.

'Family gone?' he asks.

Her whole body trembles, and she puts her face in her hands. He waits while she cries.

Then she stumbles to the loch side, kneels and splashes water over her face.

As he wonders if it is just mud on her coat, Steve comes back from the bus and gestures to him.

'She was standing at a bus stop at Knightswood,' he says. 'She just put her hand out for me to stop. So I did. She showed me her pass and took her seat. I didn't say anything, I think she must be in shock.'

The two girls wander over.

'When do you think we'll get a signal for our phones again?' asks the pretty blonde one, holding hers up to show them what she's talking about.

Sensei is about to point out that in all probability the only person she knows who is still alive is standing beside her, but then remembers what they've been through, so he bites back his sarcastic response.

'Hard to say,' he shrugs vaguely. 'Hopefully before too long.'

'I'm Joni', she says. 'This is Allie.'

Suddenly they're holding each other and sobbing bitter tears, as though the situation has just registered with them.

The two men look at each other cluelessly, then Mrs Fraser comes across and, talking quietly, leads the girls away.

They see Jack, the younger boy, turn away, and his shoulders are heaving too.

The other one, who's called Fred according to Steve, just stands and watches, expressionless.

Make allowances, Sensei tells himself, they're still young.

3

'What do you think it is?' Steve shouts at me above the noise. 'And why are we still alive?'

We are back on the road, all windows and the emergency door wide open, the wind howling through.

'All I've heard is that just about everyone with a nuclear bomb was firing it at someone else,' I tell him. 'I don't know what that is' – I point at the yellow cloud scattered across the western sky – 'but I'm guessing that the Geneva Protocol is in tatters right now. As to why we're not dead, I've no idea. How did you know that your 'debts' would be alive?'

He makes a strange sound with his nose.

'They weren't,' he says. 'I went to find a mate I knew I could trust, found his parents were the only folk alive in the street, White Street, well that bit of it anyway. And Jack, the boy there, he's the son of another mate, also dead, in Gardner Street. I told them all to bring water, and any food they could just lift. The girls had already flagged me down at the top of Byres Road, and like you say, they make sense. I told them I was going to pick up friends and they just sat down and haven't spoken to anyone since.'

'Stop on the curve before we can see the roundabout at Crianlarich,' I say, 'and I'll check it out on foot.'

When the bus shudders to a halt shortly afterwards, I move to the door.

Then I turn to Vidock.

'Stay,' I say. 'Guard.'

He stares at me like I'm crazy, looks round at the others, then pretty much shakes his head in disgust.

'Five minutes,' I tell him. 'I'll be right back.'

But he is already sitting down with his back to me.

Steve laughs aloud.

I cross the road, jump a fence, and trot up to higher ground until I can see the roundabout where our A82 is joined by the A85 from Perth, due east, and Stirling, to the south-east.

There are no barriers, no sign of any life.

'Okay,' I say when I'm back on the bus. 'Next stop Tyndrum. If they've got a checkpoint anywhere it'll be where the roads from Oban and Fort William meet on their way south.'

We stop on a curve a half mile before the Tyndrum Inn, which is about the same distance before the junction, and so seems like the most probable spot for a roadblock.

'Come,' I say, and get a quick tail wag of approval.

I soon see that the road is impassable due to a mountain of furniture being piled across it in front of the inn.

Makeshift, but effective against cars at least.

I signal to Steve, then keep out of sight by skirting round the back of the buildings, so that I approach from the opposite, or northern, side.

And I hear voices.

They are loud and drunken.

'Stay,' I say, and step into view.

I see, as expected, two soldiers from The Highlanders, 4th Battalion, The Royal Regiment of Scotland, who are based in Inverness.

They are in combat uniform, and have SA80 rifles in close proximity.

They are sitting on the front steps of the inn, half-empty whisky bottles in their hands.

Their choice of refreshment makes me smile inwardly; one is drinking Glenfiddich, an excellent single malt, and the other Dalmore 12-year old, which costs about £50 a bottle.

They start to their feet, grabbing for their weapons, when they see me.

My hands are up and open, my smile is wide.

'Man, am I glad to see you guys,' I say. 'First sign of civilisation for ages.'

They look at each other, then back at me, in some confusion. Then the questions start to fly.

Who are you? Where are you going? Are you alone?

'I'm just trying to find out what's going on,' I say, all apologetic. 'Maybe you guys can tell me what happened?'

'Well,' says the younger of the two. 'The war started, didn't it, just blew up in a matter of hours. Everyone nuking everyone else's cities…'

'Hang on,' the Dalmore guy says. 'You can't tell him all this stuff!'

'What difference does it make?' argues his mate. 'Who's he going to tell, everyone's dead already.'

'I suppose so,' he shrugs, then takes up the story. 'The next wave was the sonic bombs, the brain-scramblers we call them, they are designed to kill without destroying buildings, although they do a bit of that too!'

'You forgot the comms,' Glenfiddich interrupts. 'Everyone immediately knocked out the other side's communications capabilities, and blew all the satellites to bits, that's why television, radio, mobile phones, internet, are all gone.'

'Aye, that's right, then the scramblers, we reckon they wiped out at least 90% of the population. And as if that wasn't enough, the chemical stuff arrived.'

And he points at the yellow clouds, still crawling across the sky.

'What does that do?' I ask, playing the simple civilian.

'Makes you claw your eyes out of your head,' says Dalmore.

'And vomit your lungs out too,' the other adds.

'So is it safe for me to carry on north?' I ask. 'My old mum's in Fort William, I need to see if she's okay.'

'Aw no, no way,' Dalmore is in charge now. 'We have orders no one, but no one, can pass.'

'So where did you come from?' I ask, already knowing the answer.

'Inverness, of course, we're left here to protect the rear.'

'So where's the main body gone?' I ask, though I can guess this too.

'Not exactly a main body,' he snorts. 'One officer and three guys. Kentigern House, Glasgow, Ministry of Defence, pre-designated emergency command centre.'

'Jeez, I say, is that all of you that survived?'

'There were three others,' Glenfiddich says. 'Bolted last night with most of the explosives, so they're somewhere out there' – he waves an arm – 'roaming wild in the Western Highlands!'

'Explosives?' I say. 'What were they for?'

'We were supposed to be mining the roads behind us, keep movement to a minimum, but we hadn't enough left to do it here, had to build this bloody barricade.'

'So I can't get through, even to visit my mum?' I am whining now. 'Is there nothing I can do to persuade you?'

'Actually,' says Dalmore, pointing his weapon one-handed at my chest, and still holding the bottle, 'You're officially our

18

prisoner now. That's our orders.'
Then he laughs, quite unpleasantly.
'Lucky you're not a woman, we've to capture them and take them to Glasgow, they'll be used for breeding purposes. Aye, so we'll be starting that process as soon as we get our hands on them, eh, mate?'
He and Glenfiddich clink their bottles together.
'Perks of the job,' they laugh.
'What about their men?' I ask. 'Don't you think they might object a bit?'
'They'll either come quietly,' sneers Dalmore, 'or they'll not come at all. We already left a few in the mud on the way down, and their women are in Glasgow by now. The ones that didn't object are still alive, they'll be used for forced labour.'
'Aye,' Glenfiddich says, 'and that's the choice you've got now.'
My hands are high again, wide and open, showing that I'm not a threat.
'Whoa,' I say. 'I'm just passing through, I don't want any hassle, guys.'
'I told you you're a prisoner,' Dalmore says, then asks, 'Where'd you leave your motor?'
'I've not got a car, I'm on foot.'
'On foot?' he snaps, suddenly belligerent. 'What's your story, you've got a military look yourself, apart from the hair, obviously, are you a spy or something?'
He is shouting now, his face red with anger, suspicion and alcohol, a dangerous combination.
His rifle is still pointing at me, but waving around, and about three feet from my chest.

'Okay,' I say. 'Let's relax here, and I'll explain, right? See the houses up the back here?'

I point and whistle sharply.

Both their heads follow my gesture, so I grasp the rifle with my left hand, step in close and, slipping my right leg behind his, I push Dalmore to the ground.

I twist the SA80 from his hands as he falls and point it at Glenfiddich, who is on his back with Vidock on his chest.

'Here!' I snap, and step back to cover both soldiers.

'Nobody needs to get hurt,' I start to say, but Dalmore scrambles to his knees, hurls his bottle at my head, and lunges at me.

I smash the rifle into his face, and he goes down heavily.

Meanwhile Vidock leaps forward again as Glenfiddich reaches for his rifle.

'No!' I scream at both of them, but only the dog responds.

The man on the ground grabs his weapon and, as I again shout 'No', swings it towards me.

I shoot him in the chest.

Dalmore is on his hands and knees, shaking his head, and fumbling a handgun from under his tunic.

'Leave it!' I shout. 'Don't make me do this.'

He ignores me, so I shoot him too, then pocket his pistol, a Glock 17.

I'm furious with myself for my carelessness, wondering how I can be so badly out of shape, mentally if not physically.

I should've handled that better and I should have guessed they'd be carrying non-standard arms.

These two men should not be dead.

I curse violently, pick up the bottle of Dalmore, and hurl it across the car park.

If I'd been on my own I could have slipped by here and they'd never have seen me.

No one would have been hurt.

Except maybe the people on the bus, decent people, not in any way responsible for their situation.

So was it a mistake to stop the bus, and to get involved?

I could just walk away now, let them fend for themselves.

But I think about the deserters, and what they'd do to Steve and his 'debts'.

Then I breathe deeply, gather myself.

I drag the two bodies inside the Inn, out of sight of where the bus will stop.

Just up the road is a petrol station with a shop, actually more of a general store, which sells outdoor gear as well as the usual roadside foodstuffs.

I figure this will be a reasonable place for everyone to stock up on water, soft drinks, chocolate, and, perhaps, even cold meat and cheese.

And more appropriate clothing and footwear for what lies in front of them.

'Go get Steve,' I tell Vidock, who seems much less upset than I am, then I start to dismantle the road block, wondering if we'll be able to bypass the mined sections up ahead.

4

I'm pleased to see the bus, I need help to move a piano and a fridge-freezer.
We point the others to the shop, with Vidock guarding them, and start to heft the heavy stuff to the side.
'You have some trouble?' asks Steve. 'I thought I heard a couple of shots.'
'Two squaddies, drunk and stupid, I screwed up.' I tell him.
'What'd you do with them?' he asks.
'Inside… Hell! Fred's just gone in there!'
We look at each other.
'He might not say anything,' says Steve. 'Or he might not care…'
I'm on my way towards the door of the Inn when Fred lurches out, carrying an SA80.
'You murdering bastard,' he screams at me. 'You fucking killed British soldiers, are you fucking IRA or something?'
I suddenly realise that he's going to start shooting and I'm in the middle of the car park.
He sprays bullets in all directions, and I hit the ground, wondering how he got the weapon into full automatic mode and thinking that even an idiot can't miss me for long.
I hear the bus taking the brunt of his assault but then he starts towards me.
I crouch, hoping he'll get near enough for me to jump, but he stops, launches another foul-mouthed tirade, and tells me he's going to enjoy blowing me to pieces.
As I reach for my knife, pretty sure I don't have time to pull it and throw, there's a single shot, and he stops, staring in

disbelief at the hole in his chest.
As he falls face down I turn to Steve, who is ashen-faced, and fumbling his pistol back into his belt.
'Didn't like him anyway,' he stammers. 'Sour-faced prick.'

Vidock is looking at me with an I-leave-you-alone-for-two-minutes expression.
Behind us, Allie starts to scream.

5

Allie has finally stopped screaming, but is adamant that Sensei must leave the group.
Joni and Jack agree with her, though less vehemently.
The Frasers and Steve, of course, want him to stay.
Strangely no one is upset that Fred was killed, the feeling is that Steve had no choice, that they were all in danger.
The bus is wrecked, most of the windows and two tyres gone.
Sensei pulls Steve aside, tells him the full story with the two soldiers, and says that if no consensus is reached he'll leave the group and go on ahead as a scout.
He is unhappy, but Sensei assures him he won't abandon them.
He wants to tell the girls why Sensei had to kill the soldiers, but the latter suggests that might be a bad idea, that they are frightened and stressed enough without knowing what capture would mean.
He proposes that Steve organises a vote while he goes to search for alternative transport.
Then the two men pause as they hear a new, strong voice address the others.
The woman has reappeared, her dark blonde hair damp, and wearing a new white tee shirt with a curious image of The Tartan Army on the front.
She looks ten years younger as she speaks to Allie.
'You shouldn't be getting yourself so agitated in your condition,' she says. 'And you need to remember to breathe properly.'
Allie's mouth falls open and Joni moves to support her.
'What are you, I'd say at least six months,' the woman asks,

then, seeing their expressions, she adds that she is a perinatal nurse.

'I can tell a pregnancy from half a mile away,' she grins. 'And you look healthy enough to me. Just stay calm and remember, deep breaths.'

She turns to the rest of us.

'My name's Cathy,' she says. 'I'm sorry I was such a mess before, I'll be okay now.'

Mrs Fraser goes and hugs her, says something quietly and their heads nod.

The two men look at each other and shrug, not even pretending to understand.

Mr Fraser catches their eye, makes a pushing down motion with his hands that says leave it, it's cool.

Cathy now moves over to the girls and, with her back excluding the others, talks to them for a couple of minutes.

Then there are nods and hugs all round, and Cathy comes over to the men.

They are amazed at the change in her; her blue eyes have a confidence and a sparkle that wasn't there before, and she stands differently, her shoulders back and her arms relaxed at her sides.

'I think the mutiny's over,' she says with a smile, and Sensei suddenly realises how attractive she is.

'You won't leave us, will you,?' she asks, then turns to Vidock. 'We need you most of all!'

He shrugs with pretend nonchalance, but his tail shows that her flattery has worked.

'We plan to do whatever it takes to keep you all safe,' Sensei answers.

'Is that what happened there?' she indicates the inn with her head. 'I guess the whole country is under martial law, right?'
'We might wish it was before much longer,' he says. 'There are hard times ahead.'
She nods.
'Okay, what now?' she asks.

6

Vidock and I are on the road again, heading towards Bridge of Orchy, only 6 or 7 miles to the north.

Because of the danger from the renegade soldiers, and perhaps others, we plan to move in short controlled stages, for now at least.

The last thing we need is to meet armed aggression on the open road where we can't protect the vulnerable.

We debated whether I should take the main road, the A82, or the pedestrian trail that runs more or less parallel to it.

This is part of West Highland Way, a hikers' track that runs from Glasgow to Fort William, and is well loved and well used by Scotland's outdoor types.

We gamble that anyone coming south will probably use the road, but have Allie keeping a lookout in case we are wrong.

Steve and the others are looking for transport, but we've already discovered that all motor vehicles have been disabled.

We've been walking for less than half an hour when I see a figure in the distance, and, simultaneously, I have a memory flash,.

Pushing the thought aside I conceal myself in the roadside ditch, Vidock beside me, and watch his approach.

He's a soldier, and like his now dead former colleagues he carries an SA80 and a whisky bottle.

I decide to let him pass and follow him, to see what his plans, or orders, are.

As he nears Tyndrum he sees the bus, tosses the bottle into the ditch, and moves forward more cautiously.

I watch him assess the situation, take note of the numbers, then

turn and move purposefully back up the road.
Again I let him pass, and follow him.
But I send Vidock to Steve with an orange cloth.
Get Ready.

7

They make better time now that the guy is being a soldier rather than a tourist, but Vidock still catches them before they are halfway.
The dog's expression says that he's having fun, so his man grins and shrugs, things could be worse.
And a light rain starts to fall.
At Bridge of Orchy the soldier goes straight into the hotel, a fine old building on the left-hand side of the road.
Sensei follows quickly and carefully, and hears voices from what proves to be the bar.
He's telling what he saw, with the emphasis on the fact that there are 'lots of girls'.
The listener is quite impressed by how much the scout saw and assimilated in a short time, he also knows there's 'a boy and an old couple, and a guy who might be trouble'.
A different voice, clearly the leader, spells out the plan.
'We kill the old folk and the trouble,' he says. 'Take a look at the boy, see if he could be useful. The girls we bring back here. No discussion, we go in friendly and shoot when we're up close. Saddle up!'
Sensei dives behind a door and listens to them clatter out.
'Barry,' shouts a voice. 'You go on, I need to strap up this knee, I'll catch up, okay? And take my rifle.'
Someone shouts an agreement, and the footsteps fade off down the road.
Sensei peers round the door and sees a figure limping back to the bar.
'Guard,' he tells Vidock, indicating the front door, and moves

after his target.

He doesn't like to kill in cold blood, but he needs to follow the group, and can't have someone coming along at his back.

He slips his knife, a double-edged Fairbairn-Sykes, from its sheath, and does what needs to be done.

8

There are two soldiers and two civilians ahead of me on the road, moving quickly in diamond formation, no chatter.
Three of them have SA80s, the other carries what looks like a shotgun.
We are outmatched here, we need to be smart and lucky.
My guess is that they won't think about the guy with the knee problem until they are ready to attack, by which time it will be too late.
First blood to the good guys.
And then I have a huge slice of luck.
Just before Tyndrum the road takes a wide loop to the west, while the West Highland Way, across some fields to the east, goes in a straight line, so it's almost a mile shorter.
They stay on the road.
The rain is much heavier as I slither down a grassy bank, jump a fence, tie a red cloth to Vidock, tell him to go, and start to run after him.
By the time I hit the main road again I know Steve will be ready.
I hustle behind a thick hedgerow opposite the petrol station, find the right spot, and wait.
The two soldiers march in side by side, looking smart and efficient, the British Army here to defend the country.
The other pair check the buildings as they pass, making sure there is no ambush.
These guys are good, and cautious, but they don't expect an attack from the other side, where there are only fields.
'Anyone here?' shouts the leader, who I assume to be Barry, as

they pause at the partially rebuilt roadblock.

I move into the road behind them, and shoot the civilian with the SA80 in the back.

As everyone spins round Steve steps from behind the fridge-freezer and, with his rifle on automatic, cuts the two soldiers to pieces.

The guy with the shotgun lifts his hands, either to shoot or to surrender, and I put two bullets in his chest.

Then I see that Mr Fraser and Cathy have appeared from behind the bus, pistols at the ready.

I raise my eyebrows at Steve and he shrugs, breathing hard, clearly a bit shaken.

But he pulls back his shoulders, and points.

'I think we've just about got an army,' he says.

Jack is in the doorway of the inn with an SA80.

'He said he'd protect the girls,' Steve grins tightly. 'And I think he meant it.'

'And Mrs Fraser?' I ask.

But, looking white-faced but determined, she has appeared behind Cathy and her husband.

'You don't think I'd let him out here by himself, do you?' she says, her voice high and stressed, as she tries not to look at the four bodies.

Then she gathers herself, forcing a smile and slapping her man's arm.

'He could get himself into trouble if I'm not around to look after him. And look at you, you're soaking wet!'

9

He gazes wryly at the transport fleet that was discovered in his absence.
There are two Vespa ET2 50 Scooters, maybe 20 years old but in good condition, and two BMX bikes.
'We have fuel for the Vespas,' says Steve. 'Two full tanks and a one-gallon can. With reasonable luck I reckon a tank will last about 150 miles, and the can about half that.'
'How many of us can drive them?' Sensei asks.
'Me, of course, and Mr Fraser. He was a cop, I'd forgotten that, so he knows his way round a gun too. He might be getting on a bit, and he's got a bad leg, but he won't let us down.'
'You talking about me, huh?' Mr Fraser appears, putting on his Bob de Niro voice, and grinning widely. 'I'll take a gun and Jules, that's the missus, on the scooter, and handle anything and anybody that's out there, no worries.'
'Cool,' Sensei laughs with him. 'You take Allie, Steve, and the other two ladies can take the bikes. Jack and I will walk.'
'Actually,' says Cathy, 'Sorry to butt in uninvited, but I'd rather walk. Those things aren't really my style.'
'You two okay on them?' Steve asks Jack and Joni, and gets very positive replies.
Sensei thinks about tomorrow's walk.
'Take the bike to Bridge of Orchy,' he says to Cathy. 'Then you can walk from there. Jack, you okay walking the first stage?'
The youngster is eager to please, nothing is a problem for him.
Sensei pulls Steve to the side.
'Um, there's a body behind the bar up there, maybe you and Mr

Fraser…'

'Hugh,' Mr Fraser interrupts him. 'My name's Hugh, or Hughie, or Shuggie, all the Mister stuff is making me feel old! What are you saying about me now anyway?'

They laugh again, and Sensei explains about the guy he used the knife on.

'Better not let Allie find him, hmm, she already thinks I'm a bit of a savage.'

'No, no,' says Hugh, still chuckling. 'She thinks you're a murdering psychopath, but she's right glad you're on our side! Actually,' he becomes suddenly serious, 'Jules explained to the girls what's going on, what would happen if they fell into the wrong hands.'

'And they believed her?'

'She was a schoolteacher,' he grins. 'She knows how to talk to the weans!'

It has already been a long day for everyone, and with the heavy rain and low cloud the light is fading fast.

Steve tells them all to find what they want to eat tonight and for breakfast, and then to get a rucksack and serious winter walking gear from the shop, and to pack what they need to survive.

Then, to much hilarity, he goes through their choices one by one, throws out more than half, and advises them as to what might be more appropriate.

Like, for example, Joni, a torch instead of a hair-dryer.

While the others are inside eating, the man and his dog are in the car park at the side of the Inn.

The latter watches the road while he runs through a short exercise routine and practices Kata, during which he vaguely hears Joni asking someone 'What is he doing, some sort of

karate or something? Is that why Steve calls him Sensei?'
To his later amusement, the name sticks.
They sleep in the Tyndrum Inn, ready for an early start in the morning.

10

Jack is nervous at first, this is the first time we have been alone, and able to talk, but then asks the questions that have been bothering him.
I explain what happened with the first two soldiers in Tyndrum, telling him I was sloppy, I shouldn't have had to kill them.
The others were different.
I tell him what I overheard in the hotel bar, how they planned to kill Steve and the Frasers without a thought.
And what would have happened to Cathy and the girls.
He is shocked, struggling to believe that British soldiers would kill pensioners so callously.
'They look on it as a war now, with no rules,' I say. 'They're deserters, there's no way back for them.'
'And me?' he asks. 'What…?'
'That would depend on whether you'd go along with what they were doing. You could join them or die.'
I leave him to think for a while before I speak again.
'You got lucky with Steve, you know, he's a guy with a heart, he'll do his best for all of you.'
'And we got really lucky with you too,' he says. 'You've saved us twice already.'
'No,' I say. 'It's different. I wouldn't have picked you up in the first place. I only stopped the bus out of curiosity, and I only got on because I liked Steve.'
'You won't leave us, will you?' he asks, his voice rising. 'I'm sorry about what I said yesterday after the Fred thing.'
'I won't leave until I'm sure you're all safe,' I say. 'I owe Steve that much. He saved me yesterday, and I don't forget easily.'

'He was a friend of my dad's,' he sniffs a bit, rubs at his eyes. 'I've known him since I was that high.'

He leans a hand down towards his knees.

'Not well, y'know, but we all went to see the Thistle a couple of times, he'd buy the pies!'

'Stay close to him,' I nod. 'You can learn a lot.'

After a few minutes Jack mutters something I don't catch.

'What's that?' I ask.

'He says you're special.'

I glance at him but he is staring at the ground ahead, his face red.

We march on in silence for a spell then, when a sparrow flits out from cover almost under our feet, he laughs.

'A wee speug,' he says, and we make small talk about birds, the rain, the hills and stuff like that until we approach Bridge of Orchy.

The others are waiting impatiently, although we have made excellent time, the boy has quite a stride.

We pause outside the hotel and I hold out my hand.

'You'll be fine,' I say.

He grips it hard, staring at me, as if to decide.

Then, with a shy boyish smile, he nods.

'Thanks for everything,' he says.

11

'I wanted to talk to you anyway,' says Cathy as they head up the West Highland Way from Bridge of Orchy, the rain falling steadily. 'I wanted to explain what happened to me.'

'There's no need,' he tells her. 'We all went through a pretty traumatic experience, I'm just surprised we haven't had more problems.'

'Please,' she says. 'I need to tell someone what I did.'

To be honest, he doesn't want to know what she has been through.

Although it is less than a day since they arrived in Tyndrum he feels as though a month has passed.

His main emotion now is weariness.

He killed five men yesterday, and saw Steve kill three more.

Three of his victims, and two of Steve's, were soldiers, men he would have called brother only a couple of days ago.

He did what he had to do, but he is far from happy about it.

Seeing good men lose their way, and their morality, so quickly, saddens him.

'I'm not sure I'm much of a Father Confessor,' he says. 'But fire away.'

'I was at the mini-market,' she says. 'Just getting rolls and milk, when there was a bang that lasted for ages. Or maybe it was a lot of different bangs, I don't know. I'm not sure if I passed out, but I know my head was spinning for a while, and then I realised that the girl at the checkout was dead. Somehow I wasn't surprised, and when I went out into the street there were more dead people. I ran home, it wasn't far, knowing what I'd find there, but not believing that everything could change so suddenly.'

She stops talking, stumbles, and he realises that she is blind with tears.

He puts his hand on her arm, but she shakes it off, screams a few obscenities at herself, and marches on.

'All dead,' she says, choking the words out one at a time. 'My husband, my mother, my beautiful Karly, all dead. Unmarked, but with the same stunned expression that all the others had. But I was alive. I couldn't understand why.'

She stops abruptly.

'Why am I not dead?' she demands. 'Why are you alive, and the others?'

She waves an arm.

'Why them, why not my baby, my angel? She was only thirteen, why is she dead?'

She is screaming again, as though he should have answers, as though it is all his fault.

He stands helpless, watching her anguish, her despair, her rage. Then she is quiet.

She reaches out and touches his face.

'It isn't your fault, is it,' she is almost whispering. 'But I needed to say the words aloud. I needed to tell you that so I can explain what happened next.'

She sighs.

The tears have stopped.

Her next words come as a shock.

'I need to confess.'

And she starts to walk, and talk.

12

'When I stopped crying, I left the house. I needed to find out what was happening, to try to make sense of it all.

I went back down to the main road, where the shops are, and saw two guys there.

We stay, sorry, stayed, in Knightswood, quite a nice area, so I wasn't concerned. I suppose I had other things on my mind. But they grabbed me, dragged me into the park there, one of them had a knife.

I mean they were just young guys, barely men, but they were laughing like maniacs, and they shoved me onto the ground and one of them flung himself on top of me and started pulling at my clothes.

I was screaming and scratching and clawing, trying to bite his face, but he pushed my head to the side and I saw he'd dropped the knife.

I grabbed it and stuck it into his neck, or maybe his throat, because suddenly there was blood everywhere.

The other guy started screaming at me and I saw he was on his knees beside me with his trousers pulled down.

I jammed the knife into his stomach, well actually a bit lower, then turned away from him and twisted and wriggled until I was out from under them.

I saw that the first one looked pretty much dead, the other one was tugging at the knife as if he wasn't sure whether to pull it out or not.

He looked at me, his eyes wide open, terrified, and he started whining, asking me to help him.

I started to punch him in the face as hard as I could, just

pummelling him, completely out of control.'
She stops talking, and stops walking, turns to face the man again, barely registering his expression.
The hood from the jacket she got from the shop is pushed back, hardly covering her head, and the rain and the tears are pouring down her face.
He waits, says nothing.
'The next thing I remember,' she says, and points. 'Is seeing Vidock on the bus.'

13

After almost seven hours of serious walking through pale sunshine we hit the A82 again, this time at King's House at the eastern end of Glencoe.

Once Cathy had finished telling me of the traumatic events that had so affected her, she pulled herself together again, and the weather seemed to brighten with her mood.

Now she seems to have exorcised her demons, and shares her surprisingly upbeat views on the other women.

The two girls are 'good lassies', in her opinion, and dismisses Allie's screaming tirade as 'horror and hormones, a lethal mix'.

'And Mrs Fraser?' I ask.

'Jules,' she laughs. 'She's a real Glasgow woman, an absolute champion! She is the best person we could ever have in a situation like this, a policeman's wife who brought up three sons and a daughter in Partick, nothing will faze her, she's got the tee shirt!'

We make good time along the West Highland Way through some of Scotland's finest scenery, with views across Rannoch Moor to the east and the great pyramid of Buachaille Etive Mor – the Great Herdsman of Etive – to the north-west providing the inspiration to push steadily on to our rendezvous point as though we are marching to the sound of the bagpipes.

Less that twenty minutes later we hear the welcome sound of a scooter, and a smiling Steve pulls up and dismounts beside us.

'Get going,' he grins. 'I'll be with you in no time.'

'You coming with me?' he asks Vidock, and trots off at a pretty fair pace back the way he came.

'Keep your eyes open for anything alive,' I say to Cathy as she

climbs gracefully on, wrapping her arms tightly around me.
I am surprised how good that feels, then scowl, annoyed at myself.
'Guard Steve,' I tell Vidock, and soon overtake him as we putter down through the most famous glen in Scotland.
In a matter of minutes we arrive at our destination, the Isles of Glencoe Hotel, on a peninsula in Loch Leven only a mile or so from where the wonderful Ballachulish Bridge marks the entry to Loch Linnhe.
As we pull into the parking area two heavily-armed men step out and challenge us.
With wide grins.
Hugh and Jack are taking their guard duties seriously.
Cathy nudges me and starts to laugh.
Jules is watching from a window, pistol in hand.
I turn the scooter and head back up to find Steve.

14

While Jules prepares a meal, refusing offers of help with the words 'Away out my sight', Steve organises the defences in pairs around the peninsula, and he and Sensei take the bikes to the bridge.

Hugh is with Allie, Jack partners Joni, and Cathy has the pleasure of Vidock's company.

He hardly notices his man leaving.

The bridge is, as expected, a mess, someone having made a poor attempt at blowing it up, but it's not impassable for their light transport.

They cross carefully, examining every bit of it, then bump fists, crossing here saves them a 20-mile detour via Kinlochleven, a charming village in picturesque setting, but they're not here for sightseeing.

Then they pause to discuss the overall situation, while taking in the glorious sunset over Western Lochaber and the Morvern Peninsula on the far side of Loch Linnhe.

They talk about the yellow cloud, how they haven't seen it since Loch Lomond, but they both saw the results of it in Glasgow, and the squaddies saw it, and its effects, in Inverness.

They suppose it was some sort of poison gas, used only on critical targets, like the Faslane submarine base, and populated areas.

Fingers crossed it's behind them now.

'How was the walking today?' Steve asks. 'Anybody have any problems?'

'It was cool, Cathy did fine, and the lad could walk me off my feet! It still seems like the safest and most economic way to travel. Jack and Joni are a bit exposed on the bikes, but as long as you hold back on the scooters every couple of miles, they're not alone for any length of time.'

'Aye, you're right,' Steve says. 'But you looked right glad of the wee break at King's House!'

They both laugh, but not knowing how far the fuel for the scooters will take them is a major concern.

The Frasers are a valuable part of the team, but it is hard to see them walking long distances.

'Fort William tomorrow,' Sensei says. 'Maybe we'll get lucky there, find another bus! One that hasn't been shot all to fuck!'

'Okay, so we all cross the bridge together,' says Steve. 'Then Jack with you till Onich, then he takes the bike with Joni, and we wait for you at one of the guest houses just before we hit the town.'

'Yep,' the other shakes his head. 'And I suspect we'll have fun there. But not a lot.'

15

Vidock stands guard while they enjoy a great dinner, then he eats while the dishes are washed, dried and put away.
'I've never left a kitchen dirty in my life, and I'm not starting now,' says Jules.
But what is now interesting is the development of the group dynamics.
When Jules asks for volunteers to help with the dishes, Jack is first on his feet.
Allie is quick to tease him, and he is embarrassed enough to stammer his excuses.
'My mum,' he says. 'My mum…'
But he can't speak until he clears his throat.
'That's how I was brought up,' he says eventually. 'My mum taught me good manners.'
There is a moment's awkwardness until Jules takes his arm and speaks.
'Your mum was a good woman,' she says. 'I'd be as proud of you as I am,' – she stops and breathes for a minute – 'as I was, with any of my own.'
He puts his arm round her shoulders and they head to the kitchen, both wiping their eyes as they go.
No one speak for a while as they face their own thoughts and memories.
Then the two girls follow them, blowing into tissues, each reaching for the other's hand.
Cathy stands at the window, staring into the darkness, while Hugh sits stony-faced.
Steve catches Sensei's eye and points to his watch.

He nods and they organises a last tour of the perimeter in the light drizzle before they move inside to dry off and warm up again.

Vidock stays outside on overnight sentry duty.

Everyone shuffles around a bit awkwardly, feeling that it's still too early for bed, but not sure about how to start socialising.

'Okay,' says Steve. 'I think it's time for one of Mr Fraser, sorry, Hughie's "Tales from the Police Force"'.

This last bit he says in a deep, dramatic voice, sweeping his hand towards the proposed storyteller.

'He used to tell stories to Calum and me when we were kids,' he continues, then he pauses.

'Sorry Mrs F, I didn't mean to…'

'That's okay, son,' she says, wiping an eye. 'There's an awful lot of dead folk out there, and we've all lost somebody we love.'

Her voice is breaking, and Hugh puts his arm around her.

'Maybe this isn't a good time, love,' he says.

'Oh get away with you,' she says, smacking his arm, and trying to smile. 'You're just dying to tell them some of your whopping lies!'

'Okay,' he says, grinning. 'But I'll try to stay on topic.'

And he starts.

16

'Your husband is dead.

As a detective I often had to deliver this sort of news.

And it was never easy.

Reactions vary, of course, but grief is always painful to watch.

Anyway this one time I go to see a Mrs Oswald, at least on this occasion knowing that the wife hadn't committed the murder.

No, we found the murderer before we knew there was a crime.

Her husband's business partner, Andrew Quail, managed to get involved in a quite serious car accident, and was being tended by ambulance personnel when a police officer noticed a bloody knife in his vehicle.

I'm not swearing, ladies, the knife was covered in blood!'

Hugh is now talking in police reporting mode.

'We quickly established that he had just left his business premises where we found Jim Oswald's body.

When I questioned Quail he just shrugged, and admitted they had argued.

He said that it had escalated and, when Oswald punched and kicked him, he retaliated by stabbing his partner.

There were eight deep stab wounds and several minor cuts on the deceased, whose hands and forearms were lacerated, presumably as he tried to defend himself.

I don't tell Mrs Oswald any of this, of course.

She's a slim, attractive woman, in her late thirties, I guess, well-dressed, clothes smart and expensive.'

Hugh wiggles his eyebrows here, and Jules slaps his arm again, laughing, and tells him to get on with it.

'Aye, okay. It's a big house with a huge, well-kept garden over in Whitecraigs, poshest area in the city.

The room we're in is tastefully furnished, but doesn't contain a single item that we could ever have afforded in our lives.

I feel myself tense as she covers her face with her hands, drops her head to her knees.

Her shoulders heave, and she makes small, unintelligible sounds.

I gesture to the woman police constable to sit beside her on the settee, and wait.

When she eventually looks up her face is red with tears streaming from her eyes.

I'm a wee bit slow to realise that she is convulsed with laughter.

Mrs Oswald, I begin, concerned that she's hysterical, would you like a cup of tea?

She snorts, and drops her head again.

This time the laughter is clearer.

I look at the WPC and make a silent question with my face.

She shrugs in return.

We sit there feeling useless until Mrs Oswald lifts her head again, wiping her eyes as she does so.

Thank you, she smiles, tea would be lovely.

Is there anyone you would like to contact, someone who can be with you? I ask.

She ignores my question, asks her own.

How did he die?

I explain that I am not at liberty to discuss details, but that we are treating his death as suspicious.

Oh rubbish, she laughs, he was murdered, wasn't he? Senior police officers don't drop in to tell grieving widows their hubby had a heart attack!

You don't seem too upset, Mrs Oswald, did you and your husband have problems?

Problems! I hated him! The man is – was – a pig! And I bet that scumbag partner of his killed him, didn't he?

I'm a bit taken aback, kinda stare at her.

I take it you know Mr Quail?

Of course! I told Jim he was a crook, and violent, but he wouldn't listen. Too stupid and arrogant for his own good!

Mrs Oswald, I say, I wonder if you can fill me in with some background on the two men, and their business.

Of course, Inspector, she replies, but not now, please. I would like some time to reflect on my good fortune.

Your good fortune? I ask.

Yes, she says, standing and leading us to the front door. He was insured for… Well, let's just say a substantial amount. The house is paid for. And I am free.

Smiling widely, she shakes my hand.

Thank you so much, she says, and closes the door.

I look at the WPC.

Constable Newton, isn't it? I ask.

Yes, sir.

I've got to tell you, constable, that it's not always that easy.'

17

'They know we're here,' says Steve, when they are all assembled in a boarding house on Achintore Road, about a mile before Fort William's West End Roundabout, where the road splits into two.

The left fork is the continuation of the A82 and runs along the eastern side of Loch Linnhe, while the second exit leads into the High Street and the town centre.

'There was a wee laddie just a bit ahead, when he saw us he fled towards the town,' he explains. 'So what do you think?'

The two men walk across to the loch, which is at the south-western, or bottom left, end of the Great Glen, a geological fault which runs sixty miles north-east, all the way to Inverness. This glen splits the Highlands into two distinct parts, and is the route for Thomas Telford's Caledonian Canal, completed 200 years ago in 1822, which links Loch Linnhe, a sea loch, with lochs Lochy, Oich, Ness and Dochfour before entering the Beauly Firth at Inverness.

Standing in a steady drizzle they confer briefly, but their choices are limited.

The only good thing right now is that the clouds are low and dark, with no yellow in sight.

So they go back to the others and tell them the plan, such as it is.

'Vidock and I'll go in, suss things out. The natives might be friendly.' Sensei grins. 'Maybe we can get some transport.'

'You can't go in alone,' says Jules. 'What if they're not friendly?'

'I'll come back and tell you, and we can make another plan.'

'Hang on,' says Hugh. 'We're all in this together, right, so we should all get a say in this.'

'Let's make something clear,' says Steve. 'I'm an easy-going guy, happy to discuss everything and anything, and listen to everyone's views on any subject you choose. Except this. Two of us are ex-military, we make these decisions. This is war, not a progressive democracy.'

'I was a cop,' says Hugh again, quite forcefully. 'I want to go in too.'

'No,' says Steve. 'The decision is made for the good of all. That's why we organised the travel the way we did, strength at the front and back, protecting the cyclists between us. And, Hugh, to be brutally honest, if this is a firefight we don't want you out in the open, you're not the quickest. But here, guarding the others, you're the man, okay?'

'So why don't you both go in?' asks Cathy.

'Makes no sense,' Sensei says. 'One, it gives them a better idea of our strength, and two, if things go badly wrong…'

'If things go badly wrong we lose you,' she snaps back.

He shrugs.

'I'm dispensable,' he says. 'And you might still have Vidock. And he's the reason that I should go and not Steve, he reads my mind.'

He moves outside with the dog and they sit side by side on the steps, leaving the others to discuss, debate or argue, but they can't change anything.

Nothing else makes sense.

18

When I arrive at the roundabout there is a reception committee of four armed men and three grim-faced women.
And the red-haired boy that Steve described to me, who starts talking earnestly to the men.
'I'm Angus MacDougall,' the oldest man says, waving the youngster away. 'Who are you and what do you want here?'
He is tall, lean, hard, between 40 and 50, I guess, but with the worn, sunken features of someone who spends too much time outdoors in Scotland's harsh Highland winters.
He has the rangy look of a man from the mountains rather than the water.
He looks at Vidock, and then at the boy, not understanding, but wondering why this wasn't reported and, more importantly, what else he doesn't know.
I realise that they didn't see Cathy and me arrive with Vidock. They know there was no dog in the first group, and they have probably just heard that I wasn't there either, so now they don't know our strength.
'Good afternoon, Mr MacDougall,' I say, with my hands open at shoulder height. 'We come in peace, just passing through, heading north. But I wonder if you have any transport you can spare us?'
He lowers his brows as though thinking.
'I wouldn't go north if I was you,' he says, shaking his head.
'After the soldiers passed through, heading south, all the riff-raff headed up to Inverness, you'll not want to meet up with the likes of them.'
'Thanks for you advice, sir, we'll try to avoid trouble, as

always. But that's our road, for now at least.'

He nods slowly before he speaks again.

'Then that's your road there,' he points to the A82 that runs up the loch. 'No offence but we don't want you in the town.'

After further discussion I find that they can't or won't provide any help in the way of fuel or transport, but that we can bypass their town without any conflict.

I step forward and shake MacDougall's hand.

'We're just taking care of what we've got,' he says. 'I hope you understand.'

'Absolutely,' I say. 'We'll just move on with no hard feelings.'

As I turn away one of the women calls out.

Her hair, the fiery red of the Scottish Highlander, tells me she is the boy's mother.

'Will you take me and the boy with you?'

MacDougall is shaking his head again, more in sorrow than in anger, it seems.

'Come along, lass,' he says. 'You're better off here among your own kind, there's no chance your mother'll still be there, you know.'

'I need to find out for myself,' she says to him, with some defiance. 'I've got to know.'

Then she turns to me, tells me her mum's in Invermoriston, about 40 miles up the road.

'We've got bikes too,' she says. 'We'll be no trouble, honest.'

I look at MacDougall, who sighs.

'I've told Fiona she's not safe on that road by herself,' he says. 'But if you'll mind her on her way, then I'll not stop her. You can't keep a lass from her mother, can you?'

I tell her to wait for us at the north end of town, and I take my leave of MacDougall and his silent, watchful sentinels.

19

We move past Fort William as one group.
I lead the way at a fast trot, Jack and Vidock at my heels, then Joni and Allie on the BMXs followed by the Frasers, then Steve, with Cathy on pillion, 50 metres back.
To the left is the loch shore, to the right the rear of the buildings that face onto the High Street.
Cathy checks behind us, Jack leaps to the barrier every 50 metres or so to check the foreshore, and the rest of us watch the windows and backdoors.
Nothing.
We continue in this way until we reach the River Nevis at Fort William's northern extremity, and there we find Fiona and Malky, her son, waiting on their bicycles.
She stares at me in disbelief.
'You're on foot,' she says in a classic statement of the bleeding obvious. 'How will we get to Invermoriston tonight?'
'We won't,' I reply. 'It'll be getting dark in 3 hours and that's when we stop.'
'But you said…' She looks around in some confusion, as if she can conjure up some way for me to travel faster. 'I told you I need to be there tonight.'
'No, you didn't, so I suggest you go back there,' I indicate the town with my head, 'and ask your friend MacDougall to take you by car.'
'What? No, he um, no, he can't,' she stammers. 'He hasn't got a car.'
'I suppose I could always pop into a phone box to change,' I grin, but she doesn't respond.

'Okay,' says Steve. 'Time to go. Are you with us or not?'
She nods, somewhat reluctantly, so I make brief introductions, then ask if I can check both their rucksacks.
I brush aside Fiona's indignation, tell her I am a nasty man with a suspicious mind, and it is non-negotiable, as is the body search that Cathy performs on her, and Jack does on the boy.
After Steve and I have a short discussion, then some serious words with Jack, who is to keep the others in front of him at all times, we head off in our standard formation.
I tell Cathy to strap her rucksack on top of mine, dismiss her protestations, and set off through light rain at a fast jog.
We have 3 hours to our planned stop, almost 18 miles away.

20

This time it is Hugh who arrives on the Vespa, and takes Cathy and the rucksacks the second half of the trip.
She is exhausted, having covered over ten miles in two hours.
Without the weight on his back Sensei picks up the pace and, with Vidock trotting happily in front, arrives at their destination about an hour later.
Hugh is waiting, and leads him past a cottage and up an elegant driveway to the Corriegour Lodge Hotel, a four-star establishment only the width of the road from the east bank of Loch Lochy.
He tells the tired traveller how impressed he is by Steve's organisation and leadership, what happened when they arrived at their destination last night and tonight.

They group in a defensible position and Steve goes in first, covered by Hugh.
When he gives the all clear, the others follow, and split into groups.
The three men and Joni, who is great, says Hugh, clear away any bodies, starting with the kitchen, then the dining area.
Tonight Fiona and Malky also pitched in, working as hard as anyone.
Jules and Allie start to organise food, while Steve determines the sleeping arrangements and those rooms get cleared too.
Sensei nods to show approval, but says nothing.
He is pleased; Steve listens, and learns fast.

He showers quickly then finds Steve helping Jack carry a body

from the Residents' Lounge, a welcoming room with
comfortable armchairs grouped around a blazing fire.
'Even better than I imagined,' Sensei tells him. 'This is the way
to travel, and everything's so much cheaper after a war.'
They grin at each other and, after they eat another of Jules'
great meals, they argue about which of them will marry her
after they bump off her hubby.
She snorts disdainfully.
'None of you are half the man he is,' she declares in a voice
that ends the discussion. 'I wouldn't see either of you in my
road!'
They flee outside from the sounds of loud laughter, and make
some very serious plans.
Tomorrow they will at last leave the A82 and start heading
west, towards where they hope to find their winter lair.
Then, come spring, life will get more interesting.
But before that they expect trouble.

21

'No, no,' says Hugh, sprawled in the armchair closest to the fire. 'No more polis stories yet, somebody else can take a turn.'
They all look at each other, wondering who's got the nerve to speak up.
Sensei reckons he doesn't have any stories suitable for an audience, unless...
'Here Jules,' Hugh interrupts his thoughts. 'Tell them your wee story about your sister and her man.'
Jules lowers her eyes, shakes her head slowly.
'You think I should?'
'Yeah, go on, Jules,' says Steve. 'You used to tell us some crackers back in the day.'
'Well okay,' she says.

'It's about my sister, Maggie, she lives in Partick too, up Gardner Street, the block below White Street, a nice second floor flat.
I've been to the farmers' market, got her some lovely pears.
I chap her door and she shouts for me to come in.
And make sure the door's shut right, Roger's dead.
Roger's her husband.
Well, was, apparently.
His real name's Dick, much more appropriate.
He decided he wanted to be called Roger, because it sounded more manly, more debonair, more, what do you call it, sophisticated, like Roger Moore.
All the things he wasn't.
So I'm standing gazing open-mouthed round the kitchen,

amazed that such a wee, scrawny body could contain that much blood.
But I'm not really surprised that he met a violent end,
presumably at her hands.
I sigh and shake my head, lift my arms in a what are we going to do now sort of gesture.
Some mess, eh?
It's Maggie talking, calm as ever.
She's great, so she is, she's my best friend too.
I turn and see her smiling at me over her shoulder.
She's at the sink, rinsing the carving-knife.
There's wine in the fridge, she says.'

And Jules stops and looks around.
They're all staring at her in stunned disbelief when she looks at Hugh and shrugs.
Then they both burst out laughing.
'Gotcha!'

22

'Stop right there!'
'Lay down your weapons!'
'We have you surrounded!'
'Do it now!'
Mine is the first voice, from behind a tree in the gardens.
Steve is in the most exposed position, flat on the ground in shrubs to my left.
Hugh is in the cottage at the other side of the driveway.
Jack, the last voice, is across the road on the banks of the loch.
The group of men, and the boy, pause, uncertain.
'Mr MacDougall,' I say. 'We have eight SA80s pointing at you. One false move and we'll cut you to ribbons. Do you really want to die here tonight, and leave your town, and your womenfolk, with no men? Put the guns down now or I'll shoot you. You looked in my eyes back there, and you didn't want to fight me face to face. That's why you're creeping in at night, and why you know this isn't a bluff.'
They huddle together, muttering, then their weapons hit the ground.
'Face down, hands wide, you know the drill,' I shout.
Steve is on them in a flash, patting their sides, finding a handgun here, a knife there.
'Jack,' he says, and gestures, and our bold lad is clearing everything away, out of their reach.
'You can sit,' I say, standing with my barrel 3 inches from MacDougall's nose.
He blanches, and swallows, but is brave enough to ask about Fiona.

'Unhurt, but temporarily indisposed,' I say. 'As soon as Malky slipped away we locked her in a cellar.'

'Not quite eight of you, are there?' he spits.

'Each of my men is worth two of yours,' says Steve. 'You made the right decision, you'd all have died. And for what?'

'The girls, of course,' says our prisoner. 'We saw them right at the start, and we need young women. We'll give you anything you want, money, equipment, whatever you need.'

Steve leans down and grabs him by the throat.

'We don't sell people,' he snarls. 'Maybe we should just have shot you down like dogs. Sorry, Vidock.'

But my best buddy has got bored and gone back inside to get spoiled by Cathy.

'Get up,' says Steve. 'And try not to say anything else that might get you killed.'

'Can we chuck them in the loch?' suggests Hugh. 'See if it's too cold for a swim?'

MacDougall scowls at him.

'You don't need to worry,' he sneers. 'Nobody's interested in your old woman.'

Hugh hits him before any of us can blink, so hard that blood and teeth spray out.

The others move forward half a step, but Hugh throws his rifle to me and gets in their faces, demanding who is next.

When there are no volunteers he gestures to the prone figure of MacDougall.

'Get that piece of crap out of my way before I lose my temper,' he says, his voice surprisingly controlled again.

'How did you get here?' I ask the three guys still standing.

'Electric car and trailer, it's got no distance in it.'

'We'll take it,' I say. 'The walk'll do you good. Now take him to the water and waken him properly, I want everyone to understand something. Jack, can you get Fiona, please.'

A few minutes later MacDougall is on his feet, face lopsided and starting to swell.

Fiona and Malky stare defiantly at us, but the men have no fight left.

'Can you hear me?' I ask. 'Because this is important.'

They nod, more or less, and Fiona starts to speak.

'Shut up,' I say. 'And listen.'

I go nose to nose with MacDougall.

'If I ever see any of you, anywhere, anytime, for any reason, I will kill you without a word. I don't care what excuses you might have, because you'll be too dead to make them. Do you understand?'

I look each man in the eye, wait until they nod, then I catch Fiona by the front of her coat, and pull her towards me.

'Be sure you do too, because this includes you, and the boy. There are no rules in my world, I'll cut your throat, and his, without a thought. Okay?'

She stares wide-eyed, then turns away.

'Where are the bikes?' she asks.

'Start walking,' says Steve. 'Car keys, someone?'

23

Dawn sees me throwing sticks into the loch for Vidock, who occasionally remembers that he is a dog, and not just my partner.
The rain has stopped, the sky is the colour of Scottish blue that breaks your heart, and he emerges each time to shake a gallon or two of near-freezing water over me before demanding another reason to plunge back in.
In the morning stillness I hear soft footsteps crossing the road, and know they are friendly.
'Hello,' says Allie, standing awkwardly on one foot, and glancing over her shoulder at Joni, who waits at the foot of the driveway.
I straighten up, and smile at her.
'Good morning,' I say, and indicate the sky. 'Some sunshine at last.'
She pauses, looks again for her friend, then blurts out a string of questions.
'Did you mean what you said last night? Would you kill all of them? Would you cut wee Malky's throat? Why didn't you shoot them like you did the soldiers back in Tyndrum? Why does he' – she indicates Vidock – 'go out to the road each night and sit facing back the way we came?'
The last question catches me unawares, but I force a half laugh, and raise my hands in a gesture of surrender.
'I'll try to answer your questions one at a time,' I say, 'starting with last night. Steve and I felt we could disarm them without bloodshed, which is always our aim, whenever possible. The guys in Tyndrum were trained soldiers, three of them, with a

plan to kill Steve and the Frasers without discussion. It was them or us. Our only alternative was to give them what they wanted, you, Joni and Cathy, and hide until they left. We felt a responsibility to keep you safe.'

'I understand that,' she says, 'and we are grateful, honest. Joni and me really appreciate how you've all looked after us. So last night you kept them alive and then said you'd kill them all. Why?'

'Do you think they believed me,' I ask.

'Oh god, I did!' she says. They'd need to be stupid not to!'

'They were also here for you three, and I don't fancy looking over my shoulder for the rest of the trip, do you? They had to know they'd had their chance, there are no more. As for Fiona, she lied to me. Looked me in the eye and spun a sob story about her old mother. I didn't believe her, it made no sense, but given the situation at that moment it seemed a good idea to play it out. But, you know we all have things that bug us, right? Well, I hate liars more than anything. She got off lightly. You can relax, they won't be back, not now they've met Steve and Hugh too!'

'Can I tell you something?' she asks, suddenly very serious. She looks round for Joni, and I have to tell her she went back to the hotel.

'Hang on,' I say, picking up the stick Vidock keeps dropping on my foot, and hurling it three miles or so into the loch.

I sit on the slope of the bank, and pat the ground beside me. She sits and starts to talk.

'I was engaged to a soldier. Quite a funny story, how we met. I was going to a party, Joni's sixteenth, it was, and it was teeming down, so my mum told Rab, my brother, to give me a

lift. Well he knew Joni's brother, so he came in too, and we
were all standing chatting when I saw this guy looking at me
with great big brown eyes.
Rab, typical big brother, goes "What's he looking at?" so I say,
"Me, I think, I'm quite pretty, y'know!" Actually I was, back
then. Anyway he just growled and a wee while later he left.
The guy was still looking so I went across and just said hello.
He looked a bit nervous, asked where my boyfriend had gone,
so I laughed and told him he was a daftie, that Rab's my
brother. Well, he walked me home and that was that!'
She pauses, watching me for a reaction.
I smile and nod.
'Ronnie, that's his name, was his name,' Allie sniffs and rubs
her eyes, and stumbles over her words for a minute. 'Ronnie
joined the Royal Highland Fusiliers, based through in
Edinburgh, two years ago, just after we got engaged. He said he
could learn good stuff there, communications stuff, and get a
good job after. We were supposed to get married next summer.
He got killed in a stupid car crash near Peebles four months ago
last Tuesday. He never even knew he was a father. I've been
eating ever since, lots of chocolate, and any other rubbish I can
get hold of. I know I need to get my act together for the baby,
but...'
And she is breaking her heart, her head on my chest, while I pat
her back quite awkwardly.
Vidock, who has been sitting surprisingly patiently, gets up,
and nuzzles her with his wet head.
She looks up in surprise, then, laughing through the tears, she
wraps her arms around his neck, lays her face next to his, and
hugs the great soggy beast as though her life depends on it.

And I remember that the first thing she knew about me was that I killed two soldiers.

Aye, no wonder she screamed.

24

Steve and Sensei take the bikes and head up the last couple of miles of Loch Lochy, then follow the road as it cuts across to run up the west bank of Loch Oich.

They find the road has been blown just before the bridge over the River Garry, not far south of where the A82 meets the A87. They are puzzled but happy that the bridge is intact – Steve suggests that at least they were aware of their level of incompetence, blowing up a stone bridge isn't as easy as you might think – and they can get the scooters past the damage. The car would be a major hassle, but they don't really need it or care about it; they've managed this far without it.

By the time they get back to the others at Corriegour Lodge the rain is icy, heavy, and being driven in on a fierce north wind. The previously placid surface of the loch is now an angry churning mass.

The earlier blue sky was obviously a hoax of nature, but this is Scotland in October...

After a brief discussion they decide to spend the day here in comfort, look over the scooters and bikes, including those confiscated from Fiona and Malky, and prepare their rain-wear for the last two days of the journey, the second of which will be, for tactical reasons, very short.

25

Joni wanders over and scratches Vidock's head.
He looks at the man with a smug expression, then closes his eyes to enjoy the attention.
'She's been better since she spoke to you,' she says, moving her head in the direction of Allie and the others. 'She's a good person, y'know.'
He smiles, nods and mumbles a few platitudes, waiting for her to continue.
'Ronnie was her whole life,' she starts. 'They were mad about each other right from their first meeting. I thought she was going to die when he was killed. Thing is, he was a good guy, and perfect for her, easy-going, smart enough, and strong but gentle. In her family you need to be strong, so she will be okay, I'm sure.'
She laughs, a bit awkwardly.
'Can I tell you a story?' she asks.
He grins at her, pulls a seat across.
'My family moved to Glasgow when I was thirteen. I come from furryboots country, up near Aberdeen.'
He raises his eyebrows in a question.
She laughs again, but more naturally this time.
'That's the first question we ask anybody up there,' she grins. 'Furryboots ye fae? Where do you come from?'
He laughs with her now, and she goes on.
'I had a hard time at school, partly because I was a new girl, partly because I was a teuchter with a funny accent, and partly because, well, I was an early developer.'
She blushes, looks down at her very well formed figure.

'Yes, even then, so I got bullied by the girls and tormented by the boys. One day after school, it was pouring, what a surprise, so I was waiting for the bus instead of walking. Three boys came into the shelter and started at me, first teasing, then tugging my hair, then touching me.'

She pauses, remembering.

'I was trapped, surrounded, terrified, when I heard this deafening roar.

LEAVE HER ALONE!

We all looked and there was this tiny girl about four feet tall, and maybe six stone soaking wet. I'd seen her in our English class, but we'd never spoken.

The guys turned towards her, starting to laugh, making some vile comments in foul language about pygmies and dwarves and stuff.

WHAT IS YOUR PROBLEM? ARE YOU ALL RETARDED OR WHAT?

They were a bit stunned, as I was, until she spoke again.

MY NAME IS ALLIE SIMPSON. I'M RAB'S WEE SISTER.

The boys lost all their bravado right there.

I swear I could hear the wheels turning in their heads as they looked for a way to save face, but they were clearly terrified.

GET OUT OF HERE NOW!

She pointed, and they left in a hurry.

She was all smiles at me.

"You're Joni, aren't you?" she said, in a quite normal voice. "I see you in English. I can't really be doing with that Shakespeare, can you?"

I stare at her, trying to speak, trying to work out what just happened.

"Don't worry," she said. "They won't bother you again, my brother's a bit of a maddie, and a bit of a legend around here. But," she said, putting on a broad Glasgow accent. "Ye'll need tae learn tae talk proper an that."
I started to laugh, and we hugged each other, and we've been friends ever since.'

'So she was sort of…' Sensei says, indicating a height just above Vidock's head. 'And built like a racing pencil?'
He is struggling to reconcile this with the somewhat flabby girl he knows.
Joni laughs again.
'Yep, until she was fifteen, then she grew about ten feet in a year, and she got bumps and curves and a figure to die for. And she's beautiful inside, she's a great person, I love her, love that she's my friend. And, y'know, even when she was with Ronnie, she never forgot me, like some do.'
She nods to herself, thinking.
'When he died, she just broke, I wasn't sure she'd ever get over it. Then she found out about the baby and she was a total mess, really happy she'd have a bit of him forever and really sad he'd never know. But she was getting stronger, okay she was still eating loads of crap, but getting better, and then this.'
She waves an arm nowhere in particular
'Tell you something else. Because she's usually quiet, and thoughtful, and I'm the bubbly blonde, most folk think I'm dumb. But I'm actually a lot smarter than I look' – she laughs again – 'I'm at the uni, so you could say I'm the brains of the outfit!'
She pauses again, and he suddenly realises where she's going

with this.

'Ronnie was like Steve, I think, solid, dependable, somebody you could trust,' she says. 'Not like her brother, he was different. Nothing worried him, nothing scared him, I'm not sure anything touched him. He was more like you.'

They stare at each other for a few moments, suddenly uncomfortable.

Because he knows what she's going to say next.

'Stick with Steve,' he says at last. 'You're right, you can trust him, he'll keep you both safe.'

'I like you,' she says.

26

That night the consensus is that it's the turn of Sensei to tell a story.
You must have done…
Have you ever killed...
Wheesht! You can't ask that…
Well, nearly been killed...

'Okay,' he says. 'But no war stories. I'll tell you a wee thing that happened long ago, when I was still in my teens, a bit rough, and living in Glasgow.'

'We're on Great Western Road, high above the River Kelvin.
I think most of you know the area.
Nice suit, I say.
The guy with the nice suit and the briefcase stops halfway across the bridge.
He doesn't have much choice, Wee Tam is right in front of him.
Thanks, he says, trying to manoeuvre his way around Wee Tam.
This is harder than it sounds, because Wee Tam is not called Wee Tam because he's in any way diminutive.
No, he's called Wee Tam because his dad was Big Tam.
Wee Tam is a few inches taller than me, so maybe six feet four, and built along the lines of a bomb shelter.
You a lawyer, I say to the guy.

Um, no, accountant, he says, looking longingly over my shoulder, perhaps towards the now impossibly distant wine bar.
Even better, I say, that's good, eh, Tam?
Aye, says Wee Tam.
Why, says the guy with perhaps understandable suspicion.
Numbers, I say, you know about numbers. So, tell me, how far down is the river, d'you reckon?
Taking a step further away from the parapet, he peers out.
Maybe fifty feet, he says.
So if I drop something off here, how long till it hits the water, I ask him, quite pleasantly.
He gulps, tries again to escape, but Wee Tam is tight on him.
Couple of seconds, he squeaks.
Got your stop watch, Tam, I ask.
Aye, says Wee Tam, who could communicate wonderfully with just that single grunted syllable.
Is that your briefcase, I ask the guy.
Take it, he yelps, thrusting it at me and galloping off back the way he came.
I shrug, look at Wee Tam.
I only wanted to borrow a pencil, I say.'

He bows to acknowledge the laughter, but avoids the many questions that get asked, saying he needs to take Vidock out. Steve catches his eye, makes a wry expression, and shakes his head in disbelief.
Cathy meets him at the door.
'You're a man of many talents,' she says. 'But it's very clear

that lying isn't one of them! That was a real cop-out, wasn't it?'
He laughs and tells her it might have been slightly fabricated, then tries to move past her.
But she is persistent, catches hold of his arm.
'So where's your friend Wee Tam now?' she asks. 'Or at least before all this happened, hmm?'
Her eyes study his reaction as he feels his face tighten.
He wonders how she reads him so easily.
This is not a conversation he wants to have.
In fact it's not a conversation he has ever had.
He decides brutality is his friend here.
'His real name is Chester,' he says. 'And I haven't seen him for a while, not since the time I broke both his legs.'
She steps back, staring at him, and he slips past her into the night.
Vidock pauses at the road, sniffing the night air, then his tail droops and he follows the man to the shoreline.
As he goes off to do what a dog's gotta do, Sensei's mind wanders back to Chester, and the last time he saw him.

27

We're a team, just the two of us, and we're pretty close to the best.

I have superior weapons and fighting skills, Chester has brains, contacts and ambition.

We're making big money for hits, hits that very few others can do.

We take out gangsters and thugs, and political monsters who bleed dry their countries, and their people.

We kill bad people.

We have ethics, we have morals.

Or so I think.

He tells me our next target.

This time it's a political figure in Europe, not a bad person, but with ambitious opponents.

She's married, she's got children.

'This is wrong,' I tell Chester. 'I'm not doing it.'

'If we don't do it,' he says, 'then somebody else will, and they'll be rich.'

I flatly refuse.

I maybe can't protect the whole world, but I don't have to make it worse than it already is.

'I've accepted the contract,' he confesses. 'We can't back out now.'

'We can,' I say, 'and I do.'

'We don't murder good people, family people, for money,' I argue. 'If we do then we're no better than the scum we've killed.'

Chester has a huge house, with acres of grounds, and my Aston Martin's parked in his drive-way, nose on to his Bentley.

I'm still shaking my head in disgust and disbelief as I start the engine.

He steps in front of me, points his gun, a Smith and Wesson Special from the 1950s.

'No one walks out on me,' he roars.

I lower the window, tell him to cool it, to reconsider.

He bellows that this is the doorway to the big time, to $10 million contracts.

'Goodbye,' I tell him.

I'm betting that he won't shoot his oldest, his only, friend.

I lose my bet.

The windscreen shatters, and the bullet crashes through my shoulder as I move instinctively down and to the side.

I hit the accelerator, release the clutch.

To this day I'm still not sure if I deliberately went forward, rather than reverse.

I crushed his legs between the two cars.

He has never walked since.

28

We arrive at the damaged section of road early the following morning, and Steve, as usual, directs operations.
The rain is lighter today, but the grassy verges are still tricky to negotiate.
He supervises the passage of the ladies and the bikes while Jack and I lug the scooters around and onto the bridge.
At the other side of the River Garry the A87 forks off the A82 and heads west.
While we mount up in our usual formation – Steve with Allie, the Frasers together as always, then Jack with Joni, and Cathy and me bringing up the rear, but on bikes now – Vidock, for the first time, heads off before us, ignoring the turn-off and continuing straight ahead.
Steve laughs and points, calls him back and then, when he is ignored, he turns to me, all grins.
'Looks like the pooch doesn't fancy our road,' he says.
But I hardly hear him, I am staring at my dog and my heart is breaking.
'Off you go,' I mutter to Steve. 'All of you. Cathy, go with Jack, I'll catch up in a couple of minutes, okay?'
'I'll wait…' she starts, but I cut her off.
'Please, just do it,' I am dismissive of her concerned look.
I lay my bike on the ground and walk after Vidock, who has stopped, and is sitting looking back at me, ignoring the others who call to him as they swing into the A87 and disappear from sight.

I crouch beside him with a lump in my throat.
He has that incredible sense of direction that so many animals possess, which is a source of mystery to us humans.
He knows that we have been heading north, more or less, since we left Troon, except when we crossed the Clyde and, like now, turned west.
We had a conversation back then but, I am ashamed to say, I was less than honest with him at that point.
Since then we have, other than for brief detours, followed the same road all the way.
Now we are leaving it, and changing direction.
He knows now that we can't be followed.
'She isn't coming,' I tell him, rubbing his head and ruffling his ears.
He doesn't respond, just looks away.
I get to my feet and walk back to my bike, push it round the corner.
I whistle sharply, slap my thigh.
He just sits and stares at me with flat ears.
He has never disobeyed me in his life.
I feel the tears in my eyes.
I dump the bike, go back to him, kneel and hug him, tell him we have to go on.
I hear a noise behind me, see Cathy has come back and is staring open-mouthed.
We both get up, he looks back across the bridge for the last time, then walks off, ignoring me, and goes to Cathy.
For the second time in a few minutes I cut her off as she starts

to speak.

'What...?'

'Go!' I say. 'I'll be right behind you.'

But I push my hair back behind my ears, remembering other fingers doing it, but more gently, and stand for an eternity gazing southwards across the River Garry, to where the road curves out of sight.

I know too that she can never follow.

29

I am roused from my reverie by the sound of footsteps, erratic footsteps, coming down the A82 from the north.
I am unworried, so I don't bother to move towards the bike, where my weapons are.
A man totters round the bend only 40 or 50 metres away.
It seems he's trying to run, but is barely managing a stagger.
As he approaches I see he has blood on his face and he's about to collapse.
I move to meet him, but he lets out a wail and tries to pass me on my right-hand side.
I catch his arm, and he falls helplessly into my arms.
I lower him carefully to the ground, and see that his face is bruised and cut as though he has been in a fist fight.
He is heavily-built, overweight, but not seriously so, and probably in his fifties.
'They're after me,' he gasps. 'They're going to kill me.'
'Just rest a minute,' I say. 'Breathe slowly, relax.'
He opens his eyes wide, fear shining out of them, and clutches my arm.
'We have to hide,' he says. 'They'll kill us both.'
'Relax,' I say again. 'Nobody's getting killed.'
But I hear a noise, turn my head, and see a bicycle hurtle into sight.
I lie him flat and stand to face the newcomer, who throws his bike to the side and pulls a handgun.
He is red-faced with exertion and anger, tall and lean, in his

thirties, and wearing denims and a nondescript shirt.
He approaches slowly, waving the pistol in a supposedly threatening manner.
'Hi,' I say. 'How you doing?'
'On the ground,' he shouts. 'Face down, now!'
'No,' I say.
'What?' He stops, confused. 'Get down or I'll shoot.'
'I don't think so,' I say. 'You don't know me, and you don't look like a cold-blooded killer. Let's talk.'
He stares at me, unsure of himself now that things aren't going according to his script.
'I'm taking him with me,' he says. 'And I'll kill you if you try to stop me.'
'C'mon,' I say. 'Drop the drama and tell me what's happening here, see if we can sort it out without anyone getting hurt.'
'Who are you anyway?' he demands, still gesturing with his weapon. 'Are you a friend of his?'
'Never met him till he appeared round that bend and fell at my feet. So what's he supposed to have done?'
'Supposed to have done? He's guilty as sin! I'm taking him back up to Drumnadrochit to be dealt with.'
The guy on the ground half rises, starts to splutter his innocence.
'Shut it, Clark,' the other shouts. 'You know what you did, and you're coming back to face the music.'
Clark grabs at my arm, pulls himself up.
'They're just jealous,' he says. 'Because I've got money and the women love me. Tell the truth, Gregor, tell the guy how

you framed me out of jealousy.'

Gregor jerks the gun up again.

'I should just kill you here in the road,' he snaps. 'You deserve to die in the gutter.'

'Okay,' I say. 'Cut the crap and tell me what you're fighting about. And' – I say this to Gregor – 'nobody is killing anyone here today, understand that. Clark, what did you do to make folk this angry?'

'Nothing,' he says. 'I swear it. I let them into my hotel up on Loch Ness, and they started to take over.'

'Your hotel!' splutters Gregor. 'You just moved in ten minutes before we got there, and wanted to charge us for accommodation! And then you wanted our women!'

'Ha,' says Clark. 'You all got angry because your women saw that I was the man, the only real man in the place!'

Gregor looks at me, anger and frustration in his eyes.

'He's a liar, and much worse where women are concerned,' he says through his teeth. 'The things he tried...'

Over his shoulder I see Jack charge into view, shoulders hunched over his handlebars.

'Right, Gregor,' I say, moving towards him. 'Give me the gun before someone gets hurt.'

'Get back!' he screams, jumping back and to the side.

He still hasn't seen Jack, who launches himself from the bike onto Gregor's back.

They crash to the ground to the muffled sound of a shot.

I curse violently, and grab Jack.

'You okay?' I ask. 'Are you hit?'

'Just a bit stunned,' he grins. 'I saw him wave the gun, thought he was going to shoot you.'

I reach for Gregor who is lying on his face, unmoving.

I turn him onto his side and see the hole in his stomach, blood pouring out.

I rip my shirt off, telling Jack and Clark to do the same, and press it to the wound, knowing that it is pointless.

'What an idiot,' whispers Gregor. 'I'm so stupid, I don't know anything about guns. I'm going to die now, yeah?'

'Save your breath,' I tell him. 'I'll see what I can do.'

'Don't trust him,' he croaks, then murmurs something I don't catch, but I think I hear the word 'women'.

Then he dies.

Clark gets to his feet, and reaches for the pistol.

'Great work, guys, thanks a lot,' he grins.

I stand and smack him across the mouth with the back of my hand, pretty sure that I've screwed up again, and that the wrong person died here today.

'Get the gun, Jack,' I say.

When he doesn't move I see that he is bent at the knees and waist, long arms wrapped around himself, and shaking violently.

'I killed him,' he forces the words out. 'I killed him, I killed him.'

30

I am outside the Loch Ness Inn at Drumnadrochit, just off the A82 and only a half mile from the banks of one of Scotland's most beautiful and most famous landmarks.
And home of the celebrated Monster.
I ring the bell then step back so that I can be seen from any of the front windows.
My arms and hands are spread wide, like a goalkeeper facing a penalty kick.
The front door opens a crack, the barrel of a shotgun appears, and a voice tells me to get on the ground.
I sigh and shake my head.
'I'm not carrying,' I call back. 'I bring news of Gregor.'
'Get on the ground,' the voice shouts again. 'Get on the ground before I shoot.'
'Forget it,' I say, and walk back the way I came.
'Wait! Wait!' This time it's a woman's voice. 'Where is Gregor? Is he with you?'
I stop and look back.
A woman, barefoot, but wearing denims and a white smock, has come out and, ignoring the steady drizzle, walks towards me.
Her dark skin and long raven-black hair, which is held back in a sort of bandana, tells me that her family origins are from the Indian subcontinent.
'Kirsty, come back here,' the first voice shouts again. 'You don't know who he is, it might be a trap!'

The woman, who looks about thirty, slim but strong, stops a few metres away from where I have again spread my arms. As she starts to speak the man with the 12-gauge comes up behind her, followed by another woman and two more men. She pauses, then speaks over her shoulder.

'Shut up, William,' she says. 'Let's listen to what the guy has to say.'

William is a nervous-looking individual, probably late forties, small and thin but with a paunch. He is wearing what I can only describe as golf trousers, with an ugly quasi-tartan pattern, a two-tone Polo shirt, and hiking boots.

The second woman, significantly older, is wearing denims and a check shirt, while the older of the other men is similarly dressed.

The youngest man, scarcely out of his teens, is wearing cargo shorts and a tee shirt.

They seem unaware that it is October in Scotland, probably less that 10 C, and wet.

I figure that the hotel must have excellent central heating.

'I told you to get on the ground,' shouts William.

'Shut up,' Kirsty snaps at him. 'Let's hear what he has to say.'

I hold her gaze, nod, and ask that William stops pointing his shotgun at me.

She turns, pulls it from his hands, drops it on the ground and puts her foot on it.

'Not another word,' she tells him, then turns back to me.

'So where is Gregor?' she asks.

I take a deep breath.

'He's dead,' I tell her. 'Clark appeared with Gregor chasing him, we had a struggle, and his gun went off accidentally. The bullet went through his stomach. He died quickly.'

'I knew it!' William leaps for the gun again and Kirsty slaps him across the back of his head.

Not hard, but enough to stop him.

'Did Clark shoot him?' she asks. 'Because if he did…'

'No, it was my fault, I tried to stop him from shooting Clark and his gun went off. He blamed himself, but I take responsibility for it. It should never have happened.'

They all stare at me, the older woman wiping her hand across her eyes.

'Where is he now?' asks Kirsty.

'Just a few metres down the road,' I tell her. 'I thought he deserved to be buried by his friends.'

'We hardly knew each other,' she says. 'But he was a good guy, tried to protect us against that prick Clark. By the way, where is he now?'

'He's long gone,' I lie. 'He'll be near Fort William by now, I reckon.'

'Good riddance,' she says. 'What a scumbag. Can you show us where Gregor is, please?'

As we walk back down the road to where I'd left Gregor's corpse, she tells me about the events of the past few days, and my heart sinks.

The men lift the body and carry him to the hotel, but Kirsty lingers with me.

We discuss what has happened to the world, but neither of us can shed any new light on what the other already knows.

She tells me they hid when the soldiers passed from Inverness, and again as a number of travellers, almost all male, headed north.

There is something about this woman that makes me think of the past, and maybe the future.

'Um,' I say, somewhat awkwardly. 'You don't look too much like a Kirsty.'

She laughs, delighted, and tells me that her father was Indian, but her mother was a Scot.

'You want to stay a while?' she asks. 'This is probably not the worst place to be right now.'

'Thanks,' I say, 'but there are things I have to do first.'

'First,' she says, her voice making it a question. 'And then?'

I pause.

'Depending on how things work out,' I say, watching her expression, 'I could maybe come back this way.'

Her eyes brighten with her smile.

'I'd like that,' she says.

She stretches up, grasping my arms, and kisses my cheek.

'Take care,' she says.

I lift my hand and turn south again.

31

The rain has stopped as I remount the bicycle that I had concealed back at the A82 and head back towards Invergarry, wondering about the reception I'll get from the others when I finally rejoin the group.
There was strong resistance from most of them when I announced I was taking Gregor's body to Drumnadrochit.
The two girls and the Frasers felt it was an unnecessary risk, and a dangerous loss of time.
Steve held his counsel, watching the debate from the sidelines.
Jack felt he should do it, or at least accompany me.
Clark ridiculed the idea, saying that there was nothing to be gained from it, that Gregor wasn't worth the effort.
Cathy bit her lip and scowled at me, with an occasional angry shake of the head.
I told them to stay close to each other and that I'd rejoin them at our planned overnight stop.
And, to his utter disgust, I sent Vidock with them.
Once I was on the bike Steve helped me strap Gregor to my back.
'You sure about this?' he asked.
'Watch him,' I indicated Clark. 'Make sure he is unarmed and in front of Jack and Cathy at all times.'
And I tell her to keep Vidock close.
Now it is already afternoon, and I am 26 miles from where I left them over three hours ago.
After that I have another 35 miles to go before I reach tonight's

agreed rendezvous.

Although I ache all over from having Gregor on my back on the way up, I lean on the pedals and start to pound down the road. The hiss of my tyres on the wet tarmac is the only sound that breaks the silence as I look down at the vast cold grey beauty of Loch Ness lying low to my left.

Then the rain starts again, heavier than before, and the wind blows in from the west.

It has not been a good day.

Another man died, unnecessarily.

I miss my dog, who is hurting.

Kirsty is in my thoughts too, trying to make a space where there is no room.

I know I'll never return here.

32

It is already dark when he reaches Kintail Lodge, their planned stop, which is another high quality hotel, with a spectacular setting on the shores of Loch Duich, one of many long, bony fingers of the Atlantic Ocean reaching into Scotland's rugged interior.

The wind has cleared much of the cloud cover, and the glitter of moonlight on the water, surrounded by the vast darkness of the Kintail Hills, does much to ease his soul.

When he goes inside the others have already eaten, and Steve is about to tell a story.

They ask for his news, but he suggests that Steve go ahead and entertain them while he eats.

'Well, okay,' says Steve. 'I've got a wee tale you might find amusing.'

'I don't hate anybody, and that's the truth, but for Billy Fisher I could make an exception.

We've got a bit of history.

Sworn enemies since school, and that's not yesterday.

I've always wanted to punch his lamps in, even if that's not usually my sort of thing.

But he'll never fight, he snipes, he runs away, a right wee sleekit so-and-so.

Anyway, I've met this girl.

Well, a lady, actually, very classy.

I'm heading for the subway at Partick, that'll take me into

Buchanan Street.
I've booked us for lunch in the Rogano, the best place in town.
I've got flowers and everything.
This is the important date, I really want to impress her.'
'Hoping to get lucky?' asks Joni, and everyone laughs.
'Hmmff.
So I'm strolling along Dumbarton Road, nearly at the station, in my best suit.
I hear a horn, turn to see a white van swerve towards me.
It sends a great puddle of muddy water swooshing over me.
I am drenched from head to toe.
I see Fisher's jeering face hanging out of the window, his hand with one finger raised in the international salute.
I decide to head up to your place, Mrs F, but I'm really furious, looking for a fight.
I find one almost immediately.
I bump into Gordy McQueen, who, understandably, starts to snigger.
I throw him through the window of a butcher's shop.
Some mayhem ensues, resulting in the butcher emerging from his shop, understandably irritated, and grasping in his big mitt a meat cleaver, which he hurls at us.
Now Gordy's really a friend, so I pull him down and the cleaver wheechs over our heads.
The sound of the crash makes us pause.
Fisher's van is concertinaed against the front of a number 2 bus, which was en route to Faifley, out at Clydebank.
Quite a chunk of his ear seems to be missing, sliced off by that

flying cleaver.
Trust that idiot to came back at just the wrong moment!
I'm still laughing when the cops arrive.
As they slap handcuffs on just about everybody between Partick Cross and Thornwood, a taxi pulls up.
My date gets out, assesses the situation, and shakes her head.
Then she starts to laugh too.
She picks up the rather bedraggled flowers.
Call me, she says.'

33

The next morning Vidock and I leave Kintail Lodge on what will hopefully be the last leg of our journey before we bed down for the winter.

The others will follow in one hour.

Vidock is wearing a red flag.

If he returns to them wearing it, they need to prepare for a fight.

Our job is to ensure that our chosen destination is safe, or to make it so.

We turn off the A87 at Balmacara and follow a country road which soon becomes a single track, and leads through some of Scotland's most spectacular countryside, the sheer beauty of which would normally be enough to lift the lowest of spirits.

But my thoughts are on the previous night's discussion, when I updated the group on my trip to Drumnadrochit.

The reaction was mainly positive, with a couple of exceptions.

Clark, of course, argued volubly that I had been conned, that the people in the Loch Ness Inn were liars and thieves, and we should have nothing to do with them.

Much more surprising was Cathy, who seemed quite resistant to the idea of new blood joining us, with comments like 'done okay so far' and 'unknown quantity'.

She even asked 'how many can you and Steve reasonably defend in a crisis', which raised a few eyebrows and voices around the room.

I wonder about her reasons as I scan the countryside for signs of life but, apart from the usual choir of birdsong, there is nothing.

The road climbs and falls through the rugged but verdant landscape, until we pass a railway station and a modern high school on our left, and from there we descend rapidly into the village.

We pass a much older primary school and a church, before arriving at a parking area on the shores of Loch Carron, with breathtaking views of the Applecross Peninsula on the far side.

I pause here, staring out across the water, and feel much of the heaviness lift from my heart.

This is Plockton, often described as The Jewel of the Highlands.

However, we haven't chosen it for its scenery, but because of its strategically defensible position.

Other than minor tracks, this is the only road access.

It is not a place that anyone would wander into by accident.

There are clear views over the loch, so we will have advance warning of any approach by water.

Short of finding a habitable but uninhabited island, this is as good as it gets, and islands have their own problems.

Vidock moves along Harbour Street on full alert.

I unroll a white flag on a stick and hold it up, then drop down onto the shore and follow on a parallel course.

This gives me a wider view of the buildings, which are stone-built and solid.

The Plockton Hotel looks like a probable headquarters so, seeing that the door is open, I signal to Vidock to check inside.

He re-emerges minutes later and continues his search.
Further along, when gardens cause the shoreline and road to diverge, I move up behind my scout and follow 10 paces behind him.
Just as I am ready to believe the town is deserted he stops dead, crouches, and looks back at me.
Almost immediately a voice tells me 'Stop right there!'
I stop, my hands in their familiar open wide position, the flag held high.
'We come in peace,' I say. 'We're looking for a safe place to winter.'
'On the ground,' shouts the voice, and I almost laugh.
I whistle a signal and Vidock turns his head with a long-suffering look, then lies down on the damp ground.
'That's it,' I call back. 'I don't plan to get any wetter, I don't have a change of clothes here!'
I can tell that the voice is an older person's, and I don't feel threatened.
The accent is what used to be described as BBC English, all those years ago when the broadcaster was still deserving of respect.
I tell him I am armed, but that I will lay my pistol on the ground and step away from it.
'Then you can come out and we can talk,' I say. 'I'll tell you about the people in our group, and you can decide if you'll let us stay. We won't bother you in any way, and we'll provide extra security.'
An elderly man, stooped and wizened, comes out carrying an

enormous shotgun which might be older than he is.
I'm trying not to smile when he brandishes it, but I'm saved when a woman emerges behind him and tells him to stop being silly.
'Put that thing down and let the boy talk,' she says. 'Let's hear what he has to say.'
She goes to Vidock, bends and scratches his ear.
'You can get up now, doggie,' she says. 'He's got no bullets for that thing anyway.'
He gets up, saunters back to me, and shakes the water from his coat onto my face.
'Come away in, son,' the woman laughs. 'I'll make us a nice cup of tea and you can tell us what's going on.'
The man looks a bit embarrassed.
He takes the gun in his left hand and holds out his right.
'Rick Page,' he says. 'Sorry about that, can't be too careful these days.'
He is standing straight now, and I see he is not as old as I first thought, and surprisingly fit looking.
He sees me assessing him and tells me he's a runner.
'Well, I was,' he says. 'I haven't been further than the end of the road since this happened. Come in and tell us what you know.'
'One moment,' I say. 'The rest of our group isn't far behind us.'
I take the red flag off Vidock and give him the white one.
'Go get Steve,' I tell him.

34

That evening is a riot.
Rick and Bet are quite the double act, and she keeps prompting him to tell his tales.
'We've been worried ever since it happened,' she says. 'Well I know I have. I thought I'd have to listen to him for the rest of my life! Or just get out that old blunderbuss and shoot one of us!'
He tells the group he's from London, but he worked near Glasgow for an American computer company. When they shut up shop in Scotland he got a good redundancy payment and they moved up here and bought a house.
'As far away as possible from those thieving bastards in Westminster,' he says. 'I voted Yes the last time…'
'No politics,' his wife interrupts him. 'Tell them about your time with the Yanks, that's funnier than the Tories, and more believable. And no swearing, there are young ladies here!'
He pretends to sulk, but he is grinning behind his hand.

'I worked for a company I'll call MAD, the Mighty American Dream. They built computers and tried to import US philosophies to darkest Ayrshire. I developed software, and worked on the most significant project they'd ever attempted in Europe.
This is where my tale begins…'
And Rick switches to a comic Cockney accent.

'I'm sitting at my desk, staring in consternation at the smiling face of the chubby little man standing beside me.

Do I want to what? I ask him.

I'm going over to the warehouse. Do you want to chum me? Less than life itself, I think to myself. Hell, I'm a married man! Aloud I say I'm, uh, kind of, uh, you know, busy here, Jim, thanks all the same.

I continue to stab brutally at the long-suffering keyboard on my desk.

There's more to life than just work, my colleague announces smugly, as though it were an original thought, the first from Personnel, sorry, Human Resources, in over a decade.

Yeah, but I don't think that my lords and masters would pay me to sit in the pub and get pissed, and that is about the only other thing I'm good at, I tell him. This crap software doesn't just write itself, you know.

But Jim's one of these guys you can't embarrass, he is unshakeable.

So, five minutes later, I find myself strolling in the direction of the warehouse with my new 'chum', Jim from Personnel, sorry, Human Resources.

Hell, I effing hate Personnel, I think, then stop abruptly, wondering if I said it aloud. But Jim continues blithely on his way, blethering away non-stop about the greatness of the company.

And the best thing is, of course, the freedom, he pontificates. Here we fu... effing go, I think. He has managed to avoid the topic for about thirty effing seconds, but we're there now.

Yes, everyone can dress however they like, wear whatever they choose. Not like the old days, eh, when you wore a tie if you worked in the office.

I stop and spread my arms wide. I am fu... absolutely resplendent in dark 3-piece suit, white shirt, dark tie and black leather shoes. I know that this is the issue, the entire point of the fatuous Jim's visit.

Yeah, right, and this is what I choose to wear. Pretty damn neat, eh?

Well, yes, of course, you look very smart, but that isn't really the point, is it?

So tell me, I say, in simple language, so that even a Sassenach can understand, what it is you don't like. You, or rather your big dipstick curly-headed crony, told me at my interview that everyone was free to dress however they wanted. When I started here, you – Personnel, that is, sorry, Human Resources – made a real effort to tell me, guess what, that everyone was free to dress, yep, however they wanted. So now I am being distracted from doing my job so that you can tell me what exactly? That I can dress however I want to?

But you are missing the point! Jim is clearly exasperated. You are alienating yourself from the rest of the plant. No one else wears a suit, it's just you being different!

So, I say, determined to make this as much fun as possible for me, and as uncomfortable as possible for this bampot, if I understand you correctly, I can dress however I want as long as I dress exactly like everyone else. Is that what you're saying?

No! Of course not! He means yes. But it would be better if you did, don't you think?

Jim is desperately trying to be reasonable with what he considers to be a wretched upstart.

Then people wouldn't perceive you as being different, he finishes, on a note of triumph.

Perception.

Oh dear lord, this is it, the word that epitomises MAD's philosophy.

It doesn't matter what you do, or how well you do it, only how you are 'perceived' (Rick makes finger quotes) by your peers in this 'single status' company.

Which, of course, is all just hoo-hah. It is single status, but only the managers have private offices. And go to company meetings. And such like.

Jim, if I wanted to dress like a fu… like an effing lumberjack then I would get a job chopping down fucking trees. (Sorry, ladies, ordinary trees.) Check shirts and denims are just not my look.

He looks so crestfallen that I take pity on the poor sod.

I make a last effort, knowing that it is an exercise in futility.

I have spent the last five years, I say, working as a systems consultant. I met with CEOs, FDs, bankers and lawyers. I put systems into the Edinburgh financial sector. So you see, I had to dress professionally. I have a wardrobe full of suits.

I pause, try to smile at his exasperated face.

Look, I say, I'll make a deal with you. I won't criticise your ludicrous dress sense and you don't criticise mine. Any of my

'peers' who have a problem can either pop round for a chat, and I'll explain things, or they can go screw themselves. What do you say?
Well, I'm disappointed, he says, but not really surprised. I've been told you have a problem with authority.
This dress thing is nothing to do with authority – quite the reverse. Can't you see that I am the only person who is actually adopting the company philosophy, and not just blindly following the herd?
Aye, right, typical! Jim is angry now, all pretence at the 'chum' bit is out the window. Everybody's out of step except you. I don't think that you're going to fit in here, do you?
And I think to myself Fuck a duck, what am I doing here?'
When they stop laughing Hugh speaks.
'But you didn't leave, did you?'
Rick and Bet look at each other and start laughing again.
'No,' he says. 'We put in that system, which ran their entire European manufacturing business, took nearly two years. But we did it in phases, so they saw some benefits early, and they got off my case.
But that's not the funny bit.
After that I asked for a transfer, and they gave me a three-year two-way contract in France, in a place called Valbonne, on the Côte d'Azur, not far from Nice.
Company house, company car, upset allowance, blah, blah, blah! The wife here even got a sun tan! After three years they paid for us to come back, then they gave me my redundancy!'

They all laugh again, then Rick shakes his head.
'All that cash doesn't mean much now, does it?'

35

When I see Steve's face I know that trouble is coming.
It's late morning, the sky is blue, the sun is sparkling across the flat surface of the loch.
The air is cool but we are all sweating.
We are burying the dead.
Rick has shown us where new housing is being built to the north of the village.
Excavations have already taken place, so we have a ready-made grave.
We've 'borrowed' a dumper truck and we're going from house to house uplifting the bodies.
Because of the cold weather decomposition is not yet too drastic, although those in centrally heated homes are less pleasant to handle, even when there is no longer any functioning electricity.
We are treating them with as much respect as possible, and Jules, Allie and Bet plan a memorial service.
Every time Cathy and I cross paths she looks at me with hard eyes.
I have no idea what I've done to upset her.
But that's a problem for later.
Steve went out on a mission and has clearly failed.
We walk down to the shoreline and he faces me, shoulders slumped.
'Sorry,' he says. 'I couldn't do it.'
'You let him go,' I say, a statement, not a question.

He nods, and I sigh.

'I should have listened to you,' he says. 'But I felt it was my responsibility.'

He rubs his face with his hands.

'Back there in Tyndrum,' he says, 'that was the first time I ever fired a shot in anger.'

'No one could tell that,' I lie. 'It didn't show, you handled it perfectly. That's when the others knew you were their leader.'

'You should be,' he argues. 'But I know what you said, and I respect that.'

I squeeze his shoulder.

'He went south, yes?' I ask.

'Yep. I told him he could go west to Skye, or south, but that if he went back to Drumnadrochit you would certainly hunt him down. He shook at that thought, he's terrified of you.'

'With good reason. We need to work out timescales.'

'Maybe he won't, y'know,' says Steve, but we both know it's not true.

Because this is what happened during the night, in Joni's words.

36

'I wakened up with his hand over my mouth.

It's okay, he said, it's me. I got your signals.

What bloody signals, I thought, and I tried to wriggle away from him.

He switched on the bedside lamp, and put a finger to his lips to signal that I should be quiet.

Then he started to pull at the bedclothes, trying to get them off me.

It took me a wee while to realise what he was trying to do, and try to stop him, so at first I didn't understand the noise.

Then he turned his head and leapt back, and I realised it was Vidock growling.

He moved towards us, really low to the floor, like he was ready to leap, and his lips were pulled back, and I never knew he had so many teeth!

Clark was right in the corner by now, cowering and shaking like a leaf.

That's when I noticed the stink.

I didn't know what it was at first, then I realised it was, um, urine.

He had wet himself, peed his breeks, as we say in Glasgow!

Call the dog off, he was whining like a wee lassie, I didn't mean any harm, I thought you wanted me to come and keep you company.

Then you two came charging in and I just about collapsed with relief.

When Steve moved forward you caught his arm.
And you asked me if I thought Vidock deserved some fun, which I think made Clark smell even worse!
Then you let Steve drag him out, quite roughly, just like he deserved.
When you told us about Drumnadrochit and the people there, you didn't tell us everything, did you?
You knew stuff about him, and you still gave him a chance.
And that's why you told Vidock we were friends, and did that wee ceremony, isn't it?
And why you left him to guard me, just in case.
Okay, I need to go and give him lots of big hugs now.
But I'd rather hug you anytime.'

37

'MacDougall!' I shout.

He turns in surprise and I shoot him in the chest.

I do the same to the guy behind him, and find I am facing Clark.

He throws down his weapon and stretches his arms towards the low clouds.

I hear the rat-tat-tat of Steve's SA80 on full automatic as he comes out behind MacDougall's group, and the fight is over.

He marches across the now familiar bridge over the River Garry, stepping past the two bodies and their fallen bicycles.

'Three down at my side,' he says. 'Why is this piece of trash not dead yet?'

'Wait guys,' stammers Clark. 'It's not what you think, they made me do it…'

'Shut up,' snaps Steve. 'We knew you'd be back, we just weren't sure if you'd come to us or go to Drumnadrochit.'

'Oh not you guys, no, I like you guys, you're the good guys, I know that. I just told them about Drumnadrochit, they are thieves and liars, they tried to stitch me up with your lot, didn't they! But I'll tell you something else that'll make you happy. Now you've got rid of this shower of wasters we can be kings in Fort William! Our own town, all the women just for ourselves.'

Steve looks at me, I nod, and he shoots Clark point blank in the chest, sending him backwards over the low wall into the River Garry.

'If I'd done that the first time I would've saved five lives,' he says.

'Yeah, and if I'd listened to Gregor none of this crap would've happened,' I answer.

'Then you wouldn't have met Kirsty, would you?' he grins.

I stare at him.

'What are you on about?

'Cathy told me you've got a thing for Kirsty.'

'Cathy? How the hell would she know?'

'C'mon man, she's a woman, and she's spent a lot of time with you. And she's smart, easily the smartest of our wee collection of oddballs, she's got a degree and all sorts. That means she can probably read you like a kiddies' picture book! Also, you're her hero.'

He pauses here, looks embarrassed.

'We all know we couldn't have made it without you – no, don't argue, it's true and you know it – but she's the only one who's seen everything that you do. How your eyes never rest, how you instinctively move ahead to protect when something concerns you. Jack's mentioned that too. Hell, you even do it with me, and I'm a soldier and supposed to be the leader!'

He stops again, searching for words.

'But she reads people, it's a big part of her job, and she probably knows more about you than you can imagine. So she's possessive of you, for herself and for the whole group, and maybe a bit jealous, and worried that you'll leave us.'

I stare at him, thinking that I've been oblivious to all this. This is war, I've no room for personal feelings.

'Jeez, that was quite a speech,' Steve laughs. 'So while I'm on my soap-box I'll say this too. Way back in Tyndrum you made a promise you didn't need to. You could have walked away then and been much, much safer on your own. Now you've kept that promise, so if you ask me you're free to go.'
He looks at his feet, before speaking again.
'And what's more, I've learnt a lot from you. You always foresee situations, like when you scouted out of Tyndrum, and you devised the system with the coloured flags to make sure we wouldn't be caught out. And you explained very clearly what I was to do if Vidock brought a red! Same with MacDougall and his shower, you knew what they'd do and you had strategies to handle them. You don't want to kill but, when you think it's necessary, you don't hesitate.'
He laughs.
'Even when we got here, you crossed the bridge first, you showed me where I should hide, but let me think it was my idea, and you fired the first shots.'
'And there's one other thing,' he says, suddenly very serious. 'You're incredibly fit. I mean, I was a fair soldier, I did a bit of boxing there, and played rugby with some exceptional guys, but I've never seen anyone like you.'
He waits and, when I say nothing, he asks.
'What were you, Special Forces or something?'
I hold his gaze for a moment, then shrug.
'Or something, to be honest,' I tell him.
He nods, then half laughs and shakes his head.
'Aw jeez, we really got lucky,' he holds out his hand.

'Thank you,' he says. 'So what do you say, we'll zip up to Drumnadrochit and invite them to join us at Plockton?'
'What do you mean we, paleface?' I shake his hand and grin at him. 'If you think it's a good idea, I'll go. But it's your group, so your decision.'
'You're right,' says Steve. 'I need to get back. But yes, go get them. A few more useful bodies won't be a bad thing.'
We check out the weapons from MacDougall's crew, but there's not much that adds value to what we have.
It seems we cleared them out after the ambush at Loch Lochy. These we toss into the river, we still don't want them falling into the wrong hands.
Then we lay the bodies on their backs in a row in a field, and cover them with road signs and fence posts that we rip out of the soft earth, building a rough cairn..
'What about him,' Steve asks, nodding towards the river.
I shrug, indifferent.
'Shit, he says. 'Even he deserves some dignity in death.'
He disappears down through the trees, so I sigh and follow him.

'Want to say a few words?' he asks when we're finished.
I give a short laugh, and turn away.
We head back to our bikes at the road junction where I first encountered Clark.
Vidock is sitting there, patiently waiting for us, having played no part in the ambush other than to watch our backs.
I have rigged up a trailer for him behind my bike, because I

don't want him damaging his feet or exhausting himself running long distances at speed.
When I point to it, he turns away, pretending not to understand. Steve laughs.
'He's still not keen on his chariot, is he?'
'I'll let him stretch his legs for a bit,' I say.
We shake hands, and as Steve turns to the west, I head off north again.
Vidock bounds after me like a puppy, knowing this is the road we should have taken the first time.

An hour or so later I am standing outside the Loch Ness Inn. The door has been smashed open and the man who is not William, the older guy in denims and a check shirt, is lying inside, riddled with bullets.
His body is cold so I open his shirt and see that livor mortis has taken place, his body is livid with pooled blood just above where it is in contact with the floor.
I press his skin with my finger, but there's no discolouration, so that suggests he's been dead for at least 12 hours.
I'm no expert, and the overnight chill obviously has an effect, but my feeling is that I'm late here by maybe a day.
I do a quick search of the building.
There are no more bodies, but no one alive either.
I know they didn't go south, because they would've encountered either Steve and me or MacDougall and his men, so Inverness, less than 20 miles to the north, is the logical next stop.

As I tow Vidock up the A82 along the side of Loch Ness, lying vast and grey below, I wonder about the prescience of Cathy's words as we were leaving.
I had thought about leaving him to guard the others in Plockton, but she was adamant it wasn't necessary.
'You need him more than we do. Good luck.'

38

'Hello there!'
'Oh hello! Jeez, thank fuck, somebody else!'
'Aye, I thought I was… Oh, it's you.'
'What? Oh, it's you.'
'So, how's things?'
'How's things? Are you fucking kidding me? Everybody's dead! Have you not noticed?'
'No. Aye, it's the same where I live, they're all dead. Everybody in the street, I think, maybe the whole of Inverness.'
'Same here. Listen, I know we had a fight, like, way back when…'
'We did, yeah.'
'Wasn't really much of one, was it? I mean I'm not a scrapper, never was…'
'No, it was rubbish! Handbags at ten paces as they say, no danger of anybody getting hurt or anything. Me neither, I've never been a fighter, just had to go along with it, because, well, it was us lot and you lot, and you're one of them, like.'
'No, I'm not, I'm one of us, you're one of them!'
'Haha, aye okay, but still. A bit pointless, wasn't it?'
'Fucking stupid looking back, hardly knew each other, just different schools…'
'Aye, exactly. So where do you stay?'
'Glendoe Terrace. You?'

'Cameron Terrace.'
'Oh aye. That's a bit posh, eh?'
'Didn't make a lot of difference, did it? We're all the same now, doesn't matter where we stay or what school we went to, or where we're studying or working.'
'You working?'
'No, I'm at the uni, doing a computing course.'
'Ah, a smart bastard, eh? I'm a joiner. Well, doing my apprenticeship.'
'Good for you, aye, useful. Wish I could do things with my hands, but I'm all thumbs!'
'Wish I had a brain! So where you headed?'
'Into town, see what's happening. You?'
'Aye, same.'
'C'mon then, we might as well go in together, there might not be anybody else...'
'So, I don't remember, what's your name? '
'Graham. You?'
'Sean. Seanie, actually. That's what they call me. Seanie.'
'Okay, Seanie, you can call me Grahamie!'

39

At Dochgarroch the great loch ends, and the River Ness and the canal veer eastwards away from the A82 and run separately but in parallel until they reach the outskirts of Inverness.
Here the canal heads north-west and the road crosses it via the wonderfully-named Tomnahurich Swing Bridge, just before the roundabout with the same name.
I follow what is now Glenurquhart Road for almost a mile, pausing only to nip into a small supermarket to lift a bottle of The Famous Grouse whisky, before turning right down Bishops Road towards the river.
I hide the bike and my rucksack behind a garden hedge and saunter past the spectacular Eden Court Arts Centre where the road curves to the left.
Although there's been no sign of life until now, I bring Vidock to heel and advance with caution.
Almost immediately I see a young guy in a kilt heading towards me on the riverside walk, carrying a shotgun.
I trot back round the curve, take off my jacket, pull my shirt half out of my jeans, and empty most of the Scotch onto the ground.
I grin at Vidock who scowls at the smell of whisky.
This is something he's met before, and does not like at all.
I shrug, and get into character.
'Shtay,' I slur at him, thinking it's lucky I didn't want him to sit.
But 'sit' means relax, 'stay' means wait and watch, on alert.

Jacket in one hand, bottle in the other, I spread my arms wide and start to sing.

'*O Flower of Scotland...*'

I lurch into the middle of the road, and spot gun guy maybe 50 yards away.

'*When will we see your like again?*'

I veer across towards him, giving no indication that I see him. He tenses, swings his weapon up to waist height.

'*That fought and died for...*'

'Halt!' he shouts. 'Stop where you are!'

I pretend to have just noticed him, swing my arms to turn my body towards him.

'Hullo there,' I shout back. 'Good to see you, my friend, civilisation at last!'

I reel across to where he stands, uncertain, and I see that he's got no idea what to do.

He's older than I first thought, probably late twenties, but soft-looking, and has never held a firearm in his life.

'Are you in charge here?' I bellow at him, splashing good Grouse in all directions. 'Are you Captain of Inverness?'

'Don't come any closer,' he commands, unconvincingly, and too late.

With a drunken gesture I swing my jacket high away from me and let it fly.

As his eyes follow it, I toss the bottle and take his shotgun.

'Sorry,' I say. 'But it's okay, I'm not going to hurt you.'

'You, you can't do that,' he twitters inanely. 'That's my gun!'

'You'll get it back in a minute, after you answer a couple of questions. What's your name, son?'

He blusters and stammers, but eventually tells me his name.

'Okay, Kev, that's good,' I say. 'Now, first question, who's in charge here, who sent you out on patrol?'

'Doctor Finlay, of course,' he says, as though everyone knows that. 'He's getting us all organised, getting things back to normal.'

'Doctor Finlay?' I almost laugh, remembering a television program of that name my mum watched when I was a just a wee brat. 'And where does this great man hang out?'

I expect him to say the Cameron Barracks, the Castle, or maybe even Inverness Prison, but he just points across the river.

'Over there,' he tells me. 'In the Glenmoriston Townhouse Hotel.'

Kev recites its full title as though he's talking about Valhalla or Superman's Fortress of Solitude, and I see it in the row of fairly imposing late Victorian buildings of blond sandstone on the far bank.

It seems that the good doctor likes to be comfortable.

'Okay, Kev,' I say. 'Listen carefully, I have a message for him.'

When I'm sure he understands what I'm telling him, I retrieve my jacket and walk with him back in the direction he came.

There I lean the shotgun against a tree, and we both stroll back to where the Grouse bottle lies in the grass.

'Okay,' I say. 'It's been nice talking to you.'

He stares at me, uncomprehending.

'Go get your gun,' I say, 'then deliver the message to Finlay.' He scurries off and, by the time he reaches it and turns, I've already rejoined Vidock and disappeared.

40

'Come on, sweetheart, try and pull yourself together, okay? I know you're scared, so am I. Listen to me, okay? Like I said, I've checked the rest of the street, everybody's dead. Well, except for old Mrs Palmer, and she's just gibbering in her front garden in her nightdress. I've done all I can for her just now. I'm a doctor, so I need to see if I can help anyone else out there.'
'I know, I know. I understand…'
'So this is what's going to happen, okay? I'll go into town and see how bad things are, and you'll get a shower, and get dressed. Power clothes, okay, because something's really wrong here and we might need to take charge. We need to be ready for anything, and we need to look the part. You with me?'
'Yes, I'm with you. It's just… Well, my head's still ringing, I can't think straight. What was it? What do you think happened? I don't understand how everybody can be dead…'
'I don't know, baby, looks like maybe some idiot tried to call some other idiot's bluff when he wasn't bluffing. Hell, we knew most politicians were fucking psychopaths, just look at the lying arseholes in Westminster over the past few years. The Americans have always been trigger happy, so when you add in the Russians and Chinese, and the Koreans, and most of the Middle East…
God, even Macron is dangerous, delusions of grandeur there for sure.'

'But… Everybody dead? I don't know…'

'I know, it's not easy, but we can get through this. Okay, I'm going to check out the town, you get yourself ready. Right? See you soon.'

A quick kiss and the doctor leaves the house, closing the door quietly.

Inside, a trembling hand fumbles open the bottle of Lagavulin, and splashes two inches of peaty perfection into a crystal glass…

41

At 9 o'clock the following morning, as arranged, Doctor
Finlay strides across the Infirmary Bridge, a narrow pedestrian
crossing which spans the River Ness about 100 yards from his
headquarters in the splendid Glenmoriston Hotel.
He is a tall, angular gentleman with collar-length grey hair
swept back off a high forehead.
Dressed for a business meeting, or a court appearance, he
wears a dark suit, white shirt and dark tartan tie, polished black
leather shoes and, casually but carefully draped over his
shoulders, a dark full-length wool coat that looks Italian and
probably cost about two thousand pounds.
He is clearly making a statement.
I generally try not to be too judgemental, preferring to keep an
open mind, but I have to say that I detest this guy on sight.
He has the sort of face you wouldn't quickly get tired of
slapping.
Still, maybe he was nice to his mum.
Close behind him are two men, one a big lump of a lad, fair-
haired and ruddy-cheeked, barely out of his teens, the other
older, smaller, darker, but wiry, tough-looking.
They're both carrying high-quality, brand new shotguns, one
of which looks like the Beretta 692 that Kev had yesterday, the
other perhaps a Browning B525, both fine weapons.
Bringing up the rear, looking anxious and maybe confused, but
unafraid, walks Kirsty, alone.
I'm sitting across the road on the low wall of what I think is a

care home.

Behind me grass, interspersed with flower beds, runs up to the front of the building.

One of these little gardens is elevated on brick walls, maybe two feet high, and displays tough wee shrubs, still green.

Vidock, whose existence isn't known to anyone here, waits behind it, just in case.

Finlay stops when he reaches the road, and makes a show of looking around, making it clear that things are not as he expects.

The two men flank him, guns held in both hands, but angled towards the ground.

Kirsty waits further back, still on the bridge.

'Good morning, Mr...', Finlay says, his voice rising in a question.

'Morning, Finlay,' I say, with deliberate lack of courtesy.

'I thought you wanted to trade,' he says in a cultured local accent. 'I don't see the three ladies you offered as your side of the bargain.'

'Yeah, I lied about that, I just want Kirsty and whichever of her friends want to join us.'

'And what makes you think that Sister Kirsty would want to go with you?' he asks. 'You can see she is clearly happy here, and with an important role to play.'

'Kirsty,' I call across to her. 'Why don't you tell Finlay what you want to do?'

She looks at me, then at Finlay, uncertainty on her face.

'Sister Kirsty is aware,' says Finlay, 'that you are charged with

murder, and you'll be tried here in Inverness tomorrow.'
He steps to the side and with a sweep of his arm indicates that I should go onto the bridge.
I stare at him, unmoving.
'And just who do you think I've murdered?' I ask.
'Well, let's see now' he says. 'First of all, by your own admission, and for no reason whatsoever, you killed poor Gregor Simpson. Then, just last night, you brutally beat young Kevin Beattie to death.'
'Kev is dead?' I ask. 'So how did you get my message?'
'You murdered him when he returned to confirm this meeting, although why I don't know. Maybe you just enjoy killing, hmm?'
I shake my head, thinking that I've underestimated this man, that he is far more dangerous than I imagined.
I had pictured a local hardcase, all brawn, but he is smart, devious and apparently ruthless.
I look to my left and see two bruisers moving towards us behind the riverside trees.
They are still 100 yards away, but I need to be alert here.
He motions towards the bridge again.
'Shall we go?' he asks.
'I don't think so,' I say. 'You're not about to use those shotguns with Kirsty watching, are you? That would kinda destroy the image you're trying to create.'
From his coat pocket he pulls a pistol, a Glock 17 like the squaddie in Tyndrum had.
How many of these things are floating around post-war

Scotland, I wonder.

'Get him,' he snaps, and the others move to take my arms.

I grin at him.

'You haven't got a chance at making this stick,' I say. 'Kirsty will see right through you.'

He moves closer, so our noses are almost touching.

'You're going to be hanged from the Ness Bridge,' he snarls, gesturing down river towards the town centre. 'You'll have a lovely view of the castle while I cut out your heart out.'

I pull back against the hands holding me, whistle sharply and, as they pull me forward again, I move with them.

Propelling myself forward, I headbutt Finlay square in the face, smashing his nose, and sending him stumbling to his knees.

I take the Browning from the astonished older guy at my right side, pushing him backwards at the same time.

The big laddie is on the ground with Vidock snarling joyously in his eyes.

I call him off, tuck Finlay's Glock into my belt, toss the Browning into the river, and lift the Beretta, which I point at the two heavies who are panting up to the action.

'Just walk back the way you came,' I say, 'and you won't get hurt.'

They look at Finlay, still on the ground, blood from his nose pouring through his fingers, then at each other.

They turn and walk away.

'You two, back across the bridge,' I snap at my erstwhile captors, then finally look at Kirsty.

She is wide-eyed and wide-mouthed, trying to speak.
'He was right,' she splutters. 'You are a savage, what did he do to deserve that?'
I realise that she couldn't hear what he said up close to me, so I'm not sure how to explain.
'He's a great man,' she has found her breath and starts to shriek. 'He's trying to rebuild our world, rebuild our civilisation, so that we're safe from thugs like you. He's right, isn't he, you did murder Gregor and that poor boy! Get away from me! And take your bloodthirsty wolf with you!'
I'm pretty sure she has been drugged and manipulated, but I don't see what I can do about that right now.
'I did not kill young Kev,' I tell her, but she ignores me, goes to Finlay and helps him to his feet.
I think about throwing him into the river, but instead I shrug and turn away.

42

'Hi, sweetie, I'm back! How are you doing? You okay? You ready?'

'I'm upstairs, getting dressed.'

The doctor mutters *sotto voce*.

'Christ, two hours and still not ready.'

Calls loudly.

'I'll come up, see if I can help you… Hey, you're ready to rock! And looking good! Okay, the situation is dire. People are dead everywhere. It seems the military rounded up all the women and all the men under about fifty, and took them south in buses. About two bus loads, I think. They just abandoned the old folk.'

'So that's all that's left, just old people?'

'No, no, there are others that the soldiers didn't see, maybe just coming in from the suburbs and the schemes. But not hundreds, maybe a couple of dozen all together.'

'That's not much, is it?'

'It's enough to get organised. They need a leader, so we'll take charge, make sure everyone is safe and fed. We can start again, rebuild Inverness, and wait for the central authorities to get their act together.'

'We'll be in charge?'

'Of course, we're educated and organised, we know how to help people. We're natural leaders, both of us.'

'Do you think they'll listen to me, accept me as a leader?'

'Of course, sweetheart, you're strong, like me. You can be

persuasive, and people listen to you, don't they? People like us are natural leaders, they'll follow us without question.'
'Yes, I suppose you're right. So what you're saying is it's chaos out there, yes? No law and order? Nobody in authority left?'
'Yes, exactly. That's why we need to do this, and do it now, to keep everyone safe, to make sure that we don't get into a Wild West situation.'
'Okay, I understand. Ah yes, I really understand now. In that case I'll tell you something else. You get on my nerves, have done for years. I can't stand how bloody bossy you are. So fucking full of yourself. So you're a fucking doctor, as you never get tired of telling me, and anybody else who'll listen! And your patients all love you, because you're so fucking wise and kind. Well I'm a doctor too, remember, I've got my doctorate from Edinburgh, just like you. And now there's no one to answer to, I don't need to listen to you any longer, do I?'
'John! What are you doing? John! What's that knife for? John!'

The Doctor of Clinical Psychology drops the kitchen knife beside the body of his wife, then gets a face cloth from the bathroom to dab the spots of blood from his suit.
He checks his appearance in the full-length mirror, and smiles.
'Right, Doctor, let's go take over this town.'

43

As we hurry back up Bishops Road to where I left my belongings, a thought strikes me.
Did I ever mention to Kirsty about Plockton?
I turn back, deciding to do some reconnoitring, to assess their strength before I leave.
Because I know that Finlay won't let this rest, he'll be looking for revenge.
But as the rain blowing in from the Moray Firth turns to sleet, I know that winter isn't far away.
He's more likely to dig in until spring before setting out on any expedition.
So I pause, and turn again, while Vidock watches in confusion.
I can see in his eyes that he is telling me to make up my bloody mind.
'Okay,' I say. 'Let's go home.'
His tail goes up and he bounds off, head up, catching the sleet on his tongue as it falls.
I shake my head.
At least one of us is having a good day.
I consider taking a car but, because the roads have been mined at so many strategic points – north of Drumnadrochit and again north of Invermoriston, as well as a seemingly random point on Loch Cluanie which prevented Steve and me from driving to our ambush at the River Garry – it is hardly worthwhile.
I guess they thought they had plenty of explosives when they set out, but then had to build their ill-fated barricade at

Tyndrum.
At least the wind is behind me for now – it usually blows the other way, right up the Great Glen from the south-west – so, already drenched, I start to pedal.

44

'Well, I have to say that I didn't like him when we first met him, and I don't like him now.'
'Is it just me, or is he scary as fuck?'
'Aye, he's a nut job, barking fucking mad, thinks he's a king or general or something. What are we going to do?'
'I suppose we do what he says and go after this crazy psychopath guy. That's sounds just like us. Not!'
'Too right, but I'm not telling him no, are you?'
'No fucking way, man. Let's just get going and see what happens.'
'Aye , we'll maybe never see the guy anyway. Here, you take the gun, just in case.'
'Me? No fucking way, Pedro! I've never held a gun in my life!'
'You told him…'
'I was feart not to! I didn't want to look like an idiot, so yeah, I said I knew what I was doing. I lied, okay, fucking sue me!'
'Well I don't want it!'
'You've got it, pal, just live with it. And you're probably right, we'll never see the guy. He's hardly going to be sitting at the side of the road waiting for us, is he?'
'No, he's likely in Glasgow by now. We'll go slow just in case though...'

45

I'm 20 miles plus out of Inverness, past Drumnadrochit and heading for Invermoriston where I'll turn off to the west again. The wind is, unsurprisingly, now much stronger and in my face, and hailstones are bouncing off my teeth.

My beanie is pulled down over my ears, and I am deep in thought, wondering about Kirsty and Finlay, and why he called her 'Sister'.

Is he creating his own little cult there?

Vidock, in the trailer, barks, but like an idiot I ignore him, thinking he is just as cold, wet and miserable as I am, and wants off to run.

By the time I hear the roar of the motorbike it is too late.

Something smacks my head and shoulder, sending me off the road, over the low dry-stone wall, and tumbling down towards the loch.

When my head starts to clear I find Vidock standing across my body, in full aggressive defence mode.

I hear voices.

'Just shoot it!'

'I'm not shooting a dog, you shoot it.'

'I've not got a gun, you're the big guy with the shooter, get on with it.'

'Here, you take the gun, you shoot it.'

'No way, I'm not shooting a dog, it's not his fault, is it?'

I struggle into a sitting position, put my hand on Vidock's neck, calming him.

'Nobody needs to shoot anybody,' I say. 'What are you guys after?'

'Whoa, dude, you're not dead,' the guy with the gun says, as the other steps back, almost behind him.

Another Glock, I think, shaking my head, how many can there be around here?

I can focus now, and see they're both very young, barely out of their teens.

'Who are you?' I ask. 'And why did you attack me?'

'The doctor sent us,' gun guy says, waving the Glock in what he probably, but wrongly, imagines is a threatening manner.

'You're a murderer and we've to take you back for trial.'

'Has Finlay drugged you guys too?' I ask. 'He's the only murderer I've seen in the past couple of days.'

'Hup,' I say to Vidock, holding his neck and lurching to my feet. 'Sorry, guys, but I'm bloody freezing down here.'

'Okay, okay, don't try anything, I'll shoot, you know, I'm not scared,' gun guy lies, as his friend backs up the slope towards the road, hands out straight in front of him.

'Jeez, guys, let's relax here,' I say, patting the air at my sides. 'Can you point that thing away before somebody gets hurt?'

As he swings it away from his body, I touch Vidock's head.

'Gun,' I say, and he leaps forward and grabs the guy's wrist. He screams and drops the weapon.

I pick it up and toss it into the loch.

He scrambles back up beside his friend and they both stare at me wide-eyed.

'Why... what... why did you throw that away,' they stammer.

'C'mon, boys,' I say. 'These things can be dangerous in the wrong hands.'
'You're just acting tough 'cos you've got him, otherwise we'd still take you back,' not gun guy says.
I start to laugh.
'Vidock, sleep,' I say, and I swear he almost winked at me.
They watch open-mouthed as he wanders off a few steps, makes three circles, then lies down and curls himself tightly with his tail over his head.
'How'd you do that?'
'Training,' I say, grinning. 'Come down and I'll show you.'
'Okay,' gun guy says, looking at his mate. 'On three, right? One…'
'Two,' I say, as I step forward and swing my clenched first up hard between his legs.
He makes a noise like the air escaping from a balloon, and falls down almost at my feet.
'No fair,' the other one shouts. 'That's a low blow!'
I'm laughing aloud now.
'You guys bring a gun to a fist fight and I'm cheating! Let's get him up to the road and have a chat, okay?'
Ten minutes later Grahamie and Seanie, as they introduce themselves, because obviously Graham and Sean are not cool enough names, have decided that they're not going back to Inverness.
'I tell you, Bossman, he's really weird, the doctor, he's a psychiatrist, or a psychologist, maybe, his wife was a real doctor, medicine, y'know, we never liked him, but he's

managed to organise a few guys into his own wee army, and he's got Inverness wrapped up. To be honest' – and at this point they look at each other a bit awkwardly – 'we were pretty scared of him.'

'He's a pretty scary guy,' I say. 'Strong personality.'

'He's like Al Capone or something,' Grahamie continues. 'He sent guys up to Tain, to the gun shop up there, y'know, Macleod's it's called, to get weapons, got some quality stuff, shotguns too.'

'I know,' I tell them with a grin. 'He was kind enough to give me one of them.'

'God,' Grahamie says, feeling his wrist. 'You don't need a gun when you've got him! And you fight dirty!'

This time we all laugh.

As my bike suffered more than I did when it hit the wall, they offer me a lift.

'What do you think, Vidock?' I ask him, gesturing at the two Honda 500s.

Giving me a look of utter disgust in reply, he sets off at a trot. After a short discussion we manage to attach the trailer to one of the bikes, I get on the other one behind Seanie, and we trundle after him.

And further down the road things get more interesting.

46

We turn off the A82 at Glenmoriston, heading more directly west on the A887 which joins the A87 at Bun Loyne, just before Loch Cluanie.

This junction is halfway along a stretch of unusually straight road and, before we reach it Grahamie, who leads the way, raises a hand and draws to a halt.

He points ahead and we see two cyclists, maybe half a mile ahead, moving away from us.

Something clicks in my head.

'Get off,' I tell Seanie. 'You two wait here.'

'Come,' I say to Vidock, who leaps joyously from his personal transport behind Grahamie and bounds after me.

I hurtle after the cyclists, pass them, and swing round twenty metres ahead of them.

I hold up my hand, dismount, and pull my knife from its sheath in the small of my back.

I see the terror in their eyes.

'Hello Fiona,' I say. 'Hi, Malky.'

She drops her bike and walks towards me.

'Please,' she says. 'Please just listen.'

But I don't listen, I just snap at her

'I thought I made it clear what would happen if I ever saw you again. And no explanations will change my mind.'

She drops to her knees, hands clasped in front of her.

'Please help us,' she says. 'We don't deserve this.'

Malky steps in front of his mother.

'Don't touch her,' he shouts, raising his little hands in fists. 'You'll have to deal with me first!'
'Whoa, Bossman,' the two lads appear, looking horrified. 'What's with the knife?'
'Stay out of this,' I bark at them. 'This isn't your affair.'
'Okay,' I say to Fiona, still on her knees. 'One chance. Go back now and I'll pretend this didn't happen.'
'Malky,' she says. 'Show him your back.'
I stare at her, not understanding.
'No, mum!'
'Malcolm! Do what I say!'
He glowers at her, then at me, and lets his sodden coat fall on the wet ground.
He turns to face Fiona, and pulls up his sweatshirt and tee shirt.
His back is a mess of welts, cuts and bruises, some old, some very recent.
I swallow hard, say nothing.
She stands, pushes him aside, and drops her own coat.
Her green eyes stare into mine, then she turns quickly and pulls up her shirt.
She is wearing nothing underneath, anything rubbing the unhealed wounds would be unbearable.
The two boys step away, muttering darkly.
'McDougall?' I ask quietly, sheathing my knife.
She nods.
'And his brother, Malky's father, before him,' she adds.
'Cover yourselves,' I say, lifting her coat, and helping her into it. 'But why come here now, MacDougall's dead.'

'We know, Malky followed them and saw what happened at the bridge. Then he came back for me, and we set out here.'
'Why?' I ask again, and she starts to cry.
I look at Grahamie and Seanie, but they are, if anything, more confused than I am.
'The night we spent with you people at Corriegour Lodge was the best time we've ever had in our lives,' she sobs. 'We wanted to see if you'd let us join you. We'll work hard, do anything you say.'
I turn away and lift my face, hoping the rain will hide the tears.

47

We spend the night at the historic Cluanie Inn, in the heart of rugged Glen Shiel, and close to the site of a bloody battle in 1719 during the first Jacobite rising.

Vidock and I walk down to the loch side, to let him cool his feet.

Although he is half-husky, and has much of that great breed's ability to run vast distances at surprising speed, the tarmac of our roads is not his friend.

So, as I do every night, I check his legs and paws for any problems and, as always, he thanks me with a lick.

While he paddles in the shallow water I gaze off to the west, where the spectacular Five Sisters of Kintail are silhouetted against the darkening sky.

This is the country I love.

A country of great lochs and rugged mountains, of undulating green fields and vast beaches.

A country with a history of war and bloodshed, sometimes internecine, often in the name of national freedom.

A country of myths and mystery, of ghosts and monsters, real and imaginary.

A country of great men and women, thinkers, philanthropists, explorers, inventors, humanitarians.

A country of artists, writers and poets.

A country with a small population, but a huge impact.

And, I think bitterly, a country where a woman and child have been beaten repeatedly, relentlessly, unjustifiably, for over a

decade.
I realise that nothing, and nowhere, can be perfect.

After we eat, the two lads have a great time depleting the stocks of the bar, while Fiona and I share a bottle of wine.
'Hey, Bossman, you and the lady want a nice malt, plenty here!'
And Malky finds a freezer full of choc ices, tubs of ice cream, and various other delights for a 12-year old boy.
Every time Fiona tells him he's had enough, he grins and says 'Just one more, mum', and she shakes her head, making her long red curls quiver, and smiles back at him.
I watch the years fall off her, and see that she is actually an attractive woman.
I realise to my embarrassment that this is the first time I've viewed her as a person.
I didn't trust her from our first encounter in Fort William, and refused to consider anything other than what I saw then.
The same applied to her son, who has only done what he had to for his mother's sake, and who put himself between her and my knife this afternoon.
Added to which they were blamed and beaten for the failure at Corriegour.
My biggest regret now is that I can't go back and kill MacDougall again.
And make him suffer more this time.

48

In the morning we rise early, have porridge for breakfast, and I call Fiona and Malky into a room away from the guys, and explain to them what they must do.
I tell Vidock he has new friends.
He sits upright, watching.
'This is Malky,' I say. 'Malky is our friend.'
The boy goes forward, bends almost nose to nose.
'Hello Vidock,' he says. 'I am Malky, Malky, I want to be your friend.'
Then he holds out his open hand, palm upwards, for the dog to smell, and then lick.
He takes some time over this, then sits up again and offers his paw.
Malky takes it carefully, almost caressingly.
'Malky is our friend,' I say again, and the great tail moves from side to side.
We repeat the whole process with Fiona, who is clearly in awe of my shaggy friend.
'He really understands that,' she asks. 'We are really his friends?'
'Oh yes,' I assure her. 'He will protect you against anyone or anything that threatens you.'
'And so will I,' I tell her, looking into her eyes. 'No one will hurt you again while I am here, I promise.'
She nods thoughtfully, then takes a deep breath.
'Is it one of his 'friends' he looks for on the road at night?' she

asks.
Her eyes open wide at my reaction, and she quickly apologises.
'The two girls were talking about him that night,' she says.
'They'd noticed that he always looked back down the road before he went inside. As if he was waiting for someone, they said.'
I shake my head.
'Just girls gossiping, like girls do,' I say.
'So what did you think of them?' I ask, changing the subject.
'Oh they were lovely,' she smiles. 'Kind to me and very sweet to Malky. But everyone was, that Mrs Fraser's great, isn't she!'
I smile back, and touch her arm.
'You'll be fine,' I say.

49

Then we set out for Plockton.
The rain is steady, and cold, but the trip is uneventful.
We stop a mile before we reach the centre of the village.
'Best not charge in unannounced,' I grin. 'We don't want to get our heads blown off at this late stage.'
'Um,' says Grahamie, 'the thing is, Bossman, we're thinking it's time to move on.'
'You don't want to come in and meet everyone?' I ask.
'They're good people, you'll like them.'
Seanie nudges his friend.
'Just tell him', he says.
'Okay, we know that, Fiona says they're cool and we believe her,' says Grahamie. 'But there's two things. First, we don't want to be here when Finlay comes. He'll mean business, and he won't take prisoners. Like we said before, he scares us.'
'Okay,' I say. 'What else?'
They look at each other again, and giggle.
'Well,' says Seanie. 'When we were talking to Fiona last night she said Fort William has women and no men. That sounds like our sort of place!'
I laugh and shake hands with each of them.
'You'll always be welcome here,' I tell them. 'And if you ever need help, just shout.'
'Here,' I take Finlay's Glock from my rucksack. 'You might need this. I think you mislaid your last weapon!'
We wave them off, then I take a green flag from my rucksack

and tie it round Vidock's neck.

'Go get Steve,' I say.

I turn to Fiona and Malky, who look suddenly nervous.

'It'll be cool,' I tell them. 'Look, there's no need to worry, but stay out of sight until I call you. I feel like a bit of theatre!'

When I reach the loch side the others are already crowding out of different doorways, shouting greetings.

I'm surprised at how pleased I am to see them all again.

There are hugs and handshakes and millions of questions.

I make calming motions with my hands, and then speak quietly.

'Kirsty couldn't make it,' I tell them. 'But I do have a couple of surprises for you.'

Part 2 – North and South

Map of West of Scotland (Ayr to Inverness)

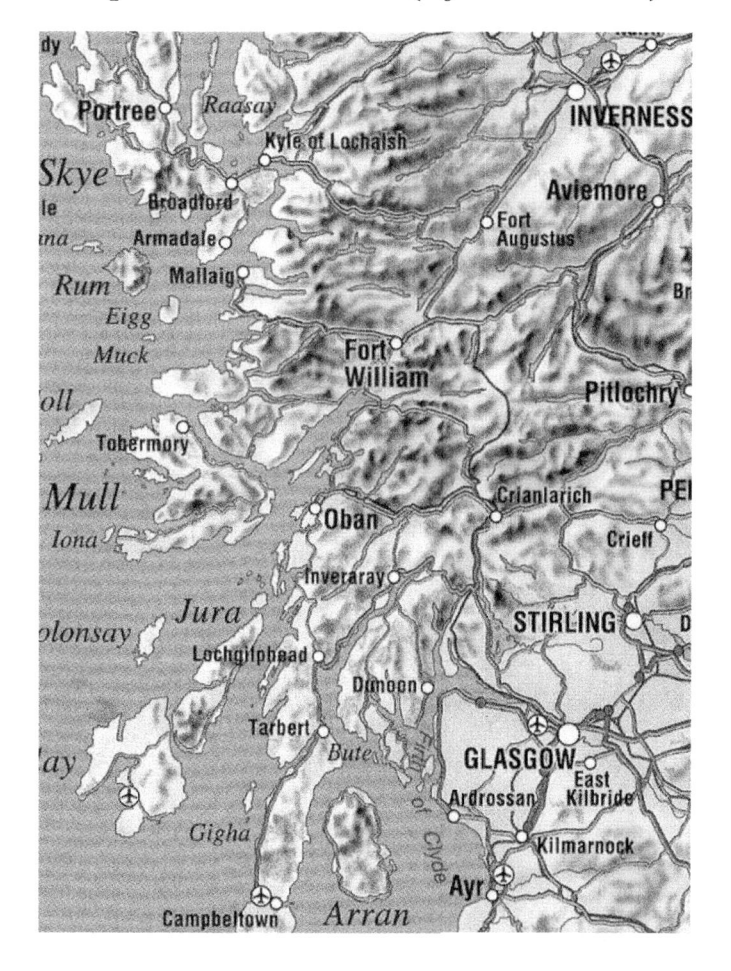

Map of Plockton

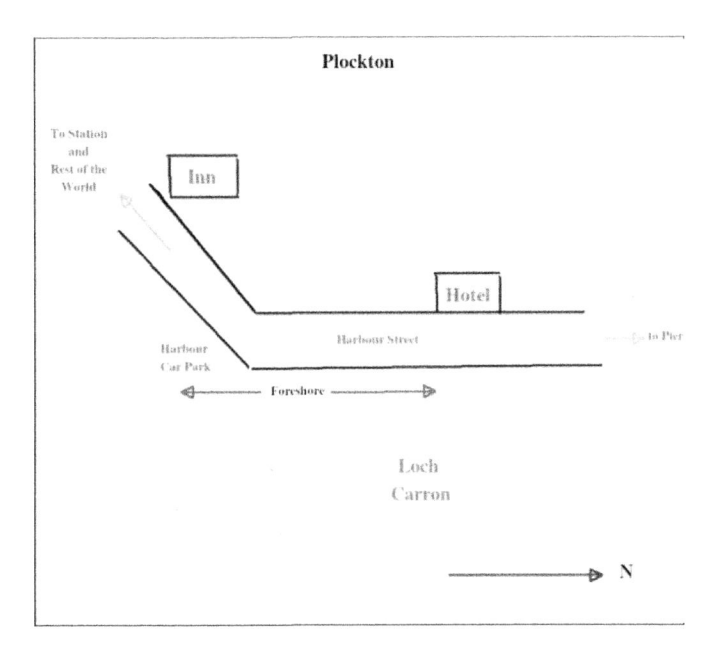

Plockton

To Station and Rest of the World

Inn

Hotel

Harbour Car Park

Harbour Street

to Pier

← Foreshore →

Loch Carron

→ N

1

'Hey Cath, have you seen the man?'
Cathy shakes her head, smiling.
'Have you forgotten, Steve, that you're the man?'
They exchange the morning hug that has become a ritual within the group before she continues.
'I suppose you mean Sensei, hmm? No, I haven't, not Vidock either.'
Steve scowls out across dreich Loch Carron, where little can be seen through the morning gloom.
The clouds are low and rain falls steadily.
'Think it's getting warmer yet?'
Cathy shakes her head again.
'Not much. Two weeks till April,' she says. 'Then we'll see a difference. Maybe.'
Steve grunts and turns away, leaves the harbour car park and heads south up the hill towards the Inn.
Cathy doesn't move, stares through the rain, seeing nothing.
She is drenched, but either unaware or indifferent to the discomfort and the cold.
The long hard months since this nightmare started haven't dimmed her memories or dulled the pain.
She misses Jim, her husband, especially at night when she finds it hard to sleep alone after fifteen years with him, but she knows she could probably get over that, and him, in time.
She has even considered seeking solace with Sensei, as they now call the strange, distant man who saved them and guided

them here, but he has shown no interest in her.

But to be fair, he seems equally indifferent to Fiona, who obviously worships him, and even Joni, who makes her ambitions there quite clear.

Cathy knows she can live without a man, but what really hurts is the loss of Karly, her 13-year old daughter, and the illogical guilt that haunts her night and day.

This is made even worse by the fact that, since her phone died, she no longer has a photo to look at, and she lives in constant terror of forgetting her baby's face.

She has spoken to both Steve and Sensei about going home to get the things her heart needs, and they both say yes, of course, as soon as it's feasible.

When she asks when that will be they shrug and tell her she knows as much as they do, but that they will investigate further when spring comes.

She has yet to decide how she feels about Allie's addition to their small band when, although not a midwife, her training allowed her to handle the birth in her usual professional manner.

The baby girl, called Ronnie after her father, is thriving, though keeping mother and child warm and well fed in these circumstances has been challenging for all of them.

Something makes her turn and watch Steve as he heads up to the Inn where Sensei and Vidock are based.

She worries about him; he seldom laughs now, and she can see the stress is taking its toll.

She shivers suddenly, and abruptly starts back to where the group gather for breakfast.

Her nerves are screaming because she realises that the tremors weren't caused by her body reacting to the cold, but her mind sensing some premonition of further disaster.

2

The winter was thankfully mild, at least by the standards of the north of Scotland.
Whether this was due to continued global warming or the effect of the apocalyptic war was impossible to say.
Plockton's sheltered position meant that it didn't actually freeze at any point, but overnight temperatures were usually in low single figures and even during the day rarely reached double figures.
In spite of having no gas or electricity supply the odd collection of survivors rescued by Steve's courage and generosity, and protected by Sensei's sometimes brutal tactics, had coped surprisingly well with their strange situation.
They had pillaged farms for diesel generators and topped up the fuel by siphoning the tanks of abandoned vehicles.
These farms, along with the petrol station outside Kyle of Lochalsh, were a great source of various necessities, including plenty of chickens and a goat, which provided a supply of eggs and some milk.
From time to time they would see a sheep wandering lonely in the fields, and it would be 'rescued' for a celebratory meal.
The supermarket on the road to the Skye Bridge, and the kitchens of local hotels supplied a mountain of canned and dried foodstuff, including flour and yeast, plus fruit juice, tea, coffee and sugar to add to the stocks already found in the village.
The pharmacy gave them vitamins and health supplements as

well as drugs, and doctors' and dental surgeries were also looted.

They trawled the district for paraffin, oil, and kerosene heaters, and the fuel for them.

They had the great fortune to discover a wood-burning stove so they could at least make porridge, bread, soup and hot drinks. As time passed they caught fish and seal, of which there were still large numbers along the shores and on the small islands just offshore, pigeons and the occasional gull, and even rabbit, as Sensei set traps in small copses where they stay warm in winter and eat the bark of trees like the silver birch.

One unanswered and probably unanswerable question that has consistently preyed on every mind is why they are alive when so many died.

It seems too that most mammals suffered a similar fate, with dogs and cats, horses and cattle, like humans, mostly dead. But birds, fortunately including chickens, as well as fish, appear far less affected.

'Sensei, can we eat seagulls?'

'The truth is, Jack, that we can eat pretty much anything if we're hungry enough. And they're pretty nutritious.'

'We catch pigeons, so why not gulls?'

'Because it's much harder and more time-consuming! But the time might come…'

'What about crows?'

'Really smart little shits, hard to catch, and they remember.'

'They remember? What do you mean?'
'Crows remember places that are dangerous, won't go back there.'
'Why don't we just shoot them, and the gulls?'
'Several reasons. Lack of ammunition is one. And a gunshot travels a long way when everything is so quiet. We'd be heard miles away.'
'Would that be a bad thing? Don't we want to meet other folk like us?'
'Sure, of course, but on equal terms. We don't want unknowns watching us, assessing our strengths and weaknesses, and thinking about the women.'
'You guys worry a lot about the women, don't you?'
'The thing is, Jack, that women have a special value in this situation. There are some who'd just use them as breeding stock, all about the survival of the species.'
'But that's horrible, it's just barbaric!'
'Aye, it is, but it's also official policy. That's what the two squaddies way back in Tyndrum were ordered to do. They were no different from the deserters we killed there when you boil it down. That's why I'd rather have Steve's law than military or any other.'
'Fuck sake. Aye, okay, no shooting things! Will you teach me how to net them?'

Sensei got his name because of his daily exercise routine, based largely on Qigong, which he neither encouraged nor discouraged others to follow with him, but taught them nevertheless, primarily by example, about meditation, breathing, body posture and movement.

He appeared to be somewhere between indifferent and mildly amused at being addressed as Sensei, as long as the practice itself was taken seriously.

Several of them found that they could manage the effects of cold better by applying these techniques, which also formed the start point of the unarmed combat training that Steve and Sensei gave them.

The two older couples, Hugh and Jules and Rick and Bet, and Allie, growing with the child inside her, concentrated on basic Qigong, but the two women, Cathy and Fiona, the two lads, Jack and Malky, and Joni threw themselves into the fighting classes with great enthusiasm.

Everyone except Bet, who refused to handle weapons, was tutored on handling knives, clubs, and guns, although actual shooting practice was limited to preserve ammunition.

The gun supply, already pretty substantial with the spoils of war from the two sets of soldiers at Tyndrum and then McDougall's men at Loch Lochy, was significantly augmented by the discovery of shotguns and other perhaps less legal firearms at farms in the area.

But even now there remains a feeling that at some point every bullet will be needed.

Two days before Ronnie appeared, with great serendipity on 25th January, the birthday of Robert Burns, the group lost its first member since Fred in Tyndrum.

Bet's death hit them much harder, as she was well-loved for her cheery nature and sound common sense.
She developed a chill in mid-January and slipped away quietly in her sleep a few days later.
Rick struggled to come to terms with the loss for a couple of weeks when, oddly, it was Malky who was instrumental in helping him recover his previous good humour.
Whether on his own, or with Fiona's prompting, he asked Rick for help with his fishing rod
and line, saying he had problems with the reel.
A couple of hours later the two of them were at the end of the pier trying to pull in some poor mackerel, cod or pollock, and Rick was soon close to himself again.

Fiona and Malky integrated easily, both being hard-working and keen to learn.
Jack takes time with Malky, at least when he isn't eating, because in the winter months he has grown and filled out as only teenage boys can do, and is already, at 16, taller than Steve.
His chest and arms are hard with muscle, as he does more than his share of the heavy work, trying always to take the load off the Frasers and the women.
And his look of boyish innocence is long gone.
Everyone except Allie is leaner and harder than before; she has been cosseted
throughout these hard times by everyone, as if by mutual agreement.

Steve has watched for any hint of resentment, and seen none. His hair, which Allie cuts for him, shows flecks of grey, and his face is lined with constant worry; he takes his responsibilities seriously.

The others too have aged visibly, with the possible exception of Sensei, who seems immutable.

The absence of fresh fruit and vegetables, added to the lack of sunshine, has left a greyish tinge on their skin, which conflicts strangely with the ruddiness caused by the exertion of outdoor work.

This being Scotland, there is an abundance of available alcoholic beverages, which are consumed in moderation.

The Frasers and Rick, and occasionally Steve, like to partake of what Jules calls 'a wee medicinal dram', usually of a quality single malt whisky, while Bet, Cath and Joni often share a bottle of wine.

Fiona always refrains, citing a husband who was a mean drunk, the full truth of which only Sensei knows.

She explains to him that she only shared the wine that first night because she felt that, under the circumstances, it would be rude to refuse.

And she was scared.

They are both laughing by the time he tells her that he only offered because he knows he lacks social graces, and felt that it might help to reduce the tension between them.

On the odd occasion that he joins the group socially he invariably asks Jack if he fancies a beer.

The lad dives off and returns promptly with two cold bottles,

which they chink together and '*Slainte*' each other.
Some evenings are tolerable, even for Sensei, with the two older couples, and sometimes Steve, telling stories, and Joni, who is a drama student, singing to Fiona's guitar accompaniment, or delivering soliloquies from Shakespeare. On occasion Allie is also persuaded to entertain them, as they have all heard her singing lullabies to Ronnie.
Her voice is strong and clear, and she often performs the old Beatles song 'Yesterday', a nostalgic piece that invariably causes deep reflection among the vulnerable survivors.
Sensei contributes rarely but, to universal surprise, does remarkable recitations of Robert Burns' poetry, in particular the magnificent Tam o' Shanter.

Personal hygiene is rigorously enforced.
This is necessitated by the fact that they gather nightly in the warmest room in the hotel, and Steve insists that anyone with a hint of body odour removes themselves until the problem is resolved.
Joni's hair now has a decidedly punk look, as she decided that her lovely long waves were too much hassle to keep clean and brushed, so Allie gives her much the same treatment as Steve gets.
She applies the same approach to Jack and Malky, although Hugh has Jules cut what's left of his, insisting in the face of strong evidence to the contrary that she knows what she's doing.
Rick is bald.

Cathy keeps hers long, usually tied up gypsy-style in a scarf, and is phlegmatic about the grey streaks appearing through the auburn.
Fiona's mass of red curls are apparently untameable so she doesn't even try.
Sensei ties his back with string or anything else to hand, and avoids most of the social niceties, only joining the group for an occasional meal.
He works, forages and trains for eighteen hours per day, often swimming off the pier to the impressed horror of the group.
Steve and Jack join him occasionally, and briefly, finding it unbearably cold.
Malky is forbidden by his mother, who thinks he'll get cramp and drown.
Sensei raises an eyebrow, and smiles, but doesn't disagree.
He guides the others with a word or a gesture, but little conversation.
Sometimes he walks with Steve, their voices low; when Hugh joins them they sit close together.
He never refuses to answer a question if it is a matter of fact but, when an opinion is sought on topics that involve the group, he carefully suggests that Steve is better able to discuss the issue.

3

I wait in the grounds of the Church of Scotland on the north side of Somerled Square, Portree, on the Isle of Skye.
I am very close to the Portree Hotel which my earlier observations tell me is the focal point of this community.
Long before daybreak which, this far north in December, especially with today's low, dense cloud cover, is somewhere around 11 o'clock, there are signs of life.
I watch and listen long enough to spot the guy in charge, wait until he is alone, tell Vidock to 'Stay' and step out.
'Hello there,' I say, in the voice of someone about to ask how to get to the Post Office, 'You got a minute?'
He turns quickly, dropping low, his hands disappearing inside his heavy jacket.
'I'm not armed,' I say, and that's nearly true, 'I come in peace.'
I walk towards him, arms wide, hands open.
'I'm from Plockton,' I tell him, 'We saw your boat seeing us the other day, so I thought I'd drop by and make friends.'
When we are close enough to see each other, he holds up his left hand, the right one still hidden.
'What do you want? Why are you here?'
He is a big man, broad-shouldered, dressed like that he looks enormous.
'I figure we're neighbours, don't want any unpleasantness. I guess we both have troubles enough right now, don't need any more hassle. Thought I'd see if we can arrange a truce.'

'We've got things under control here,' he growls, 'What makes you think we'd be looking for trouble? Not that we couldn't handle it, we're ready for anything.'

'I can see that,' I tell him, 'I've been watching how you go about your business, pretty impressive.'

'You've been watching?' He is mocking me. 'What, for about ten minutes? So what have you discovered, eh?'

'I've been here since this time yesterday, just observing how your people do things. I saw your fishing operation, it's obvious some of you have a background there. I know where you sleep' – I point to a window of the hotel – 'and where your sentries are posted. I'm a bit surprised you've no one before the cemetery. Would you like more details?'

'Nobody's reported seeing a stranger to me. How'd you manage to not get seen?'

We're close enough now that I can see the confusion and concern on his face, and the tension in his body.

I grin at him, shrug with my hands open in front of me.

'I'm not bad at that sort of thing. I wanted to see how things were before we spoke. You seem like a reasonably civilised bunch, so I figured we'd get along.'

'And you really walked in here unarmed? You've got some balls, I'll say that!'

'To be honest, I've got a knife. And a secret weapon.'

He snorts, amused.

'A secret weapon? What the fuck's that?'

'Well, Alex, if I told you that it wouldn't be much of a fucking secret, would it?'

He half laughs.
'And you know my name. You've been close in, eh? Want some tea?'
'I thought you'd never ask, it's bloody freezing out here!'

An hour later we are comfortable with each other, up to a point.
I don't tell him how many we are, just that we're a tight-knit band, that we've fought two battles, and wiped out our enemies each time.
He asks if I'm ex-military and I answer with a half smile and a shrug of my right shoulder.
'You all military?' he pursues it.
'Not all, one guy's a cop, old school, hard as nails.' I don't say that Hughie's retired. 'A guy from Fort William crossed him and got a broken jaw for his trouble.'
I tell him our observation system (I don't admit it's just Rick with binoculars) spotted their boat, which Alex confirms saw our smoke and got nosier than was sensible.
'I tell you, Sensei, they should never have been that far down in the first place,' he grumbles, 'We knew you were around, of course, you pretty much cleaned out the stores in Kyle! But we saw that you cleared away the bodies, too, saw the big cairn on the building site, that was well done.'
'We didn't want the whole place overrun with rats, little bastards breed like rabbits, only faster, so we buried what we could, dropped some in the water with weights, and shut doors.'

Alex nods, still studying me.

'Aye, good. The guys had their orders to stay close, but they were following the fish, they say. They've been chastised, a wee smack on the wrist, like, but it seems there's no harm done'

'Quite the contrary,' I say, 'Now we've agreed to coory in for the winter, I think it's a bonus to know we have friends not far away. Because come spring I think trouble will come looking for all of us.'

I tell him about Doctor Finlay, who I feel sure will be gathering forces to move southwards, although whether he will swing this far west I have no way of knowing.

But Skye might be a temptation for him.

We agree that a winter campaign would be stupidity on a 'March on Moscow' scale unless, of course, power gets restored to the grid, in which case things will change dramatically.

'And this doctor guy doesn't like you, eh?'

'Well, I broke his nose, embarrassed him badly enough that he sent two lads after me and then I talked them into not going back. So yeah, I'm probably not getting a Xmas card.'

Before I leave he asks what we are doing about finding meat to eat.

I tell him honestly that we are struggling, that we catch some fish and a few rabbits and birds, and we have some chickens and sheep, which we plan to ration.

He shakes his head and laughs at 'city folk'.

Then he takes me down to the port and shows me where they

skin and butcher seals.

'You say there's not many locals left alive down there,' he says.

'Just the two incomers,' I confirm, and he shakes his head.

'Pity about Calum, a good man that. But you've got his boat, the Sula Bheag, that he used for seal trips for the tourists, yeah? It's a 38-footer, reliable, perfectly good for this.'

I get a quick lesson in how to do what is necessary, and what is the best way to cook them.

He gives me a slab of meat that must weigh 5 or 6 kilos, and a harpoon.

'You'll work out how to use it,' he grins. 'You seem like a pretty resourceful kind of guy! Are you walking back?'

I laugh, tell him I left my bike at the cemetery.

'I thought even your guy there might have heard a bike going by! And the one at the Guest House seemed more awake.'

I don't tell him that my bike has a trailer for Vidock; I prefer to keep my secret weapon a secret for now.

Alex shakes his head, then my hand, and tells me, half-joking, what he'll do to the sentries.

I leave him there before circling round to get my sleeping bag and Vidock, who is curled up asleep with his tail over his head.

'Is that you on alert?' I ask him, but he just sniffs at the bag of seal meat, gives me a sort of old-fashioned look, and follows me out into the murky twilight.

4

The group gathers in the lounge bar of the hotel, where a wood fire provides warmth and light.
When Sensei arrives he is asked where Vidock is, and replies, to smiles all round, that Steve has asked that he stand guard, as he is least susceptible to the cold.
Hugh coughs, and announces that the meeting is under way.
'It has been suggested,' he starts, 'Now that we've been here nearly a week – yes, Joni, it seems much fucking longer to the rest of us too, but we're still in October, remember – and we're pretty much all settled in, right, so it's time to agree on some rules and some roles. First thing is to appoint an official leader of the group. I'll start by proposing Steve.'
'I second that,' says the man who has always been viewed by most of them as the de facto leader. 'I don't see that there's any rational alternative.'
Steve meets his eye and nods an acknowledgement with a small grimace.
'Okay,' says Hugh, 'Does anyone else want to put themselves forward or are we all in agreement?'
The three men have agreed this in advance, there is to be no debate.
Jack opens his mouth as if to speak, then changes his mind.
But Cathy and Fiona are not so reticent, both starting to speak at once.
'One at a time,' interrupts Hugh. 'Cath, d'you want to stand for the leadership?'

She throws him a scowl that would melt steel, and snaps back at him.

'Don't be so bloody obtuse, man, you know what we're all thinking. We all love Steve, and admire him, and are grateful for everything he's done, but we know he's not the real leader here, don't we?'

'I might be new here,' adds Fiona, 'But I agree with Cath. Don't get me wrong, Steve is great, but he's not the guy who makes the decisions, is he?'

Steve looks awkward, as though he doesn't know what to say. 'The thing is,' he starts, but it stopped by a hand on his shoulder.

'You should all remember a couple of things. Steve is the guy who saved all of you, well, all of the original group' – a nod to Fiona and Malky – 'he's the guy who with insane creativity – or maybe creative insanity - stole the oldest bus in Scotland, stopped to pick up every one of you, every one of us, and saved you from death, slavery or, in the case of the ladies, something probably worse.'

Apart from the crackling of logs in the fire there is total silence in the room.

'And you might remember that way back in Tyndrum, a hundred years ago, or maybe just two weeks, some of you wanted me to leave. I made a promise at that time to stay with you until you were safe. Now that might be a relative term here, but I think this is as good as it gets in the short term. So I consider that I've kept my promise.'

This time everyone starts to speak, all trying to shout each other down.

'Shut up, everyone!' shouts Hugh. 'Cath, you still have the floor.'

'So are you saying you're leaving us now, just like that? You don't feel any loyalty or' – she chokes slightly – 'or any sort of affection for anyone here? You can just walk away after all we've been through?'

'All I'm saying is that I'm not a fixture here. I'm not a gregarious person, and Vidock and I have our own longer term objectives. But no, I don't plan to leave right now, I imagine I'll be here through the winter, at least. But to go back to the issue at hand, Steve is the obvious and logical choice. He is smart and brave, he's hard-working and organised, and he'll do everything in his power to protect you all because he cares about you, all of you.'

There is a pause and various quiet conversations take place until until Cathy goes to Steve, puts her hands on his arms, stretches up and kisses his cheek.

'I'm sorry, Steve,' she says, 'That must have sounded like I don't think you can do it, but I do. I trust you completely, and I'll help you as much as I can, I promise. I spoke out of turn and I was wrong. It was just…'

She pauses, searching for words, and Steve says them for her. 'It's just that I'm not him, right?'

'Fuck sake, Steve, you're a great guy, we're all behind you, me most of all!'

'That's good, Cath, because I'm appointing you quartermaster. I know that Jules is our Master Chef, and Bet her main

assistant, but I want you to control all our consumables. That is not just the food, but everything else we use, especially fuel for cooking and heating. You can commandeer any of the others to help you – Joni and Fiona especially, and Allie until you decide she needs to put her feet up. I have other duties for Jack and Malky, but if you need them we can discuss it. Okay?'
Cathy looks surprised for a moment or two, then nods.
'That makes sense, Steve, I can do that.'
'You just let me know when we're running low on necessities, and we'll go foraging. First thing is we decide what we need to stockpile, I expect everyone's input on that, so we can prioritise. We all want different things, but what we need is pretty much the same for all of us.'
Hugh speaks again.
'If anyone at any time has a problem either with their duties or with anyone else, they should come to me or, if it's more of a woman's thingy' – he makes a wee embarrassed face – then speak to Jules or Bet. And if I'm the problem, hmm, I don't know. Ach, you can just go to hell!'
The mood lightens again as everyone laughs.
'We're in a pretty unique situation here,' adds Steve, 'We're back to subsistence living, something we're not used to, so there will be problems. I don't want them to be allowed to fester and develop into anything major. Speak to one of us early, and we'll resolve them. We are totally dependant on each other, we need to have trust and belief in our system.'

5

I hear running footsteps and know it is Jack.
Vidock and I are in the Plockton Inn, at the entrance to the village, but only 5 minutes from the hotel where most of the others sleep.
I am at the door when he arrives, panting.
'Something's bothering the chickens, probably a fox!'
'Go to Steve,' I tell Vidock, pulling on boots, and following the galloping boy and joyously bounding dog.
As I race along Harbour Street, I hear Malky's shrill voice and Steve shouting to Vidock.
Slowing momentarily, I take a breath and whistle, one long, one short and high.
I repeat it, and start running again.
The hens are cooped overnight in what were gardens on the shore side of the road.
In the dark I see Steve's shape and then Vidock, crouched and quivering with rage.
'Wildcat,' says Steve. 'Malky spotted it, says they're lethal.'
Malky is, of course, a Highlander, who went on hunts with his father and uncle, so we trust his judgement here.
'Here Vidock,' I say, and get a furious glare in return.
I'm pretty sure he could take a wildcat, they're not that much bigger than a domestic cat, but they are feral beasts, and fierce, and I don't want his eyes anywhere near those claws.
Hugh appears and hands me a shotgun.
Steve, already holding one, gestures that I should circle right,

down onto the foreshore, while he moves along the road.
Fiona appears behind me carrying an improvised torch, cloth wrapped round a branch, and I see Cathy behind Steve with another.
Vidock growls, a deep savage rumble that I've never heard before, something atavistic, and I see the flash of the cat's eyes in the flickering light.
But a shadow moves and is gone before can pull a trigger.
When I meet Steve he shakes his head.
I nod, and indicate Vidock, who is still taut with anger.
'It was there, he smelled it and wasn't impressed. I saw a flash, then nothing. Whose idea was the torches?'
'Fiona,' says Cathy, 'These teuchters are smarter than they look.'
She and Fiona grin at each other and Steve herds them back to the Inn.
I crouch and talk to Vidock, who sulks until I'm asleep, and probably long after.

6

'Um, er, how do you feel about procreation?'

Cathy looks at Steve with raised eyebrows.

'That's just about the worst chat-up line I've ever heard,' she laughs. 'What are you trying to say here?'

Steve stares at the ground, red-faced.

'That maybe didn't sound quite the way I meant it,' he stammers. 'But it's a follow-on from last night's meeting, honest!'

The previous evening the group had gathered to review the bigger picture, as Steve put it.

He laid it out as best he could.

'We're settled in and relatively secure, with enough food, although a less than perfect diet, and plenty of water. Well, it tumbles from the skies on a pretty regular basis, sometimes ready frozen!'

When the laughter and comments subsided he continued.

'The probability is that the military have set up their base as planned in Kentigern House in the centre of Glasgow.

From there they will control the city, and then start to spread out.

We figure that most people will drift there looking for leadership, while others, like ourselves, will prefer to go it alone or in small groups.

The military will want total control, that's the nature of the beast, so as their numbers grow they will gradually annexe the

Clydeside conurbation and the major Lanarkshire towns.
The Clyde valley is a centre for market-gardening, they'll need that, and Renfrewshire and Ayrshire are important for sheep and cattle, assuming some have survived.
So they'll forage south to Kilmarnock and Ayr, that's only a question of time.
Eventually they'll want to get to Edinburgh and Stirling, but any opposition there will be a challenge, given their castles.
There are, or were, military installations in both, but we have no way of knowing if they'll be as compliant as Inverness and centralise in Glasgow.
Or even if they have the same emergency orders.'
To further laughter he added 'Sorry to disillusion you, but that was above my pay grade. No, Jack, I wasn't a bloody general!'
He gave them a couple of minutes to consider all this before speaking again.
'No questions, yet, please, I'm nearly done.
The point is, and all this will take time, they will have control of Scotland, and will hopefully start to rebuild the infrastructure, and get the energy back online.
We should assume this will take years, and maybe decades.'
He waited again until the outburst died down, waving aside questions.
'We don't know how widespread this is, we gotta think most of Europe is in the same situation as we are, maybe the whole world is.
And if not, if people are still living happily untouched in Australia or Japan or Argentina, it's not likely that they'll be

thinking "Gosh, we better go help those folk in Plockton!"
The point is this, we should expect to be here for the long haul.
You each have the choice, of course, to stay or to go.
We have friends on Skye, in Portree, with Alex and his people, who are sound, according to Sensei, and in Fort William, where we believe Graham and Sean, sorry Grahamie and Seanie, are settled.
Apparently though, Inverness is a less popular tourist destination this year, thanks to Sensei.'
To renewed laughter and mock applause he made a sweeping introductory gesture and got a bow in return.
'As I've said before,' said Sensei, 'I have serious concerns about the good doctor in Inverness. I think he'll try to expand his empire, or maybe cult would be a better word. His people already raided as far down as Drumnadrochit, and that was just a scouting trip. The two lads told us' – he indicates Fiona and Malky – 'that night in Glen Shiel that Finlay has delusions of grandeur, sees himself as a great leader of men, maybe president of the new Scotland. I doubt he'll come here, but I think Fort William is a likely target, and maybe even Skye, that would give him control of the Western Highlands.'
'If he goes to Skye,' asked Hugh, 'D'you think he'll go in peace?'
'I think he'll ask if they want to be part of his plans, and contribute to them, and he'll want the women. Alex won't buy that, so there'll be trouble.'
'And *they* know we're here,' said Cathy.
'Yep, so if Finlay finds out, he'll come looking, for sure.'

'So what do we do?'

'We get ready. Or…'

'Or what?'

Steve took over again.

'Or we go to Portree and join up with the folk there. Like I said, anyone is free to do that individually, or we can vote to do it as a group.'

Once again everyone started to shout their views until Hugh established calm.

'This is not a now decision,' said Steve, 'We should all think carefully about it, discuss it with each other, consider the benefits of our small group where we all trust each other against the added security of a larger operation where we'll have a smaller voice. And probably their rules.'

'Another thing,' Sensei added, 'They're not city people like most of you, they're islanders, fishermen and women, not better or worse but a bit different. Pros and cons there too. Like Steve says, you should give it serious thought. And ask us your questions, we might even have an occasional answer.'

'Is going to Fort William a possibility,' asked Fiona, her voice worried.

'I can't see any benefit in that,' replied Steve. 'It's much more vulnerable, and the benefits are not obvious.'

Fiona and Malky hugged, their relief clear.

'But,' added Steve, 'We should probably contact them, tell them our concerns, and ask if any of them want to join us.'

He looked at Fiona.

'Doesn't mean we'd accept them all, okay?'

So now a tongue-tied Steve is trying to squirm his way out of his embarrassment, while Cathy laughs at him.

'You mean if we're here more or less forever we need to consider breeding, is that it?'

'Well yes, consider it… I wasn't suggesting you and me… You know what I mean, don't you?'

She is still laughing.

'Hmm, I suppose I could do worse. You, on the other hand, could do much better, all those younger women idolising you, you big sex symbol!'

'Don't, Cath, please. I know it's early days still, but is it something we should be thinking about or do we just let nature take its course?'

'I'm guessing that you see yourself with Allie… oh don't be silly, none of us are blind, at least not the women! And she obviously likes the idea, so that's cool. But Sensei won't be here forever, so Jack is going to have to grow up fast to take care of Joni, Fiona and me!'

She is giggling like a schoolgirl now, while Steve just stands, speechless.

'Hmm, I guess I didn't quite think it through, did I?' He pauses, looks at her closely. 'You really think he'll go?'

'Of course. God, men see fuck all! He – and Vidock – have got someone somewhere, he'll have to go and find out if she's still alive.'

'You think so? He's never said anything to me.'

'Yeah, and you guys share so much personal stuff, don't you!

What do you know about him?'

'Lots! He's ex-military, something serious, and he lived in Troon, I think…'

'Bravo! I know Fiona's parents' names, why she married MacDougall's brother, what happened to her sister… I know Joni's life story, where she went to school, how she and Allie met, about her first boyfriend… You guys just don't talk about anything except fighting!'

'That's right, Cath, we just talk about how to keep all of you alive. Sorry we're so insensitive.'

Cathy falls against his chest, her arms tight around him.

'I'm sorry, Steve, I need to go home, I need to see where it happened, I need her photos, I need closure!'

'Soon, I promise, we'll take you home soon.'

'Don't you see, none of this is fucking real! It's not our life, it's certainly not my life! I'm a nearly middle-aged mother, a wife, not a fucking warrior! I can't do this any more!'

'You can, sweetheart, because you *are* a warrior. You've been through hell, maybe the worst of any of us, but you're strong, you've held us together, you're the most important person here. You're the glue, the link between the generations, and between the men and women. I need you more than anybody. Yes, more than Sensei.'

He holds her until she stops sobbing.

She wipes her face.

'Soon, Steve, okay? Soon.'

7

Sensei settles back into a rhythm as he pedals along the north shore of Loch Cluanie through the steady rainfall.
A sodden Vidock is perched grumpily in the trailer behind the Genesis Croix de Fer gravel bike.
Neither he nor the man are happy about the arrangement, but the distances to be travelled are such that the latter is more concerned about the dog's well-being than his humour.
He let him run most of the way from Plockton to Loch Duich, but had him on board before they passed picturesque Eilean Donan Castle, which was invisible in the darkness of night.
On the mountain stretch between Lochs Duich and Cluanie the dog cantered the uphill stretches, partly for the benefit of the rider, and hopped back on for the long downhills.
After a brief stop to stretch and refuel the cyclist at the Cluanie Inn, they set off again.
Sensei's mind drifts back to his last visit there when, with Grahamie and Seanie, he accepted Fiona and Malky into the fold.
He now considers that to be among the best decisions of his life, as they have contributed greatly to the group dynamic.
Not only that, she is a very attractive woman who, in a different situation, he might have offered more encouragement when she made her charmingly subtle approach.
But the situation is far from simple, with Cathy also in the equation.
His feelings for her are dangerously troublesome; he admires

her sharpness of mind and mental fortitude as well as her physical attributes, her strong, lithe body and intelligent face. He smiles as he remembers how she took control of things after being appointed quartermaster way back at the end of October, nearly five months ago...

At the next group meeting she laid out the 'rules' quite clearly.

'I am responsible for the food and Jules is responsible for the cooking. We have agreed some, ahem, let's call them guidelines,' she told them with a smile.

'These apply to everyone, everyone except Allie, for obvious reasons. We will provide set meals every night, where everyone will get the same fare. Not the same amount, of course, because Jack eats as much as the rest of us put together!'

There was laughter as Jack turned very red.

'It's okay, Jack, we already know that you do as much work as the rest of us put together, so it's a fair trade! No, my point is that we have a limited range of stuff, so there will be no special meals. No pescatarian, vegetarian or vegan, no gluten-free without a doctor's note. We will try to provide you with as healthy a diet as possible, because we can't afford for anyone to get ill.'

She paused and looked around.

'There will be no snacks between meals, and no food will be wasted. If anyone has any questions I am always here. Hell, where else could I be!'

She stopped and looked at Steve, who nodded once.

This had been a prepared speech, agreed in advance, and

delivered with conviction and humour.
The message was clear: we're all in this together, no rank, no favourites.
It left no room for debate.
But, Sensei reflects, she is still a deeply tormented woman, in no way ready for a relationship, although he has long been aware that she was available for comfort and warmth during the long winter nights.
Add Joni to the mix – young, lovely, bubbly, energetic Joni – and they have the makings of a British comedy film from the nineteen-fifties or sixties.
He is aware that he is no Brad Pitt (or whoever the current male sex symbol might be, he is hugely ignorant of such things) but Steve seems to have an agreement with Allie, and Jack is still a boy, so there's not much in the way of competition, unfortunately.
He pushes these thoughts to the back of his mind, along with the mystery of the enigmatic Kirsty from Drumnadrochit and her conflicting behaviour during their two encounters; he has his own ancient demons to battle before he can face new ones.

8

'He's gone, isn't he?'

Steve and Cathy start at Fiona's question, and look at each other nervously.

They are back in the hotel, where most of the group is eating porridge before getting on with their tasks.

'I know things,' says Fiona, 'Always have done. Lost it for a while there, but it seems to be back now. When were you going to tell us?'

'Jeez, Fiona,' says Steve, 'He's not home right now, it's not the end of the world. Hell, we've already had that!'

His attempt at humour falls flat as everyone watches, waiting.

'It's true,' says Malky, 'Mum's some sort of spey-wife, sees things nobody else does, usually before they happen. Used to drive my dad and my uncle spare!'

Fiona touches his head.

'That's all gone now, sweetheart, we're safe here. So, Steve, what's the plan now?'

Steve reddens, his temper rising.

'Fuck sake, the guy's not at home, he's often not at home, how is this suddenly a bloody crisis? Has nobody got any work to do? Will I find some for you?'

'I didn't mean to upset you, Steve, but I think you've just confirmed what I said, that he's gone and you know it.'

Steve's shoulders slump; he looks at Cathy, so she answers.

'He's not there, yes. But we don't know more than that. We do know that he has his own plans, but he promised to stay at least until the end of winter, didn't he!'

'It's the middle of March,' says Joni, 'How long does winter last up here?'

'Hell, Joni,' Steve tries again to lighten the mood. 'You should know that better than any of us, you come from the frozen north, don't you?'

He catches her eye and, to his surprise sees understanding there.

'Aye, fit like,' she says in a self-mocking Aberdeenshire accent, before putting the back of her wrist to her forehead in best melodramatic style and continuing in a posh BBC voice. 'Woe is me, I have forgotten my roots! I have been seduced by Glasgow's balmy Mediterranean climes.'

The laughter is a momentary relief, before every eye turns back to Steve.

'Aye well,' interjects Hugh, 'It still feels like bloody winter to me. He'll not have gone far, he'll not abandon us without a word, that's for sure.'

But the look in his eyes reflects back the doubt in Steve's and Cathy's.

'Right,' snaps Steve, 'Everyone on their toes, even more alert than usual until our friend gets back.'

Good advice that sadly was not universally heeded.

9

Before long Sensei has other problems to occupy his mind.
The rain is heavier and, as they leave Loch Cluanie and climb again, he realises that the absence of traffic is a double-edged sword.
Sure, he is in no danger of colliding with an impatient motorist trying to overtake a camper van, or a reckless white van man straightening out the tight curves, but the roads have the whole winter's precipitation uncleared.
Nearer the coast the salt on the wind means that the roads are fairly clear, but here there are large puddles of water edged with snow.
The real danger is unseen as, even with the relatively mild weather, there is some black ice lying under patches of snow, or in spots where successive rainfalls have frozen on top of the previous ones.
After one particularly hair-raising skid which left Vidock sprawled on the white-crusted grass verge, he determines that caution is preferable to speed, a decision ratified by Vidock's flat refusal to climb back onto his chariot.
By the time they once again reach the bridge over the River Garry, the scene of the one-sided skirmish with MacDougall and his crew, it is, despite their early start, already afternoon.
He realises he has seriously misjudged the state of the roads, with the trip taking almost twice as long as it did with Steve back in October, but he reckons to make good time from here as the road is fairly flat, running along the banks of Loch Oich

and Loch Lochy.

But as he reaches the Well of the Seven Heads, near the southern tip of Loch Oich, he is stunned to hear a loud bang which he immediately recognises as a gunshot.

This is a place with a bloody history, as the seven heads commemorated on an obelisk belonged to a family of MacDonalds, a father and his six sons, who were decapitated over 350 years ago in reprisal for an earlier murder committed by them.

The heads were washed here by Bald Ian Lom, Gaelic Poet Laureate of Scotland, before being sent to Edinburgh for public display.

Leaping from the bike, Sensei sees a figure jumping up and down brandishing a rifle on the far shore, a bit over 300 yards away.

He shakes his head, there being nothing more useful to do, wonders what the hell the point was, remounts and continues without stopping until he reaches the Commando Memorial outside Spean Bridge.

This is a monument in honour of British Commandos who trained in the area during World War II, so he pauses briefly to pay his respects and to sift through some memories of his own.

With only a passing thought for the rifleman of Loch Oich, who he guesses is a branch or two short of a family tree, he gazes through weak sunshine at the great rounded peaks of Ben Nevis and Aonach Mor to the south before coaxing Vidock back on board and tackling the last few miles into Fort William.

He had intended dropping in to see Grahamie and Seanie, and warning them to watch out for Finlay come springtime, but as he hadn't made the progress he hoped today, he decided to push on and visit them on his return journey.
Two or three days, he thinks, won't make a lot of difference.
If only he knew…

10

The rain is, as we say in Scotland, fair chucking it down when I cross the River Nevis and arrive at the roundabout where Fiona and Malky met us as we were heading north.
I send Vidock on ahead and follow him as far as the supermarket on the right-hand side of the next roundabout, from where the road runs south along the banks of the loch.
I am not surprised to find that its shelves still hold some supplies; it is close enough to the town centre to make it as good as any place to store tinned goods and other non-perishables.
I pick up cans of peaches and dog food – not his favourite brand but we all have to make do – and, a bonus, some Mature Scottish cheddar cheese.
'Want some biscuits, they've got Bonio?' I ask, but he has already wandered off to sulk elsewhere. 'Look, I've got you some mild Scottish cheddar, your favourite.'
I shove some in my pockets, whistle once, and leave.
Fort William is a strange town, lying as it does on the east shore of beautiful Loch Linnhe, but with no view from the main street of the rugged splendour of Lochaber across to the west.
Instead this road, the same one we were directed to use by MacDougall, is a bypass, so that any traffic or otherwise unwelcome folk passing through don't intrude on the town centre.
This suits my purpose, as there is little chance of anyone

peering through the rain and low cloud and seeing me peching by.

With Vidock leading the way we reach the West End Roundabout, where I first encountered MacDougall, without sighting anyone.

Then he climbs reluctantly on board and we zip past the hotels and boarding houses on Achintore Road, where I am angered to see that the bodies have still not been collected and buried, so there are rats everywhere.

Not yet my problem, I think, and we soon leave the town behind us.

In a couple of hours we'll reach the Isles of Glencoe Hotel which I know is, if nothing else, corpse-free.

11

It seems to Cathy that when Sensei left he took harmony with him.
The formerly tight-knit group is suddenly riven with small squabbles, and alcohol consumption has increased significantly.
Minor annoyances which would have been laughed off a day or two ago are now the trigger for arguments.
For the first time since they arrived here people are questioning their duties, their workload, looking to see who is not doing their share.
Steve is edgy and curt, seemingly devoid of any warmth or humour.
Joni takes offence at everything, falls out with everyone, even Allie, who retreats into a Ronnie-shaped cocoon.
Jack speaks to no one, answers Malky's offers of help with a series of grunts.
Fiona works harder than ever but, except when necessary, speaks only to her son.
Except at dinner time, Rick stays at home, ostensibly on lookout duty, but who knows if he is even awake.
Cathy watches through narrowed eyes, says nothing.
Hugh and Jules, too, watch with growing concern, until they feel action is needed.
They call a formal meeting and are forced to decree that attendance is compulsory; this has never happened before.
Hugh has the floor.

'Speaking as the oldest and wisest among us,' he starts, and pauses waiting for the laughter that never comes, 'I have to say I have never been more disappointed in my friends than over these past days. I look at all of you, people I love and respect, and I see a bunch of spoilt brats. I'm ashamed to be one of you.'

Stony silence.

'I'm not surprised you've nothing to say, your collective behaviour says everything about you. Joni, where are you going?'

Joni mutters something under her breath, lifts a half-full bottle of wine and storms out of the room, slamming the door behind her.

Steve and Cathy start to speak at the same time, then stop, looking at each other.

'Fucking shambles,' snaps Jack, 'I'm on lookout duty. Again!' And he stomps, only slightly less dramatically, out into the night.

12

The light is fading as we cross the Ballachulish Bridge, but the clouds are higher and lighter now, which lets me hope for good weather for the climb up through Glencoe tomorrow.

Less than a mile from the hotel is a war memorial where I let Vidock off to stretch and trot ahead.

The view across Loch Leven touches me, and reminds me that the world is not yet completely lost.

I pedal on, weary as hell now, when Vidock stops abruptly and crouches into his spring position.

I slip off the bike, grab my Glock 17 and, bending low, run to his side.

We are still maybe 100 yards from the turn-off to Ballachulish village, and over the low hedge I see some cabins and a Fiat service station.

What I don't see is a reason for his behaviour, but I trust that his ears or nose have picked up some indication of life.

Then two men appear from behind a metal container, close enough that we can't avoid each other.

I figure that they can't see Vidock for the hedge so I snap 'Hide' and motion him forward.

Then I push the pistol into my jacket pocket, stand tall and, with my left hand high, call to them.

They look up from whatever the taller man is carrying, the surprise evident on their faces.

I have reached the gap in the hedge now, Vidock low to my right, and I see the older, stockier man move towards a motorbike leaning against the container.

'You don't need a weapon,' I say, 'I'm just passing through, not looking for trouble.'

He grunts, lifts a rucksack from the bike, holds it in front of him as he moves to meet me.

'Donald McLean,' he says, 'My son, Donnie.'

A fleeting thought about pairs of survivors skims across my consciousness, but this is not the moment to ponder such things.

'You down from the Fort?'

I nod.

'Just left there two, three hours ago, on a bike.' I gesture with my head towards the road. 'Heading south, Curious about what's happening. You?'

'Oban. Scouting for parts.' He indicates his son's hands, which holds something oily in a rag. 'There many left up there?'

I'm reluctant to give up any information about my friends in Fort William, so I keep it vague.

'Aye, quite a strong wee community. You thinking about a visit?'

'I think so, I've another bike I want to get running.'

'Good luck with that. If I'm not there, just say that Bossman sent you. That's what they call me, for whatever reason.'

The older man nods.

'Aye, I can believe that, you've a look about you right enough. You might even give Donnie here a bit of competition in a square go.'

Donnie still hasn't spoken, just keeps staring at me.

I've been watching him, assessing him, and figure he's strong enough to toss large chunks of tree about in traditional Highland fashion, but probably moves at the pace of the great glaciers that shaped this landscape over 10,000 years ago.
I laugh, arms wide.
'He looks way too big and strong for me, I'm kind of old for that sort of thing. You head man in Oban?'
'Not quite, more second in command. We're like you, not that many, but we're tough, well-organised.'
He tells me how the soldiers arrived with guns drawn, captured everyone they saw, disabled whatever vehicles they didn't take with them, and mined the A85 going north and the A83 south at Inveraray.
In return I tell him about Finlay, but he's not interested.
'He'll not come away down here, and if he does he'll get sent home again with his tail between his legs! We weren't ready for the army back then but we're ready for pretty much anything now, eh, Donnie!'
Donnie grunts, his sole contribution to the conversation.
This is a guy who thinks that a fruit drink is half a banana in a cup of warm water.
We part on good terms, open invites on both sides, but when they turn back to their Honda Rebel, I point to the shrubs across the road, tell Vidock 'Hide', and head back to my bicycle.
They don't need to know about my secret weapon just yet.
A few minutes later they roar past with a wave and a toot of the horn, and I summon my chum from his place of

concealment as I cycle wearily towards food and a bed.

13

'Fiona's all agitated,' Cathy tells Steve, 'She says something bad's about to happen.'
'Oh c'mon, Cath, you can't believe all this second-sight fortune-telling shit, she's just jumpy because Sensei's not around. Hell, we all are, you saw that fiasco last night.'
'She knew he was gone before we did, and nobody could have told her. Some folk do have a gift, I knew a girl down in Ayrshire who was like that. Fuck it, she had red hair too! And green eyes, just like Fiona…'.
'Okay, let's stay calm. How are we going to get things back together if you lose the plot too? Come on, please, I need you to sort out the girls, the women. Get Jules to help, she's solid as a rock, just what we need. I'll talk to Jack and…'
He stop abruptly as two things happen almost simultaneously. Something cracks off the wall of Meghan's Ice Cream shop behind where they are standing in the harbour car park.
And a boom echoes across the bay.
Steve's eyes widen then he grabs her arm and pulls her down behind the low wall.
'Gunshot!' he snaps, looking round frantically for the source.
A few seconds pass before the second bang shatters the shop window.
'Fuck sake, it's coming from the other side of the bay,' he yells, 'Let's get out of here.'
Heads low, with Steve trying to shield Cathy, they sprint the hundred yards back to the hotel.

The others are in the street, looking around with puzzled expressions.

'Inside, now!' roars Steve, 'We're under attack!'

He hustles everyone in, stands panting with his back to the door.

'Is everyone here?'

'Malky!'

Fiona appears from the kitchen, takes in the frightened faces, and screams for her son.

'I'll get him says Steve, grabbing her as she dives for the door. 'Where is he?'

'I'll go myself, he's fishing with Rick, let me go!'

'It's okay,' says Cathy. 'There won't be any more shots. We're not in danger.'

They all stare at her in disbelief, Steve especially.

'How can you say that? We just had two shots fired at us?'

'They weren't trying to hit us, they were a warning.'

She waits until the clamour of voices quietens, before she continues.

'We were behind the wall when he fired the second shot. And it was further away than the first.'

'Do you think it was Sensei?' from Joni. 'Making sure we're on our toes.'

'I wish I did,' says Cathy, 'But it wasn't him. Definitely.'

Steve asks the obvious question.

'What makes you so sure? You can't possibly know that.'

'The first shot missed. He was aiming at the window.'

Fiona disappears out the door as the others stare at Cathy.

Then they jump as Jack barges in carrying a mountain of logs. The silent confusion turns to relieved laughter, which causes him to dump the wood loudly at his feet.

'You lot talking about me?'

And they all hug him as the laughter becomes more natural. When Fiona comes in with Malky they are all chatting and joking with each other.

She scowls at them for a long time before she speaks.

'Aren't we all forgetting something?'

14

Although the sun has not yet risen, there is some light in the eastern sky as Sensei starts the long haul up through Glencoe. He has several miles of steep climbs, so plenty of time to think, not something he wants to do too much of at this stage.
He is concerned about those he has left behind, wonders if he should have told them he was leaving, but that would have led to all sorts of questions he has no intention of answering, and they would seek reassurances he is not in a position to give.
So instead he looks for the positives in the current situation.
Well, the Tories are finally out of Westminster, that can't be bad!
He is a firm supporter of Scottish independence, not because, as the main stream media want people to believe, he is anti-English, but because he despises the lying, corrupt, self-entitled psychopaths who have dominated UK politics for too long.
He has trained and fought with English soldiers, as well as those from many other countries, and he does not differentiate on nationality, colour, gender, ethnicity or anything else.
If he trusts someone in this situation, they are a brother (regardless of gender), and if not, they are nothing to him.
His only gripe with the English is the bastards they vote into office.
The sky is turning slowly blue up ahead as he reaches the heart of the glen, one of Scotland's most atmospheric spots, the scene of the infamous massacre more than three centuries ago,

the spirit of which still hangs heavily over these hillsides.
His country's reputation as a land of mystery, myths and mists, of monsters and ghosts, is nourished by such places, and although today there is, remarkably, no low cloud to heighten the atmosphere, the road surface is treacherous enough that he has to take care not to add to the spectres that haunt this magnificent glen.
But he feels there is less snow, and the road is less hazardous, than might be expected, although why this should be he cannot say.
Vidock trots happily ahead, enjoying the banks of snow, untroubled by any such thoughts.
By the time he reaches the stunning view of Three Sisters to the south of the road the worst of the climb is behind him, so he gets Vidock on board and ploughs on through the snow and slush.

15

There is much debate about who could have fired the shots, and why.

If they were designed to cause unrest, they have had the opposite effect, the group has gathered together again.

Like any people anywhere, whether a family or a nation, fighting among themselves is normal, but if any outsider threatens, then they stand united.

They consider the different possibilities.

Their neighbours in Portree are a possibility but, according to Sensei, an unlikely one.

And they can't believe anyone who has met him would willingly start a fight with him.

A lone wolf, a hunter trying to make a point, makes no sense either.

Why announce yourself in such a way if you want to make contact?

And, if you don't want to, then why make yourself known at all?

So they come to Doctor Finlay.

Again, they know only what Sensei has told them, and none of that is good, but questions remain.

For a start, as far as they are aware, he doesn't know they are here.

And again, why a warning shot?

They ask Rick what there is across the bay, where they have figured the shot must have come from.

'Nothing. There's no town there, no village, nothing. I don't think there's even a road. Ah no, wait, there's a railway station, so there must be something, I guess. There's only about one train a week, I think, but I suppose it must have some access.'

Steve determines that he will go and investigate, but is immediately shouted down by the others, who are adamant he needs to stay here in charge.

'I'll go,' says Hugh, 'I don't see who else there is.'

'Well there's me,' says Cathy, full of indignation, but she is immediately overruled by Steve.

Jack speaks up.

'Needs to be me, doesn't it? Sensei's been training me, I can take care of myself. And I've been round to the wee station, such as it is, that's one of the runs he takes me.'

Steve nods in agreement, but Fiona interrupts.

'Malky will go, he's the best at this sort of thing. He's been going hunting and tracking since he could walk, he can see and not be seen. And he's been there already too. Training, they call it!'

She has her arm around her son's shoulders, trying to be brave, but he has no fear.

Steve starts to argue 'He's just a boy…'

But Malky just grins and moves to the door.

'See you in a bit!'

16

By the time Sensei reaches the Rannoch Moor Viewpoint there is a definite feel of spring in the air.
As they lunch on cheese and water he gazes across this wild, almost desolate, yet beautiful landscape and thinks that it looks less forbidding than before, but maybe that's just relief at having put Glencoe behind him.
There are plenty of climbs ahead, but nothing on the same scale, so with Vidock unhappily on his trailer he fairly hurtles past Loch Ba, Lochan na h-Achlaise (which means 'loch of the armpit', thus called due to its strange shape) and then Loch Tulla before starting the climb into Bridge of Orchy, where he murdered a soldier on his last visit.
He remembers with no pleasure that he killed five men that day, and Steve killed three more, one a lad in his teens.
Judge and jury, he thinks to himself, I just picked a side and killed anyone who threatened my choice. Did I ever pause to consider that I might be wrong? I've come to know these people now, and they are in the main good-hearted and well-meaning, but I know nothing of those I shot down. Or, in one case, stabbed from behind in cold blood. All because I caught a bus.
He goes through Bridge of Orchy without a pause, but stops before Tyndrum and sends Vidock in ahead.
It is abandoned; the military have not replaced the two soldiers he killed here.
He stops for a nature break, raids the shop for bottled water,

then sits with his arm round his best friend as they share dog biscuits and tinned shortbread for energy.

One huge benefit of the long winter nights was the time they spent together talking and training, as well as out in the dark, running and cycling.

He knows a time will come when their understanding and trust will be the difference between life and death.

He is right about that.

17

'While we're here, waiting for Malky, maybe it's time to discuss our hero, who he is, why he's here, or why he was here, what makes him so bloody special anyway. And what he expects to get out of hanging around with us.'
Joni spins round in the middle of the group, challenging each of them with her eyes.
'Yes, I know we've all talked about him in our own wee cliques, but I think we'd all like to know the truth. So, Steve, how about you spill the beans, dish the dirt, hmm?'
'Hold on, Joni,' says Hugh, 'Don't you think that the guys got the right to some privacy, after all he's done for us? None of us would have made it this far if not for him, you know that.'
'Aye, love, that's true, but I agree with Joni, we've a right to be curious about what he's after.'
Hugh stares at Jules in disbelief, but says nothing.
'Whatever it is, it's not sex!' snipes Joni. 'Unless maybe Cath knows something different?'
Cathy spins towards her, eyes blazing, fists clenched, but before she can speak Steve steps in, catches her arm, turns her back towards him.
'Let it go, Cath, please. None of this is useful. Help me here.'
She moves towards the door but Jules intercepts her.
'We know that's not true, love, we know you've had maybe the worst loss of all, your man and your wee Karly. And you've been a credit to them and to their memory, you've done more than your share of keeping us all alive. Sorry, Rick,

nearly all.'
Rick nods in acknowledgement.
'That was nobody's fault, she was just getting old,'
'Joni has got a point,' say Allie. 'What do we know about the guy? God, he does yoga and karate and that other thing, cheap pong or whatever you call it. He catches fish and rabbits and birds and seals, he works all the hours God sends, he never seems to sleep, he kills lots of folk, and he's got that dog that he talks to more than he talks to us.'
Everyone starts to talk at once, some agreeing and some challenging what she said.
'Shut up,' roars Hugh, 'One at a time, please. Joni?'
'I'll not have anything said against Vidock, he saved me from that pervert, I won't forget that. I think he's wonderful.'
'Jack? You have something to add? This is a surprise!'
Jack blushes, looks at his hands.
He rarely speaks in front of the whole group.
'When we were walking up the West Highland Way, going to Bridge of Orchy, we talked about birds. No, Joni, the wee feathered ones!'
When the laughter quietens, he continues.
'It started with speugs, sparrows, y'know, and sort of went on. I talked about these lakes in Africa where millions of flamingos go to breed. I said that the male would walk through thousands of them till he saw one he liked. And I wondered what the difference was, because they all look the same. Does he just see one girl and think "Wow, nice legs!" or what?'
Everyone is watching him, smiling but silent.

'He didn't laugh at me. You know what he said? He said that they might look the same to us, but not to each other. And then he said maybe they weren't that superficial. Just because so many people judge each other by the colour of their skin, or by their shape and size, or where they come from, doesn't mean that animals and birds are so stupid. Maybe they see more than just the outside, maybe they see something to trust.'

He stops, looking embarrassed,

'What I mean is he's deeper than we think. He knows about stuff because he thinks about everything. He's not just a soldier or a killer. And trust is important to him.'

There are murmurs of agreement.

'Thanks, Jack, that's very good. I think you've given us a lot to think about there. Steve?'

'Allie, I know he killed a few folk getting us here, but so did I. We were all in it together at Tyndrum, remember? And he tried talking to MacDougall and his shower of bampots, they just wouldn't take a telling.'

'Yes, Steve, I know, but you're a soldier, like my Ronnie was. You're strong and brave, that's one of the things I love about you. You're not like Sensei, you care about people.'

'He was a soldier too, y'know, just maybe a bit further up the food chain than I was!'

'So tell us, Steve,' Rick doesn't speak often, but his words are usually thoughtful. 'What sort of soldier was he, do you know?'

'Well, no, not exactly, but he was a bloody good one, I'll tell you that. He sees problems in advance, gets everyone organised and ready for action, like at Tyndrum. He knew there were rogue soldiers out there, and he told me how we'd need to handle it. He sent the pre-arranged signal with Vidock that told us it was war. He'd already explained to me what I'd need to do if the shooting started.'

'Kill them all,' says Hugh.

'Yes, we had no choice. We did have a choice with MacDougall and we let him live. Much good it did us.'

Rick asks again.

'Was he Special Forces or something?'

Steve looks at Rick sadly.

'I asked him that exact question back at Invergarry bridge.'

'And what did he say?'

'Something.'

They stop and think until Joni speaks again.

'That doesn't answer any of the questions, does it? Why he's with us, and what he wants from us? We don't even know for sure if we'd have been better off without him.'

Steve looks at her sadly.

'Joni, without him we'd all be dead, or maybe even worse than dead. We'd have been killed or captured at Tyndrum, either by the two soldiers or by the deserters we fought later.'

'How would that be worse than being stuck up here in the bloody freezing cold with no idea what's happening in world? We've no phones, no internet, no telly, nothing, we don't know what's going on, do we? Everything might be back to normal in Glasgow.'

'Joni, try to understand, if things had gone wrong in Tyndrum you'd have certainly have been raped, and then maybe taken back to Glasgow as breeding stock. You'd have been sex slaves, sweetheart.'

'Chance would be a fine thing', she spits back, then recoils as Cathy explodes in her face.

'Shut the fuck up! We all make allowances for you, because you're just pretty Joni, so young and so sweet, but that is the stupidest thing I've ever heard anyone say in my life! It's time you stopped playing the cute teenager and started to grow up because you have no fucking idea what you're talking about!'

'Fuck sake, Cathy, keep your shirt on, I didn't know you were the world's expert on this as well as every other bloody thing!'

'Have you forgotten what happened when you first met Allie?' asks Cathy, struggling to contain her rage. 'Because the rest of us,' she sweeps her arm around the room, 'remember it well, you've told us often enough. And now it's a bloody joke to you?'

'Christ, Cath, you don't have to be like that, it was me it happened to, not you.'

Then she sees the expression on the other's face, and goes white.

'Oh Jesus, what happened?'

'I fucking killed them, that's what happened!'

Cathy is right in Joni's face, screaming, 'I fucking killed two boys!'

'Because...'

Steve puts a hand on Cathy's arm, but she shakes him off. Then she breathes.

'They tried to rape me. Dragged me into the park, tore at my clothes. They were near hysterical, with a knife, I was terrified. But I got the knife and killed them. Just boys.'

Joni's face collapses, drenched in tears, and she sinks to her knees, arms over her head; no one else breathes.

Then Jules speaks, understanding at last.

'Was that the same day you got on the bus…'

Cathy's head drops in what might be a nod.

'I told Sensei when we left Bridge of Orchy and went up the West Highland Way. He just listened, didn't judge, didn't say anything. When I finished, and stopped crying, he reminded me what he had said back on Loch Lomond. When we stopped after that yellow gas stuff, remember? He knew something had happened. The first thing he said to me was that no one would hurt me again. And I believed him. I still believe him. Well, most of the time.'

Then she falls into a chair and sobs into her hands.

18

The road from Tyndrum down through Crianlarich to Loch Lomond undulates a bit, but there are no serious climbs and lots of long gentle downhill slopes. We make good time past the Falls of Falloch, Inverarnan and Ardlui before we hit the loch-side and see Ben Lomond ahead, majestic against the bright blue sky.

We hurtle through Tarbet, past Luss and the Helensburgh turn-off, and the loch is behind us before I realise that I've passed the point where I flagged down the bus all those months ago. I'm not a big believer in what-ifs, but my smile is wry when I consider how different my winter would have been without that out-of-character impulse.

Hell, what would the situation have been by the time I'd reached Tyndrum on foot?

We pass the turn-off for Dumbarton, with its ancient castle on an elephant-shaped rock, and follow the A82 as it runs parallel to the River Clyde until we reach the Erskine Bridge.

I can't believe there will be a military presence here after all this time, but my caution overrides my expectation, and I climb the off-ramp, my shortest route, slowly, staying close to the trees and shrubs that line the road.

Just before the bridge itself sits, quite bizarrely, a telephone box.

I leave the bike here, and follow Vidock along the pedestrian lane behind the protective rails.

He is almost at the halfway point when he again stops and

crouches, indicating trouble.

I move to his side and peer onto the road.

Up ahead someone is sitting, or rather sprawled, in the fast lane with his back against one of the wheel-less cars that block the carriageway.

I approach quietly, still behind the rail, until I am directly opposite him.

He is sound asleep.

I step up and over the rail, walk across to the guy who looks maybe eighteen years old, long and lanky, and lift his rifle, an ancient weapon of dubious provenance.

Then I kick his foot.

He wakens with a start, his eyes widen, and he leaps to his feet, shouting.

'Whoa man, you can't touch that, that's mine, that's official government property.'

I laugh, and step back, holding the rifle at arms length away from him.

'Calm down and let's talk,' I say. 'I'm not going to hurt you.'
'I'll bloody hurt you, you prick! Think you're fucking Rambo with your headband? Well, I'm a soldier and I can fight!'

I had forgotten that I wear a bandana on the bike to keep my hair off my face, so this makes me laugh even more.

So he lunges at me with the inevitable result that he lands quite hard on the tarmac.

I point the rifle at him.

'Do you want me to shoot you,' I ask, still grinning, 'Or can we have a wee chat like grown-ups?'

'Man, you're in all sorts of trouble, y'know, when I tell HQ what you did. *They'll* probably shoot *you* for interfering with a military operation. Give me the gun now, before you make things worse.'
'Aye, talking about your gun, what is this, it looks like it was last used at Culloden.'
'That's not funny, just give me it,'
'Okay, but tell me first, what's your name, and what are you doing here?'
He looks at me like I'm a moron.
'I'm Private McPhail, and I'm guarding the bridge!'
'Against what?'
'What?'
'What are you guarding the bridge against?'
'People crossing it, of course.'
Now it's my turn to not understand.
'What?'
'No one's allowed to cross the bridge. That's my orders.'
'So what happens when someone comes along, just like me, and wants to go to the other side? I mean, that's kinda what bridges are for, isn't it?'
'I stop them and send them back.'
'In which direction?'
'Depends where they came from. They go back where they came from.'
He is speaking slowly, as though I am thick as mince.
'So if someone comes from the north,' I indicate where I've come from, 'You send them back to the north, and if they

come from the south, they go back there, is that right?'

'Aye, you've got it, it's not hard, is it?'

'Why?'

'What?'

'Why do you send them back, why not let them cross?'

'That's my orders!'

I stare at him for a bit thinking that, even by military standards, this is stupid.

'So how long have you been doing this?'

'Couple of months.'

'And how many folk have you had to send back?'

'You're the first.'

I burst out laughing again, then try to stop when I see how offended he is.

'I've got bad news, son, I'm not going back. I'm heading south.'

'But you can't, they'll court martial me for dereliction of duty. Then they'll probably shoot *me*!'

'How will they know?'

'What?'

I grin at him again.

'What's your first name, son?'

'Ian.'

'I'm not going to tell anyone, Ian, are you?'

He stares at me for a while, then his shoulders slump.

'But you're my first customer,' he says, causing me to laugh again, 'I'm a rubbish soldier, so I am.'

'Well, to be fair, you were sound asleep when I arrived, so

you're not the world's top sentry, are you?'
'Man, it's so fucking boring, nothing ever happens, I'm cold and hungry and tired, and I'm wasting my time out here.'
'You're wasting mine too, I need to get moving. Yes, south, sorry. Give me a hand to make room between these cars – JUST DO IT! – thank you, now climb over the rail there.'
He looks at me strangely then, as he clambers up, he asks if I'm going to kill him.
'I don't need to.'
'Jesus Christ, there's a fucking wolf there!'
'Get over, sit down, and don't move. He won't chew you if you stay still.'
Struggling to keep my face straight at his terror and Vidock's oh-come-on-you-can't-be-serious expression, I ask him a few questions about what is happening at what he calls HQ, then head back for my bike.
I leave his gun there and call out as I cycle past.
'You're blunderbuss is at the phone box. Have a nice day!'
I whistle for Vidock and head towards the M8.

19

There is a long pause while everyone digests this, before eventually Fiona breaks the silence.

'I think he's very sweet. He's thoughtful and caring and gentle.'

Hugh once again has to calm the uproar that follows her words.

'Well,' snarls Allie, who is feeding Ronnie, and usually never raises her voice, 'Now we know why he let you join us, don't we?'

She is apparently bitter on behalf of Joni, who remains slumped on the floor, staring at her fingers.

'No, Allie, you don't. We all know that you two fantasise about some sort of post-war heaven where the four of you live happily ever after in big houses and raise families, so you don't actually see reality, do you? That's not how it was. Malky was with me the whole time, so he never so much as touched me.'

'So what made him change his mind? Neither of you ever said, did you?'

'If he chose not to tell you, it's not up to me, is it?'

'Steve, you must have asked him why. What did he say?'

'He said we all make mistakes, and sometimes we're lucky and we get the chance to make things right.'

'The thing is,' Allie says, 'I asked him the morning after you betrayed us if he meant what he said about cutting your throats and he didn't say no! We all believed him, why didn't you?'

'Because I'd met all of you, and I thought you were wonderful. That night at Corriegour made me realise that life could be different, be better, didn't have to be the nightmare we'd always lived. I had to take the risk, for Malky's sake as well as my own. He understood. I'm not denying he has faults, and he's got violence in him, but inside he's a kind man. And you have all been more wonderful than I deserved, kinder than I ever hoped. This winter has been the happiest time of my life, and Malky's too.'

Allie pulls the baby from her breast and hands him to Steve without a word.

Covering herself with her shawl, she goes to Fiona and hugs her, murmuring apologies.

Jules clatters off to make tea, and the four men catch each other's eyes then look at their feet in embarrassment.

This time the silence lasts until the next surprise.

20

They fly along the M8 – thinking how great deserted motorways are for cyclists – and turn off onto the A737 just before Glasgow Airport.
The occasional roadblock has been erected to prevent the movement of cars, but the bike and trailer pass through with ease.
Sensei is happy to avoid Paisley and, a few miles later, Johnstone, both sizeable towns which, although they're only a dozen or so miles from Glasgow, might still have population bases.
The Highlands are well behind them now so they make good time down the relatively flat A737, and reach Kilwinning, which has quite a history, without a pause.
It has a population of around 15,000 and is known for its strong Orange background.
It is home to the original Lodge of Freemasonry in Scotland, which legend says has existed since the building of the abbey in the 12th Century, and which is reputed to be the world's oldest masonic lodge.
They squeeze past the barricade of cars, then avoid the town centre by turning off the main road at McGavin Park and, with Vidock out in front, follow follow Old Woodwynd Road and then Woodwynd until they rejoin the A737 just before the bridge over the River Garnock.
After another barrier, this time constructed mainly of washing-machines and other white goods, they are pretty much clear

and on the Irvine Road, nearing the coast.
At Eglinton Country Park with its ruined castle they turn east onto the A78 in order to bypass Irvine, a town of over 30,000 people.
At the Meadowhead Roundabout they slip off to the west, past the first of the golf courses for which Ayrshire is world-famous.
Now only a few miles from their destination, near the Old Loans Inn, they are again delayed by an encounter with other survivors.

21

Malky bursts in, breathless and full of excitement, the words tumbling incoherently from his mouth.

Fiona pulls him to her and, to his great embarrassment and the laughter of everyone else, smothers him in relieved kisses.

'Mum, geroff me! I've got news, it's important, let me go!'

'Okay,' Steve grins, 'Put the boy down, Fiona, and let's hear what he's got to tell us. Well, Malky, what did you find out?'

'I saw the rifle, one like they use for hunting stags.'

He pauses as Fiona interrupts, then goes on.

'I saw them in dad's magazines, mum, he was always talking about getting a good gun, a real hunting rifle, instead of that old piece of krap – sorry, mum, but that's what he said – that he'd got from grandpa a hundred years ago!'

Everyone is laughing now, apart from Fiona, who is shaking her head.

'Let's stick to the point, okay,' says Steve. 'Where was this, Malky, and was the shooter there?'

'No, but listen. Well, I followed the railway line like you told me, it goes right along the shore, right over the water in some bits, and into the wee station. It's really small, just a platform at one side and a wee pointy-roof hut thing, but there's a bridge over the railway right there too. At the other side of the bridge there's like steep cliffs at each side of the line, so I knew he couldn't be there, you can't see anything! So I climbed up to the bridge, and there's a dirt road, big enough for a car, so I followed it towards the sea.'

'Were you being careful like you were told?'

'Aye, mum, obviously, I'm here, right! Anyway not far along this track there's a house. That's where I saw the rifle!'

'In the house?'

'No, just wait, I'm trying to tell you! In front of the house, just by the door, there's a table under a big umbrella. The rifle was leaning against it, beside some muddy boots. And there was a waterproof draped over the chair.'

'You didn't go any closer, did you?

'No, mum! I was still hiding, but I didn't want to go any further or I'd have been out in the open in front of the house. There's flat grass and a wee jetty down below, quite near the big castle we can see over there.'

Hugh chips in some questions.

'There was nothing to tell you if he was inside the house, Malky? No smoke from the chimney, nothing like that?'

Malky shakes his head ruefully.

'Nah, I couldn't really see from where I was, I should have explored more, I'm sorry.'

About five people shout 'No!' simultaneously, and then start to laugh at each other.

'So,' Steve speaks slowly, thinking. 'There are lots of places he could have fired from, d'you think? Even the castle itself, hmm? But probably not, that's adding even more distance to a shot that's already about a half mile.'

'I think so, yes,' Malky nods. 'You can see here from there much easier than you see there from here, if you know what I mean. It's all trees and bushes, but here it's a street.'

'Exactly. You did brilliantly, Malky, and you were right to stop where you did. Can you imagine what your mum would have done to me if you'd got into trouble! No, we need to think carefully now, decide on our next move.'

22

We are only a couple of hundred yards from the turn-off which will take me into the heart of Troon and the place I still think of as home when I sense something.
At the same time Vidock who, the last time I looked, was asleep in his carriage, emits a low 'Wurruff', more a cough than a bark, which is his way of attracting my attention.
I slow down and look over my shoulder to see him struggling stiffly to his feet.
He is more alert when he is asleep than I am awake.
I pull up and dismount as he stumbles off and looks at me with bleary eyes.
We've been on the road for around twelve hours, and he doesn't travel well in his trailer.
I think for the millionth time how lucky I am, how I've done nothing in my life to deserve him.
'What is it?' I ask, and he turns away, moving slowly and staying close to the stone wall until he reaches a cottage on a corner.
He lifts his head, on full sensory alert, then crouches and looks at me.
This is it, he is saying.
I check the Glock, make sure my knife is in position, and step into a small, near-barren garden.

23

Steve, normally so easy-going, is on the verge of losing his temper.

'Like I told you long ago, way back at Fort William, this is not a democracy! I'm the elected leader of the group, and I'm a soldier, so I am going to investigate this guy round at Duncraig station. That's the end of it, okay?'

Hugh raises his voice to control the ensuing hubbub.

'One at a time,' he thunders. 'And I'm going first! Steve, we need you here, you're the guy in charge, we can't have you off site at a time when we might be under attack. That makes no sense.'

'And we can't risk losing you,' chimes in Cathy. 'Most of us weren't happy back at Fort William, but you overruled us. But things are different now. We didn't know each other then, we were just a collection of individuals, but now we're a unit. And we have a united voice.'

'If Sensei was here, he'd go without any discussion, wouldn't he? I've taken the time to tell you what I'm doing, maybe I should just have gone, eh?'

'Like he did, you mean?' snipes Joni. 'Then we'd have no big brave men to protect all us poor wee lassies!'

'That's enough, Joni!' Hugh is loud again. 'That is not useful. We know that you ladies are very capable, but I agree with Cath, Steve should be here, in charge of our defences.'

'But Cath can do that! I'll only be gone a couple of hours. Like I say, if Sensei was here we wouldn't be arguing, but you seem

to think he's the only one who can take care of himself.'
Reassurances of trust and belief are shouted from all sides, but Steve turns away, shaking his head.

'Steve…'

'No, leave it! You think I don't know I'm not him? You think I didn't see how everything changed when he disappeared? I know just how exceptional he is, but that doesn't mean I'm not capable. I'm a soldier too, y'know!'

'Steve, we know that, and we trust you completely. But the big difference is Vidock. He adds something that no one else has, he can smell things and hear better than any of us. And it's like they're bloody psychic!'

'I know that, Cath, but they're not here, are they?'

'How did they get like that anyway?' interrupts Joni. 'He just says a word or moves a hand or makes a wee whistle and the dog understands everything! I think he's the smartest of us all. Vidock, I mean, not Sensei!'

'Training,' answers Steve. 'They are working all the time. When the rest of us stop to eat or sleep or just to take a breather, they keep working. Have you noticed how Vidock sometimes starts to do something just before he's been told? That's because he watches Sensei, and senses how he's going to react, even to the small things. He reads him like a book. And it's all training.'

'Hell,' says Jules, nudging Hugh with her elbow. 'I've been trying to train this one for thirty-odd years and he still doesn't do as he's told!'

The laughter is more subdued than usual, so Cathy tries to

involve them all in something that might interest them.
'I know how he got his name.'
'Who, Vidock?'
About twenty, or maybe four, people ask the same question simultaneously.
'Yep, so I'll try to remember exactly what I was told. He's named after a remarkable 19th Century Frenchman, whose name was Vidocq, but spelt with a 'q' which Sensei changed to 'k' because he didn't want to be too pretentious! His first name was Eugene, I think, and he was a criminal who was in jail lots of times, escaped lots of times, and became a police informer and then a policeman. He was probably the first Private Investigator, and he's recognised as the father of modern criminology.'
She laughs.
'I'm starting to struggle now! Ah yes, he did stuff with ballistics, matching bullets to guns before anyone else, and he made special ink and paper to stop forgeries of banknotes! And he was in lots of books! Victor Hugo based two major characters in *Les Miserables* on Vidocq, and his, um, let's say, interesting career also influenced writers like Dumas, Poe, Melville and Dickens! That's all I remember. How did I do?'
'So he's named after a criminal?'
'Well yes, but a kinda creative and brave guy. Sensei told me he always thought that the French dude was just about worthy to give his name to his best friend.'
There is some laughter and chatter for a bit, then Steve speaks over it.

'Okay, Cath, that was great, thanks, so I'll tell you what. I'll wait till tomorrow, and go first thing, before it gets light. Until then we stay on full alert, I want everyone carrying their binoculars and scanning the far side of the bay constantly. Jack, you'll stay up at the Inn for now, watching the road. Meanwhile I'm going to take a wee hurl up the road on my bike, make sure there's nothing going on. Okay, let's get to it.'
'I'll come with you,' says Cathy. 'I need to stretch my legs anyway, haven't been keeping up with my exercises since…' Her voice trails off in embarrassment.
They all understand.
Discipline has fallen badly without their main motivator.
Steve reddens and leaves without another word.
She runs after him, furious at her stupidity, wondering how to help him regain control of the group.

24

There is no sign of life at the front of the house so I move soundlessly round the side.
I hear noises from what I guess is the kitchen and peer in through the open door.
A woman is at a worktop, prodding at something inside a pot.
It takes me a few moments to realise that she is in some sort of harness.
'Guard,' I tell Vidock, and knock on the door jamb.
The woman's head jerks round and I see she is just a girl, skinny as a rake, maybe 14 or 15 years old.
Her long hair is matted and filthy, and her skin is covered in sores.
Her eyes and mouth open and she lets out a small scream.
I hold my hands up, fingers open, and tell her I mean no harm.
'I just heard a noise and thought I'd look in.'
'You can't be here, Gerry will kill you!'
She is shaking in terror, but when she turns fully to look at me her movement is strange.
'What is that?' I ask, indicating the straps around her body which, behind her back, seem to be attached to a nylon rope.
This, I now see, is attached to a heavy wooden dining chair.
'You need to go, you need to go! He'll be back soon. He'll kill you and it'll be my fault.'
'What's in the pot?' I ask, peering in at what looks like dirty dishwater.
'Soup, I'm making soup, you need to go!'

'Looks a bit thin, don't you have any vegetables?'
She stares at me like I'm crazy, tries to push me towards the door,
She has no strength, she's just a shell.
'No tins of stuff you can put in, peas, beans, carrots?'
'We finished all that in the first week! There's no more here!'
It seems that Gerry is an adherent of the Kilmarnock Credo, which says 'We don't eat vegetables, we eat the things that eat vegetables.'
'What about next door, the other houses, the Inn along the road? You exhausted all them too?'
'I don't know about that!' She is almost hysterical. 'Gerry gets the food, I can't go anywhere. He's really big, he'll kill you!'
I think for a moment, then call Vidock inside, and sit him in the corner hidden by the door.
Then I pull my knife and she screams again, but longer and louder.
I put my hand over her mouth, turn her slightly, and cut the rope.
'You won't be needing that krap again, I promise you.'
I realise with wry surprise that I have made more promises to strangers since the war than in my entire life before that.
'No, no, no,' she whimpers, fumbling at the cut rope, 'Gerry will punish me for this, and it's not my fault.'
'You will not be punished…' I stop speaking as I hear heavy footsteps on the path outside.
I pull her behind me, telling her 'Stay back.'
Gerry stomps in, a large solid ruddy-faced lad, early to mid-

twenties, carrying some raw meat and a bloody axe.

His face tells me this won't be a friendly chat, so I sigh, and show him the Glock.

'What the fuck… Susie, who the fuck… Who the fuck are you? What're you doing here?

I'll fucking have you, ya…'

He has lifted the axe and taken a step when I fire into the floor between his feet.

He stops dead, the colour draining form his round fat face.

It's pretty clear who gets the bigger share of whatever food they have.

'Outside,' I say, feeling that we're all a bit close together in the kitchen. 'And leave the axe.'

He hesitates, and I see him thinking about taking a chance.

'Don't', I say, snapping my fingers. 'You can't win.'

Vidock's deep growl makes his head turn, so I step forward, twist the axe from his hand and push him out the door with the barrel of the pistol in his stomach.

'Okay,' I say. 'Explain this situation to me, and no lies. I can't abide liars.'

He holds up the bloody meat in his left hand.

'I take care of her, feed her, keep her safe. She cooks and cleans. That's all.'

'Why is she tied to a chair? Why is she terrified of you? Why is she so thin, and you're a fat pig?'

'I don't need to take this shit from you, asshole. You're a big man with the insults when you're holding a gun.'

I have a serious urge to damage this guy.

'You really want to do this? I have to hurt you to make you see sense? Fuck it, okay.'

I toss the Glock down towards the gate and tell Vidock to guard it.

Gerry immediately charges at me, hands out and head low.

I sway to the side, catch a wrist, and send him sprawling off the path onto the patchy grass.

He scrambles to his feet, breathing heavily, and lurches towards me again.

This time I move to meet him and hit him with a straight left to his nose.

Taken by surprise, he stumbles backwards, blood spurting over his face.

He wipes it away with the back of his hand, screams a torrent of obscenities, and lunges forwards again.

I catch his other wrist, spin him round to smash him face first into the wall of the house, but change my mind and hold him a split second longer so he hits at an angle, his shoulder taking the brunt of the collision.

He bounces off and crumples to the ground.

A sharp bark alerts me to the girl who is coming at me with the axe high above her head.

I reach up and take it from her; she barely has the strength to lift it.

'Do you have tea, Susie,' I ask.

25

'Malky's late down this morning,' says Jules, dolloping porridge into a plate for Fiona.
'What do you mean? Hasn't he been in for breakfast? He's not in his room…'
'Sorry, love, haven't seen him…'
She stops when she sees Fiona's expression.
'Oh no, love, he wouldn't! Would he…'
But Fiona is already out the door, shouting for her son.

Twenty minutes later they are all at the Inn, where Jack swears Malky has not passed him 'unless it was dead of night, I do sleep sometimes!'
'The path,' says Fiona. 'He'd take the footpath, it goes all the way to the castle, and doesn't come up by here. He only went along the railway line last time because that's what we told him.'
'Okay,' says Steve, 'I'll get after him. I need your rifle, Jack, get another from the hotel. No, Fiona, I'll go alone, I can travel faster that way. I want everyone else back at their posts on full alert again. This is not a fucking debate, just do it!'

Four hours later he stands grim-faced in front of Fiona and the others.
'No sign of him. I did the full circular route, nothing. I searched the house, there has been someone there but it's empty now. Judging by what's left our man's been gone a

couple of days, so I don't understand the rifle there yesterday. I went to the castle too, it's still closed up, no sign of any entry.'
He pauses to gather his thoughts, holds his hand up indicating they should wait.
Fiona is pulling at his arm, frantic.
'I found where I think the shots were fired from. There's flattened grass and cigarette ends in a spot with a clear view across to the car park here. He must have waited there until he saw us talking to get maximum reaction.'
'I told you something bad was going to happen, didn't I, but nobody listened, and now my son's gone!'
'Fiona, I'll go back along the railway now, that's the only other place he can be. He might have twisted an ankle or something. I'll find him, don't worry.'
But Steve doesn't convince anyone, least of all himself.

26

The story that Sensei hears angers him at some primeval level.
Gerry and Susie met not far from here soon after what they call
the Big Bang.
They agreed, according to Gerry, or Gerry said, according to
Susie, that he'd get food and she'd cook it.
Asked why she was attached to a heavy chair, Gerry claimed it
was for her own safety, so she wouldn't wander off and get
lost.
Asked why he hadn't foraged for canned foods and drinks,
pasta, rice, cheese and such like, he said he didn't want to
disturb the dead.
Asked why they picked this house, he said because there were
no bodies in it. Apparently Gerry doesn't like bodies.
'Unless you kill them yourself?' asks Sensei.
Asked what the meat was that he had brought today, Gerry said
it was rabbit, as always.
Asked where he found this endless source of rabbit, he said on
the golf courses, that he was a good hunter.
Asked why the rabbit smelled like rat, he got embarrassed and
defensive and hotly denied it.
This caused Susie to go into near hysterics again and scream
that she said it tasted funny, that's why she couldn't eat it,
that's why she's so thin, and lots of unpleasant but possibly
true attacks on Gerry's parentage.
After hearing this Sensei makes some decisions.
'Sit still,' he tells Gerry, then tells Vidock to smell the

sweating young man.
He then explains what is going to happen next.
Gerry will go to neighbouring houses and/or the Inn and bring back a supply of foodstuff.
The corpses will not bite him.
Sensei will take Susie with him for now while he does what he came here for.
They will meet back here in one hour to enjoy the results of Gerry's searching.
If Gerry decides to do a runner, Vidock will find him and Sensei will make him suffer more than he can imagine.
'And I'll enjoy it,' he adds.
As they prepare to leave, with Susie in Vidock's trailer, Sensei asks Gerry how far he can run in an hour.
Then he ties a kitchen chair to his back.
'Yes, you'll be able to get it off, but it'll take time. See you soon, sonny.'
And then to Vidock he says one word, that sets the dog haring off on their original course.
Home.

27

Hugh and Joni are at the Inn, guarding the entrance to the village.
Rick and Jules are outside the hotel with Allie and Ronnie.
Everyone is armed and ready to fight.
Steve and Fiona follow the footpath, each checking a side for any sign that Malky has passed there.
Cathy and Jack walk the railway in exactly the same way.
All of them carry weapons.
They meet at the little station after a couple of false alarms, but with no trace having been found.
There has been no rain for days, and the ground is still hard with winter cold, so any tracks would be difficult to spot.
They move carefully along the track to the house, where Steve and Fiona search each room while the other two remain watchful outside.
They find nothing more than Steve did on his first visit, so continue on to the castle, where the story is similar.
It is closed up, with nothing to suggest that any of its doors or windows have been tampered with.
There is also no sign of Malky, or that he has been here.
They go back to the station and follow the line under the bridge where they find, as Malky said, it immediately enters a high-sided cutting.
There seems little point in pursuing it, so Hugh and Fiona take the longer, more circular route back to Plockton, while Cathy and Jack are delegated to scrutinise the coastal path one more

time.

Out of Fiona's hearing Steve tells Cathy to pay particular attention to the rocky shoreline below the path where, unlikely though it seems, the agile boy might possibly have fallen.

On the road the only point of interest is a stone-built, square-shaped structure with an inner courtyard, which they later discover to be Duncraig Square, built in the mid-nineteenth century to house castle servants and stables.

It has been converted to modern apartments, and is an appealing getaway in this near idyllic, if very remote, location.

The remains of a body is lying beside a car, its appearance suggesting it's been here since the bang.

They search inside, find more bodies, but no sign of any recent intrusion.

Moving on their track joins a bigger road where they discover, quite bizarrely, a small glass bus shelter.

This road, still narrow with rough passing places, climbs away from the coast, providing more spectacular views across Loch Carron and as far as Skye to the west.

After another half mile or so another road forks off to the left, towards Duirinish, but as that is a further two miles in the wrong direction they can see no reason for Malky to have gone that way.

As they are still almost an hour from Plockton and evening is advancing fast they decide to head home, Fiona still hoping that her son might have returned by this time.

A different choice here might have changed so much.

28

'I got a phone call today.'

'Oh yeah. Anyone interesting?'

'It was John.'

He waits to see if she'll say more; she waits to see if he'll ask. Although John is among the most common names in the anglophone world, he doesn't need to ask who.

He knows it's the man whose code name is John.

'So?'

'So what?'

'You started the conversation, don't you think you should finish it?

'There's not much to say.'

'What did he want?'

'To meet.'

'And you said?'

'You know I could never refuse him anything.'

'And now?'

'And now what?'

He now understands she's being deliberately awkward, trying to provoke a fight.

'And can you refuse him anything now?'

'What's that supposed to mean?'

'C'mon, Dee, it's a fairly simple question.'

'Are you asking if I plan to sleep with him? Is that all you think about?'

He sighs, defeated.

He knows that, when she's like this, there's nothing he can do except wait it out.

'When are you going?'

'Tonight.'

'Can I ask where?'

'Best not.'

'Can I ask for how long?'

'I can't answer that.'

He almost asks her not to go, but doesn't.

He knows he'd get no response.

He stands abruptly, exasperated.

'I'm going for a run.'

'Are you taking…'

'Of course I'm bloody taking him, he's my dog. He might love you best, but he's still mine.'

When he returned the house was in darkness, and silent.

He couldn't tell if she was still there, or if she had already gone.

She had the ability to live in absolute silence and to take up no space.

She'd learnt that from him, although he hadn't taught her.

He showered, lifted a bottle of 12 year old Glenmorangie, which was there for the benefit of visitors, and, leaving Vidock slumped miserably on his rug at the front door, went to bed…

29

'Cath…'

'Problem, Jack?'

She is peering down from the path to the shoreline below, not believing there's even the slightest chance that Malky could have fallen.

'No, not really. No, it's nothing. I just…'

'What is it, sweetheart, you know you can talk to me. And you know it'll go no further. Ask what you want to know.'

'Do you think he'll come back? I mean, I know he liked us, especially you, but me too, and Steve of course, and Fiona and Malky, haha, that was a surprise, and Hugh and Jules, and the two girls of course, well, I mean he liked all of us, Rick too, then he just disappeared without a word. He did like us, didn't he?'

Cathy laughs.

'Is that the end of your questions now? Okay, in reverse order, yes, he liked us, all of us, I think, but he's not a man who shows his emotions much, is he? But you've heard the saying, actions speak louder than words, yes? Well, he has shown us every day since he got on that bus that he cares about us, even if he's never said the words. He has told me, no, promised me twice that no one will ever hurt me again, and he was right, because now I can look after myself, even if he's not around.'

Jack thinks back before he speaks again.

'The first time we spoke was when we walked from Tyndrum to Bridge of Orchy and I was scared stiff, totally terrified of

him! And he spoke to me like an adult, explained what had happened, why he did what he did. I asked him what would have happened to me if that bunch of soldiers had taken us and he didn't try to fool me, he told me straight. He's very honest, isn't he?'
'He hates liars, he's always made that clear. That's why I don't understand about Fiona, he just did a complete u-turn, and that's not like him at all!'
'You don't think, y'know, he and she…'
'Not for a second. He has his own code of honour, he doesn't take advantage of anyone. No, I think he has a woman somewhere, and he thinks she might be alive. Or at least he doesn't know that she's dead.'
'You think so, really?'
'Do you remember how we all noticed Vidock on the way up here, how he always watched the road we'd come? He's waiting for her too.'
'Yeah, that's right, I'd forgotten. I wonder what she's like, hmm?'
'Extraordinary.'
'Why do you say that?'
'To have those two love her like that, she has to be something special. Although Vidock's more of a flirt than his man, he lets anyone stroke his ears!'
Now Jack laughs, but only briefly.
'You didn't answer my first question, did you? Will he come back?'
She smiles at him.

'If he can, yes. My guess is he's gone looking for her. If he finds her, he'll bring her here, because it's as safe as anywhere. If he doesn't find her, he might as well be here, because he won't be happy anywhere anyway.'
'You don't think you and him will...'
She smiles again, this time quite sadly.
'No, I think we are both too damaged. You're probably old enough to hear the truth now, I've thought about going to him some nights, just to be held again. But I don't, because nothing's really ever that simple.'
'What do you mean?'
'Well, emotions get involved, and we're all still coming to terms with the end of the world, at least as we knew it. My feelings are on the edge all the time, it wouldn't take much for me to break completely.'
'You, Cath? You always seem so strong, so in control...'
She shakes her head and puts her hand on his arm..
'Inside I'm all mush, honey. I have so many regrets, so many memories of things I didn't say or didn't get round to doing.'
'I know what you mean, I miss my mum so much, and I was never as good to her as I should have been. And I never told her... Well, y'know...'
'You don't need to worry about that, Jack, I'm sure she knew exactly how you felt, mothers do. And I'm pretty sure she was proud of you, you're a good lad, you care about people, and you show respect. Everyone here adores you. Hell, Jules wants to adopt you!'
'Thanks, Cath, you really think she knew? That's something I

regret, always, that I didn't tell her.'

'She knew, never fear. Jules has often said "That boy'd make any woman proud to be his mum". And she's right, as usual!'

'Thanks, Cath. Well, that's us back at the start of the path, and we've found nothing again. What do you think's happened to Malky?'

'Let's just check he's not come back himself before we start guessing, okay?'

'Do you think he'll be back now? I don't, where could he have been?'

'If he's not here, Jack, then it looks like he's been caught by the guy with the rifle. Although we don't know who he is or what he wants, so it's not obvious why he'd take Malky, is it?'

'No, I guess not... I wish Sensei was here, he'd know what to do...'

'You and me both, sweetheart, you and me both.'

30

He was wakened by the bang, his head pounding.
He hadn't taken more than a single drink of anything in ten years, all the time they'd been together.
But the whole decade had disappeared at the mention of that name.
He stumbled downstairs and saw Vidock trying to stand.
Leaning against the wall, he ruffled his ears, croaked out a few words, trying to make sense of what was happening in his head.
Knowing it was more than whisky causing the dizziness, he staggered through to the kitchen and threw up in the sink.
He splashed water on his face, then stuck his head under the flow of cold water which, in October, was pretty bloody fresh.
He got orange juice from the fridge, saw it wasn't working.
Flicked a light switch.
Nothing.
He had to find out what the hell had made that noise, so he reeled out the front door into the street.
Mrs Wilson from two doors down was lying on the pavement, morning rolls scattered.
Dead.
Across the road a few doors down a man and a child he didn't know lay hand in hand.
Dead.
At the bottom of St Meddans Street, at the junction with South Beach, a car alarm was wailing.

There was not a living soul in sight.
Looking back he didn't know how long it had been until he packed water and supplies in his backpack and set off.
But, incredibly, it was much later, on the A82 road north of Tyndrum, when the thought flashed through his head that he hadn't checked to see if she was in the house, alive or dead. And by that time he couldn't turn back; he had already made a promise to Steve.

31

'Morning everyone, great day, isn't it!'
Heads turn to Fiona in astonishment.
'Malky's okay, he's fine! He's with someone who's taking care of him, so it's all good!'
She brushes aside all the questions with a laugh.
'I saw him during the night. A dream, maybe, but I know it's true, they always are. Anyway he's safe, unharmed.'
She sits beside Hugh as Jules puts plates of porridge on the table.
'He makes me laugh, y'know, kids have a way of doing that, don't they?'
'They do that,' agrees Hugh. 'One or two of ours got up to some mischief in their time, I can tell you!'
'They see things so clearly, don't they, and they're so honest about things we pretend not to notice.'
Hugh grins at her.
'You got something in mind?'
She laughs.
'I remember when he was about four years old, he was walking about with his finger about two knuckles up his nostril.'
'Aye,' Hugh nods. 'They do that a lot.'
'So of course I tell him to take his finger out of his nose. But he just keeps poking it up there. So I tell him again. And he says "I've got a snotter."'
Jules is smiling, remembering her own at that sort of age.
'So I tell him to come here, I've got a tissue. And that's when

he comes out with it, the thing that makes me laugh.'
Joni has come over to hear the punchline.
'It's not a tissue snotter, it's a finger snotter!'
Joni screws up her face with a 'Yeuch!' but still laughs with the others.
'You sure he's okay?' she asks.
Fiona nods, but then frowns.
'There's a darkness coming too, but then a bright light. I think that's Sensei coming back.'
'And what's the darkness, do you know?
'Not exactly, but there's going to be something bad, very bad. A death, I think.'
'One of us?' Joni clutches at Fiona's hand. 'One of us is going to die?'
Fiona drops her head and Hugh intervenes.
'Calm down, Joni, it was just a dream. And we're all going to die some day, just not yet.'
'Think about it, love,' says Jules. 'We're still here when so many have already gone. I think there must be a reason for that, don't you?'
But Joni turns away, and goes to help Allie with the baby.
Fiona sighs.
'I should just keep quiet, shouldn't I?'

32

Vidock is waiting at the front door, his face long and his ears flat.
Sensei takes this to be a good sign and a bad sign.
She isn't here, that's clear, but if she was dead he'd know, and be howling.
At least, that's the theory.
'Wait here,' he tells Susie, opens the door with the key that hangs round his neck, and steps inside.
Vidock pushes past and disappears towards the kitchen.
He returns looking just as depressed and looks up the stairs towards the bedrooms, forbidden territory to him.
The man sighs.
'I'll go,' he says, and with legs of lead, starts to climb.
The house is empty.
The spare room where, depending on her mood, she might have slept that night if she had not gone, has not been used.
He goes through to the kitchen and calls Susie, pointing her to the cupboard where there's coffee and sugar.
Lifting the key that hangs at the back door, he goes out to the shed where he keeps camping equipment, including a Cadac Safari stove, wondering why he didn't take it with him before.
He hasn't previously realised how utterly disorienting the Bang must have been, but is annoyed that his training didn't equip him to manage it better.
Although, he thinks ruefully, the bottle of Glenmorangie might have been a contributory factor.

While they drink their coffee he asks her about Gerry, and his mood quickly darkens further.

When she finishes talking and crying, she asks if he thinks Gerry will be there when they get back.

'Do you care?'

'Well yes, I think so, he's all I know, all I've got now…'

He shakes his head sadly, once again amazed at the power of the Stockholm Syndrome.

'I'll take you back with me,' he says, feeling that he might regret this, but seeing no viable alternative. 'You won't be a slave, and you won't have to do anything of that sort against your will ever again.'

She has doubt in her eyes when she asks 'But why? Why would you do this for me?'

He has been asking himself the same question, but he knows the honest answer.

'Because we might have obliterated mankind, but we have to retain our humanity. If we don't, then we're just savages, like Gerry, feeding our own appetites at the expense of others. I don't claim to be a good man, but I try not to do bad things. I can hardly leave you here alone, and if I left you with him I couldn't live with myself.'

She thinks about this for a while.

'I thought you were going to kill him back then when you threw him against the house. You were angry, weren't you?'

He nods slowly.

'I was fucking livid. I hate abuse, I hate bullies, and most of all I hate liars. Yes, I nearly put him through that wall.'

'Why didn't you, if you were so mad?'

'I still might. Okay, do you want to go back for him or will we stay here tonight? There's plenty of food, and comfortable beds.'

'Do you think he's there waiting for us?'

'Frankly, my dear, I don't give a damn! You want me to go for him?'

When she nods, biting her lip, and looking away, he shakes his head, turning for the door.

'Okay, I'll go get him. I'll leave Vidock here with you. You'll be safe with him. While I'm gone I want you to heat water and wash yourself. All over. Yes, strip and clean everything, you look and smell like you haven't washed in months. I'll get clothes for you and leave them here outside this door. Okay?'

Then he pauses, thinks for a moment, and lifts scissors from a drawer.

'We need to get rid of your hair, it's pretty disgusting, and there could be all sorts of things living in it. Is it okay if I just hack it off?'

When she looks awkward and frightened he shakes his head.

'I'm not going to touch you, I told you no one will ever again do anything to you against your will.'

She nods, embarrassed, and in minutes she has what might be the world's most atrocious trim.

'That'll make it easier to keep yourself clean, okay?'

'Okay. You're not going to kill Gerry, are you? I don't want you…'

Her voice trails off.

'Only if I have to. Back shortly.'

He didn't have to.

Gerry was sitting on the kitchen step, with the chair still on his back.

He looked anxiously for Susie, stammering apologies for not getting more food.

The kitchen was piled with canned pasta, vegetables and fruit, as well as dried foodstuff, chocolate and salted snacks.

He acted quickly when told to load it onto the trailer, pointing out that he hadn't even touched the chair, that he was doing what he was told.

So when Sensei cycled off without a word, he was taken aback, and ran after him, asking if he could tag along.

'You can run in any direction you want. I'm done with you.'

But Gerry followed him back to the house.

33

Although Dee is, or was, quite small and slim, her clothes hang loosely on Susie's painfully undernourished body, so they spend the next days feeding her, building up her strength for the journey ahead.
They find her a bicycle and let her exercise on that for half an hour at a time.
They go to the pharmacy on Templehill in the town centre and get creams for her broken lips and bad skin.
At the end of each day he takes her to South Beach and, while she cycles back and forth along the road, he and Vidock run a couple of miles on the sand as far as the Pow Burn, just before Prestwick Airport.
When he gets back she stops to watch as he strips and swims vigorously for ten or fifteen minutes, before drying himself brusquely with a small towel.
Then he stands on the beach, looking out across the Clyde to watch the sun slip behind the Sleeping Warrior, the highest range on Arran, and feels that ache in the heart that is a mixture of love and longing…
'Don't you feel cold?'
He looks at her with what might almost be a smile.
'Yes.'
Before they leave Sensei adapts her bike, and his own, to carry provisions; she will need to eat properly and rest regularly.
He reckons the trip back will take at least twice as long, probably four or five days.

Gerry is forbidden to approach her or to speak to her.

During the day, under Sensei's direction, he gathers wood, lots of wood, and builds great pyres.

Then he gathers the partially eaten human remains from the neighbouring streets and piles them onto the pyres.

He uses a wheel-barrow salvaged from a garden for this, and for collecting food from the supermarket near the port.

He carries his axe at all times and kills whatever rats he can.

He is told what he can eat from the store of provisions.

He does not question, does not think of questioning, any of Sensei's orders.

He sleeps in the kitchen while Susie is upstairs in the spare bedroom.

Vidock is in his customary spot by the front door, at the foot of the stairs.

He is miserable, restless and edgy.

Sensei is worse.

Back in his own bed, but without Dee beside him, he can no longer keep the memories at bay.

He recalls every moment of their time together, and how happy they were, even when they fought.

He also remembers each painful element of how they came to be.

For which he deserves the death penalty.

'John' was a terrorist, or a freedom fighter, depending on your point of view.

He was a man of great charm, who seduced and recruited women for the cause.
Just after her sixteenth birthday she became one of these women.
After a very brief training period she was assigned her first task.
She was to place a bomb in the factory which produced goods vital to the other side.
This was to be on the eve of their biggest festival, so there would be no one there.
They did not deliberately take the lives of non-combatants.
She wasn't too worried about any of this, she hardly knew anyone from that side, and none of them well.
Except for a near neighbour, 'Mag', who had the good sense to marry one of the good side, the rebel side.
Mag was a lovely woman, with a darling little daughter, called Lily.
Lily visited them often, being the same age as a small cousin who she often looked after while her mother worked, and the shrieks of joyous laughter from the two little girls made the world a better place for everyone.

The factory was only two streets away, so she waited at the window to hear the blast, and hoped she might see flames in the night sky.
She had been told how to evade the security guards, how to set the timer, and where to leave the package.
Everything had gone according to plan.

When she heard the explosion her heart danced.
She had struck her first blow for the cause; the intruders would be driven from the land!
She stayed at the window, watching with a smile as the streets filled with people, some angry and some elated.
Fights broke out and she remained unconcerned.
Her people were strong and brave, they would have no concerns about a few bruises or the odd broken bone.
Then she saw Mag, shrieking hysterically, running round in circles, pushing and pulling at random people, screaming in their faces.
'Mag,' she shouted, running outside, fighting her way through the chaos to her friend. 'Mag, what's wrong?'
'It's my dad, he works at the factory, he went down there to fetch something he'd forgotten, a wee present for tomorrow.'
'Oh no, he wasn't inside, was he?'
'You don't understand! You don't understand! He took Lily with him!'

34

The authorities knew John was behind the blast, and the two tragic deaths, but could prove nothing.
He had people who could provide a cast iron alibi, three or thirty-three or three hundred and thirty-three of them, saying he was three or thirty-three or three hundred and thirty-three miles away, depending on how intense the interrogations were.
He walked.
She was never connected to it, her association with John wasn't known by anyone outside a small inner clique.
One of that clique was an undercover operative.
He knew she had planted the bomb.
He told no one, didn't ever report it to his handlers.
He loved her.
Soon afterwards he left the trouble zone, retired from his position, and went home.
His conscience wouldn't let him continue, so he did freelance 'security' work.
Within a year she had followed him and they lived passionately ever after.
Well, until the night before the bang.

35

He leaves a one word message in the house that will let her, but no one else, know where he is.
He writes a letter 'to whom it may concern' and folds it in a plastic waterproof zip-bag.
He packs the two bikes, grabs a Glasgow street map, and they are good to go.
He tells Gerry to lift the wheelbarrow and ties his hands to the handles in such a way that he can't free himself without awkwardly gnawing through thick climbing rope.
He can basically do nothing other than push it in front of him.
He ties a bottle of water to his chest so he can drink and tells him to start walking.
'About 8 miles to Ayr,' he says. 'You'll almost certainly find people there. I suggest you try to act like a human being again because, if not, they'll surely kill you.'
'They might kill me anyway! How am I supposed to protect myself?'
'You have the same chance Susie had with you. Be grateful I don't put you out of your misery right here and now. If I ever see you again I'll kill you on the spot, no questions, no discussion. Do you understand me? Do you believe me?'
Gerry nods, wide-eyed, lips quivering.
'Okay, good. Now go. Look on the bright side, at least it's not raining.'
When Gerry turns away Sensei attaches the message to his jacket under the pretence of slapping his back .

Susie starts to say something and he silences her with a gesture.

'We can find another wheelbarrow, if you like?'

She watches Gerry stumble away before she asks the question.

'It says what I found when I met you at Loans. Whoever reads it can make their own decision to give him a chance or not. He's a vile piece of shit. I wouldn't wish him on anyone, they're entitled to know what he is.'

He sets fire to the funeral pyres, stands for a few moments, then turns his back on his home for what he knows will be the last time.

Vidock makes it clear that he knows it too, as he climbs onto his trailer with an expression of utter misery.

Sensei kneels beside him, hugs him and speaks softly, but the dog lies down and covers his head with his tail.

'That went well,' says Susie, trying to lighten the mood.

'Keep up,' he says, as he moves away.

36

The first complication on the way north is that I want – no, I feel I need – to go to Cathy's home in Knightswood, situated on the west side of Glasgow.

There are a number of different routes we can take, but the key issue is the river crossing.

The shortest way is through the Clyde Tunnel, but I figure that will be more difficult to negotiate than the Erskine Bridge, which means a more circuitous but, I feel, safer route.

The Tunnel means passing through what might be inhabited areas of Glasgow, which I'm not keen to do with Susie, we are too slow-moving and vulnerable, so it's back the way I came.

Although we've only been travelling for an hour, we rest outside Kilwinning, the first potential obstacle, to let Susie steel herself for the charge.

I'm still trying to understand what it must be like for her to be free again after all this time, and to find herself in a whole different terror situation.

She still doesn't trust me fully, I feel, which is not surprising given that she had seen no one, not one living soul, other than Gerry since the bang.

Then suddenly I was there, and her whole life, miserable though it was, changed abruptly.

When I look at her I'm relieved to see she doesn't look like a girl.

She is wearing a heavy jacket, denims and boots, with a beanie pulled down to her eyebrows, all gifts from Troon's stores.

Her skin shows some improvement, but is a long way from clear.

'Remember there's only one rule, Susie. Tell me again what it is.'

'I do whatever you say, no argument, no hesitation.'

'Good girl. Ready? Let's fly.'

I lead the way, checking constantly that she is close, and Vidock lopes along behind us, starting to enjoy himself again. We zoom through the narrow gap between the fridges and washing-machines, hurtle across the River Garnock and clatter into Woodwynd.

Out of the corner of my eye I see a large brown dog of indeterminate breeding emerge from a garden and charge with bared teeth towards Susie's feet, but Vidock intercepts it by simply running through it, sending it tumbling and howling away again with its this tail between its legs.

I see her face bright red with effort, so I slow down and ease round the corner at the top, and then we are turning back onto the A737.

Then I hear the roar of a motorcycle.

'Go!' I tell her, dismounting and pulling my Glock.

As the bike approaches I fire a short burst into a parked car just ahead of it.

It brakes, skids round, and heads back into the town centre.

I see Susie moving slowly until I'm alongside her.

'Are we having fun yet?'

She looks astonished, and then laughs, and we keep going but at a more sustainable pace.

Despite making a couple of brief stops we reach the bridge before noon.

I lift her bike over the low barrier onto the pedestrian/cycle path, tell her to move up behind the higher barrier, and hide until Vidock comes for her.

Then I cycle cheerfully up to where I hope Ian is waiting for me.

He is and, as expected, he is asleep in the same spot as before.

I lift his weapon and kick his foot.

'What the… Oh fuck, not you again!'

'Hi Ian, I've got good news for you! I'm going back to the north side like you told me to.'

'Aw no, you don't understand…'

'Help me make space for my bike and I'll be on my way. No, don't fucking argue, I haven't got time for your nonsense! Look.'

I whistle and Vidock saunters through the small gap.

Ian hurries to the car we moved before.

'It took me ages to put this back by myself, y'know.'

'Go fetch Susie.'

Vidock trots off and Ian's eyes widen.

'Susie? You found a lassie? Is that where you were going? How did you know…'

We make room for the trailer to pass through and I get on my bike.

'Usual place for the blunderbuss, if that's okay?'

'Will you be back here again or is that you done now?'

I laugh and gesture towards Glasgow.

'Anything happening I should know about?'

'I don't know, nobody tells me anything.'

I pat his shoulder and shake his hand.

'You're in the army now!'

I find my companions at the phone box, lift the bikes over the central barrier onto the south-bound carriageway, and we enjoy a long free-wheel in a northerly direction down to Great Western Road, which would be much more fun if the rain had stayed off.

We are now the start of the A82, so we do an about turn, head west very briefly, and take the slip road off to Old Kilpatrick. Sounds daft, maybe, but the shortest way to get here.

We turn off into Mount Pleasant and pull the bikes into the driveway of a large red sandstone villa.

I check inside and find one body, which I wrap in bedclothes and leave in the back garden.

I will bury it later when, hopefully, the rain has lightened.

'I'll only be a couple of hours,' I tell Susie. 'Don't go out under any circumstances. You are quite safe, Vidock is here to guard you. Okay?'

She nods, not altogether convinced.

I don't tell her that Vidock is there mainly to make sure she doesn't leave the house.

I don't need the hassle that will surely come if she is seen.

37

Vidock's scowl is ferocious, leaving me in no doubt that he considers me not safe to go out on my own, but he understands his duties.

I check the Glasgow street map, and plan my route, reckoning the trip is only about 20 minutes each way.

I unload her bike, it is easier to handle than mine with the trailer attached.

The rain is now lashing down, which I see as a mixed blessing. Visibility is poorer for everyone, and my vision as I cycle is going to be blurred at best.

But it is what it is, so off I go.

I find Cathy's home without incident, use the front-door key I stole when I checked through her pockets for her address, and walk in.

I find the three corpses, daughter on the carpet in her bedroom, husband in the kitchen, coffee cup on the floor beside him, and mother, still in bed, and wrap each of them carefully in bedsheets.

It has been a long winter, perhaps not as bitterly cold as usual, but it is still Scotland, so the bodies are less decomposed than I feared.

They are still pretty ghastly, and I am not sure what words of comfort I'll be able to find for Cathy.

I then search the house for photographs, finding several including a large shot of the daughter wearing a hockey strip with proud parents at either side.

Perhaps more importantly there are a number of paintings and charcoal sketches, signed by the daughter, which look to my admittedly untutored eye to be very good.

I put several of what I consider the best with the photographs in the cardboard tube I brought for the purpose, then go out to the garden shed and find a spade.

The rain is still quite heavy, so at least the ground is softer, and I make reasonable headway until I hear a noise.

A man with a seemingly ubiquitous SA80 is at the corner of the house.

He is a solid-looking guy, maybe 40, with sharp blue eyes, who looks like we all do, as if the past winter has been hard on his body.

I shake the rain out of my eyes and ears, cursing myself for being so sloppy, so used to Vidock covering my back.

'What you doing? We shoot looters, y'know.'

My jacket, containing the Glock, is inside the kitchen door, too far away to matter.

'I'm digging a grave.'

'You from here? You know these folk?'

'I know the family. It seems a small thing to do.'

'Where've you come from? You've not been seen round these parts before. We keep a pretty sharp eye out.'

'I'm just up from Troon. Who's we? You the authorities?'

'Close enough. You armed?'

'No.'

I step out of the hole, which is not yet a foot deep, and move towards him, exaggerating tiredness and stiffness.

'Drop the spade!'

Okay, he's not dumb.

I look at the spade as if I'd forgotten I had it, then toss it aside. Arms wide, I grin at him, indicate his rifle.

'Bit pointless, don't you think?'

'What do you mean? I still don't trust you.'

'You might just shoot at a looter, if you were threatened, but not if he's unarmed, and face to face. And looters don't dig graves. Come inside, I'll show you the bodies.'

'Who are they?'

'Daughter, husband and mother. But mostly daughter. She was special. That's the one that's destroying her.'

We go inside and he sees the bodies neatly wrapped.

He puts down his rifle, tells me to get the feet.

'The hole's not deep enough yet.'

He walks outside, looks at the hole, then goes to the shed and finds a garden fork.

'I'll loosen it for you,' he says.

When we've got the bodies covered over he tells me to follow him.

We go a couple of doors down and he points to a rockery.

We go back and forward with laden arms until there is a cairn of sorts over Cathy's family.

As we stand there with the rain running through us, he asks if I want to say some words.

I hadn't thought about this, so I'm a bit hesitant, but I breathe and speak.

'Cathy loved you all, and she's a great person, so I guess you were good people too. I hope that whatever god you believe in takes care of you.'

I look up and see him nod.

'Amen,' he says.

And then 'I know a poem.'

I wait.

'Well, we've had plenty of time and too many occasions like this. Would you like me to…'

I close my eyes and lower my head.

'What was her name?'

'Karly,' I tell him. 'She was an artist.'

He takes a deep breath, and sings in a soft, warm baritone:

'Today there is no humour

Today we breathe our fears

Today brings only heartache

Immersed in floods of tears

One of life's great tenets

Is that we all must die

Today we look at who has gone

And ask the question why

We see bright youth removed too soon

We hear the song too quickly sung

The world is now less beautiful

Because the good die young.'

He pauses for a moment, before finishing.

'Goodbye, sweet Karly,

We weep for you, and for those you leave behind.'

As I listen the lump in my throat grows, making it difficult to swallow.
We stand for a few moments without speaking, without looking up.
When I gather my stuff he asks about the tube.
He listens and rubs his hand over his face.
'Of course, all the phones are dead. She's starting to forget…'
He wipes his eyes and holds out a hand.
'Thank you. It's good to know there's still some goodness left. Tell her… Tell her if she ever comes back, if things are nearly normal, if she asks for me, Andrew Brownlie, she'll find a friend. That goes for you too.'

38

When he gets back to the house in Old Kilpatrick he finds the girl and the dog sitting glowering at each other, and knows immediately what has happened.

'All okay?' he asks, and the two frowns are directed at him.

As he repacks the provisions onto her bike, he tells her she can go out now.

She looks at him wide-eyed, then lowers her head.

'One rule,' he says. 'There was only one rule.'

'I didn't know I was a prisoner!'

'You're not. I just didn't want to come back and find trouble. You can go exploring now. Take care of yourself.'

He gets on his bike and sets off back to the A82.

She runs after him, shouting for him to wait.

When he turns onto the main road he sees her chasing after him, so he stops.

'Were you really going to leave me here?' she shrieks, in tears.

'You wanted to go for a walk, so go for a walk. You made your decision, and that's cool. You're on your own now.'

'Please! I'm sorry! I was stupid, I know, but I haven't been able to do anything I wanted for so long, I just wanted to be free for a few minutes. Please, take me with you, I can't survive without you. You know that!'

'You have now run out of chances. There will be no more, and that's another promise. There is only one rule, and you can't break it again.'

'I won't, I promise you…'

'Save your promises, I don't believe them. Now keep up or be left behind.'

And he pedals off through the rain towards the west.

39

We spend a miserable hour and a half getting to Luss on Loch Lomond, arriving drenched and bad-tempered.
To my surprise the streets have been cleared of bodies so I break into a picturesque stone cottage near the pier and build a fire in the grate.
We dry off and change our clothes, then heat soup and eat it with biscuits and cheese, with hardly a word spoken.
I strip down to shorts to take Vidock for a run; he has spent most of the day in his trailer.
When I'm at the door Susie eventually speaks.
'I really am very sorry, it was stupid, I don't know what I was thinking. But do you realise this is the first time I've been free of Gerry since that bang? I just got all excited, I won't do it again, I promise.'
I gesture at the door.
'Wrap up well and try not to get lost,' which is close to a joke, as there are about three streets in the village.
She thanks me and starts to cry, so I pat her shoulder and leave, feeling like shit.
But there was only one fucking rule!

In the morning the rain is off; we have porridge with honey and are ready to leave as the sun starts to creep across Scotland's largest and most romantic loch.
The thaw in our relationship leads Susie to ask if we'll 'take the high road', referencing the song about The Bonnie Banks

of Loch Lomond.

I grin at her and say I hope so, explaining that the low road is that taken by the spirits of the dead!

Fort William, where I plan to visit Seanie and Grahamie, is only 75 miles away, so on my own I'd be there by lunch-time or early afternoon.

But, after all those months of barely life-sustaining meals, Susie is weaker than I thought, and struggles badly as soon as we hit the hills, meaning we make frequent and lengthy stops. By the time we reach Glencoe she is wiped out; I try sitting her in the trailer but her bike with its load is too awkward to manage, so we end up having to walk the steeper parts.

We coast down out of this magical place and for the third time in three trips I stop at the Isles of Glencoe Hotel, where Susie is asleep before I have our meal prepared.

Vidock and I exorcise our frustration with a fierce run and I have an almost violent swim in ice-cold Loch Leven.

We also reconnoitre the village of Ballachulish where I met the father and son from Oban, but there is no sign of life until I hear the fading noise of a distant motorcycle.

We look at each other and shrug.

There is nothing to say or do about it.

I waken Susie gently, feed her pasta and tuna, and let her sleep until morning.

But Vidock and I go to sleep with the proverbial one eye open. I am looking forward to Fort William and seeing the boys again, not knowing that, bad as today was, tomorrow is going to be much worse.

It starts just after 1 a.m. with Vidock's low growl.
Glock in hand, I go outside, and I'm unsurprised to see the McLeans, Donald and Donnie, and two other bruisers standing in a half-circle in the car park.
'You don't need the gun, my friend, we're not looking for trouble. Just a friendly chat, like.'
I cross my arms, so my weapon is clearly visible.
'You just zoomed up from Oban and dropped by in the middle of the night for a friendly chat, did you? Well, we've had it, thanks for looking in.'
I know why they're here, know I'm wasting my breath, but it's already been a long day and I really don't need this krap.
'The thing is,' McLean goes on, 'Donnie's a bit of a fighter, always has been, made a bit of cash locally, y'know, bare knuckle stuff. But opportunities are, you might say, a bit more limited these days, and we figure you to be a bit useful. So we had a guy keep a look out for you coming back. Took you long enough! What do you say?'
'I'm not interested,' I say, understanding that they know I'm not alone. 'Me and the lad' – I point over my shoulder with my left thumb, glad that Susie's sound asleep inside – 'have an early start in the morning, and I need my kip.'
'So do you plan to gun us all down, rather than have a square go, like? I thought you were more of a man, and you'd fancy a wee bet on the side.'
I've known from the start I'd have to do this, but the 'wee bet' gives me an idea.
'Tell you what, I'll have a shot at it, but my rules, okay?'

'Like what?'

'If I tell you my rules you either accept them or you fuck off now. And if you decide to wait down the road, I'll need to kill you all. Is that understood.'

The four men stare at me in disbelief, before McLean laughs.

'Sure, no problem, what's your rules?'

'Make a square, you three and him' – I indicate Vidock – 'five yards apart, so smaller than a boxing ring. If Donnie can't lay a hand on me in two minutes, he loses.'

'You think you can run and hide in a space that size? You're crazy!'

'I didn't mention running, did I? If I win, you leave now and I never see you again, okay?'

'And when you lose, what do we get?'

'That won't happen, so just say whatever you like, I don't care.'

I see doubt in all the eyes now, except Donnie, who has probably been punched in the head once too often.

'We'll take the dog, he's a beauty.'

'Whatever,' I say, 'Get in position. Vidock.'

I point, he sits, and the others step out five short yards.

I smile to myself, it makes no difference.

Late March in Scotland, middle of a cold damp night, and Donnie strips to the waste, flexes his giant muscles to intimidate me.

'Two minutes,' I say to his father. 'Or when you say enough.'

His eyes show fear now.

'Careful, Donnie…'

But Donnie charges forward, grabs thin air, tumbles over my leg, goes down hard on his hands and knees, and scrambles up again.
This time he lumbers towards me more slowly, breathing heavily, hands up in classic
boxing stance, and throws a punch with a two-minute warning.
I duck under it, and hit him a brutal blow between his legs.
All four of them make the same sound, somewhere between a whine and a whimper, which nearly makes me laugh.
I grab him by the head, which is now at waist height, and pitch him face first onto the car park tarmac.
I put my foot on the back of his neck, press down not too gently, and look at McLean.
'Well?'
He nods, eyes wide, and motions to the others to help Donnie to his feet.
'Don't let me see you again, okay?'
And I go back inside.

40

Once again the sky is clear as we eat a hearty breakfast.
Susie is much recovered, with a greatly improved appetite, as her body continues to regenerate itself after months of inadequate diet.
We set off at daybreak, so it is still early morning when we reach our destination.
As usual I let Vidock scout ahead, freeing him to run about a mile before the West End Roundabout, by which time I already have an unsettling feeling that all is not well.
A hotel sits on the right-hand side of the High Street, and about 20 yards past that is the formidable barricade set up by MacDougall.
There is only space to pass through it on foot, so we leave the bikes there and follow Vidock into the town centre.
He looks back at me, indicating his unease, and pauses frequently at doorways, sniffing and scowling.
We pass the Official End of the West Highland Way and walk the length of High Street, half of which is pedestrianised, until we reach the open space known as The Parade.
We cross this somewhat warily, and arrive at the Alexandra Hotel, outside which Vidock stops and crouches, indicating that there is someone inside.
'Stay away, I've got a gun!'
The voice is old and frail and female, so I tell Susie to speak, and what to say.
'Hello there, my name's Susie, I'm with Bossman, he's a

friend of Seanie and Grahamie.'

She makes a face at me.

'Seanie and Grahamie? Really?'

I shrug, and the old woman speaks again.

'They've gone now, dead and gone. Everyone's dead and gone. There's only me here…'

Eventually we convince her that we mean no harm and venture cautiously inside.

The poor old dear has no weapon, and is weak with hunger, fatigue and stress.

We make her comfortable on a settee in the public area and I leave Susie to console her while I go for our provisions and then heat some soup on the Cadac.

I wait impatiently until she has eaten, and then dozed for a while, before I coax her to tell us what happened.

Her name is Agnes, and this is her story.

41

'I was in here doing the cleaning, that's my job, when I heard lots of bangs.

Not like the great big one that killed everybody, that's when I lost my Geordie, y'know, and the grand-weans and near everybody I knew.

No, I think this time these were just guns.

I looked out the window, I was upstairs in the front bedroom, that was Seanie's, y'know, he liked it tidy.

Aye, I looked out there and there were lots of people, men with guns, and one of our lassies lying dead.

Mrs MacPherson, I think it was, she was a grandmother too, but bad-tempered, y'know the kind, always moaning and griping.

I suppose that's why they shot her, just to shut her up, and I can't really say I blame them, she was an awful greeting-face, so she was, but killing her's a bit severe all the same.

Anyway, I heard shouting that they were to get everybody outside on the Parade there, and I was dead feart, I didn't like the look of them at all, so I hid in the cupboard where we keep the hoover and the brushes and cleaning stuff.

When they got everybody out and it was quiet for a bit I had a wee keek to see what was going on and there was a man with a loud voice asking questions.

He wanted to know where the rest of the men were, there must be more than two, because he was looking for someone, said he'd kill everybody to find him.

There was one old fellow, Archie Thompson it was, he's even older than me, and they dragged him out on his knees and said they'd shoot him right there if nobody spoke up.

Well, Grahamie said there were no more men, they'd all got themselves killed up at Glengarry a while back, and the loud voice asked who'd killed them and Grahamie wouldn't say any more even though we all knew who did it.

See, we'd been told so often about this man they called Bossman, that's you, isn't it, he was a legend here, him and his dog, how he'd beat Seanie and Grahamie when they had guns and he didn't, but he didn't hurt them, just made friends, and how he'd beat the men from here twice, and just sent them home the first time, but when they went after him again with that slimy creep from Drumnadrochit – I didn't like him one bit – he killed them all single-handed, just him and the dog. And you're really a nice big doggie, aren't you?

Anyway one of the men punched Grahamie for not telling them anything and knocked him down and kicked him.

Then Seanie tried to stop them and they battered him too until eventually one of the women started to talk, it was Lizzie Ingram, and said the folk that killed them were away up north, maybe in Inverness.

The man hit her himself, didn't get somebody to do it for him, maybe she was wee enough for him, I don't know, and said if they didn't say where this killer was he was going to start shooting people.

Grahamie shouted that they'd never tell him anything and the man shot him with a wee gun that was in his pocket.

Then everybody started screaming and saying Plockton, he's up in Plockton, honest, don't kill us.

There was only one of them didn't like it, big rough-looking fella with a big grey beard, and those things on his legs, he shouted a bit, then they said something to him and he was quiet again, but not happy, I could tell that even from over here.

Then I realised that somebody was watching me, a dark-haired lassie, and she made a sign to get away from the window, so I went away up to the top floor and hid in another wee cupboard there.

I knew they were downstairs, I don't know how many of them, but a lot, they made plenty of noise, and the women, that'd be our women, I think they had just the one with them, were screaming a lot too.

I was away up the top but I could hear them, so I think the women were getting dragged upstairs to the bedrooms, y'know.

Then I got a terrible fright when my door got opened, but it was the same lassie, the dark-haired one, she had dark skin too, like them in the Tandoori restaurant in the High Street used to have, they're all dead now too, a shame, they were nice folk.

Anyway she just told me to wheesht, not make any noise and I'd be okay, and she gave me a couple of bottles of water, a cup of soup and some biscuits.

She said they'd be gone the next day, she'd come back to see I was okay, but that I wasn't to come out at all, no matter what I heard.

She didn't come back so I just stayed there in the dark for a

whole day, or maybe even two, I couldn't tell how long, I just did the toilet in a plastic bucket, and waited till it was quiet for a long time then I came out and found they'd all gone.
I didn't know what to do so I just stayed here, I haven't got the strength to go anywhere else now.'

42

Sensei looks out at The Parade where these events took place, the open space they walked across, and wonders what happened to the bodies.

Then he nods, figuring that Finlay hadn't fully believed anything he was told, so he'd cleared away the corpses and waited to see if any more men appeared.

He goes looking for the dead, and finds them in a heap in what was probably a laundry room.

He swallows hard when he looks at Grahamie's battered and murdered corpse and thinks of the poor lad trying to protect him.

He promises the boy's body that he will be avenged, then counts the others, a few older women and two old men, one of whom would be Archie Thompson.

He asks Agnes how many people were living here, and although she is tired and confuses a few names, he reckons that Finlay has probably taken three women, one of them presumably Lizzie Ingram, and a young girl, 'Chrissie MacLeod's lassie, Tina, I think', as well as Seanie.

He remembers seeing a cemetery not far away on the road out of town so he empties his bike of supplies, tells Susie to store them inside, and starts to transport the doctor's victims there.

He is pleased and relieved to find a large wooden shed adjacent to the burial ground, so he builds a pyre and deposits his cargo on it.

He stands for a moment and, in memory of Grahamie, recites

the words that Andrew Brownlie sang, before burning the whole structure to the ground.

Taking into account how much faster he can travel alone, and feeling that she is probably safer here than with him, he shows Susie how to fire the Glock, tells her to wait until he returns, or sends for her, and ignores her pleas.

She complains that he made a promise, to which his only answer is that this is the best way for him to keep it.

She and Agnes are standing close together when he leaves.

Agnes' uncertainty as to how long she stayed in hiding means he has not been able to ascertain how long Finlay has been gone, nor does she know how he travels.

He is confused about Kirsty's role, but strangely comforted to hear that she has retained some humanity.

Time will, as always, reveal all.

43

Jack rushes breathless towards the hotel, calling for Steve and the others as he runs.
'Calm down, laddie,' Steve snaps. 'What's going on?'
'There's some men at the Inn with a white flag, say they want to talk. I don't like the look…'
'They're here,' barks Cathy. 'And with guns.'
A tall, elegantly-dressed man with long grey hair, flanked and followed by men with rifles, strolls down past the Harbour Car Park, white flag discarded on the wet road.
His nose has been broken and reset badly.
'Doctor Finlay, I presume,' mutters Cathy.
He smiles at the group who are starting to gather before him.
'Take me to your leader!'
'That'll be me,' says Steve, stepping forward.
'Nice try, big man,' Cathy shoves him aside. 'I think you mean me. What can I do for you?'
'Now, now, children,' Hugh pushes forward. 'The old guy doesn't need your protection. I'm in charge here.' he says. 'What's your story, eh?'
'A touching little Spartacus moment,' Finlay sneers, 'But where is he? Where's Bossman?'
'I told you already,' says Steve, still calm. 'I'm the boss around here.'
Finlay laughs unpleasantly.
'I like a joke as much as the next man, but this krap stops now. Where is he?'

Now Rick speaks up.

'You like a joke? I suspect, dear boy, that you have as much jocularity as a rancid hedgehog. And whoever you're looking for isn't here. So why don't just do a wee about turn and go back where you came from, there's a good little laddie?'

Finlay explodes.

'Where is he? The one you call Bossman. Is he hiding in a corner, behind these women and old men? Come out, you coward, wherever you are!'

He gestures to his followers.

'Bring that thing forward!'

And Seanie, his face bruised and cut, is dragged from the back of the group and thrown to the ground at Finlay's feet.

'Just hold on,' says Steve. 'Don't think you can just charge in here and take over, We're independent, we don't need or want you.'

And there are multiple weapons pointing at his face.

'You were saying?' asks Finlay. 'He told me Bossman was here. Did you lie to me, little man? You know what happened to your friend down the road, don't you!'

'We called him Bossman,' gasps Seanie. 'We never knew his name. And we were never here, we never met these people.'

'More lies!' Finlay pulls a handgun from his pocket, levels it at Seanie's head.

'Wait!' Fiona speaks up. 'What he says is true. We met him on the road, and they left before we got here. As for your Bossman, he's long gone, he wasn't really one of us. Said he was heading for the Stauning Alps in Greenland.'

'Aha, another carrot-top! I wonder if the little brat we have imprisoned belongs to you, hmm? He doesn't stand up well to torture, the poor wee soul!'

Fiona stays calm.

'He hasn't been harmed, so I guess you don't have him.' Then she spits out her words. 'And if you ever think about hurting him then understand I will tear out whatever you have in place of a heart and eat it in front of your eyes.'

Finlay leans back, startled by her ferocity.

'A Highland wildcat, impressive. I look forward to taming you very soon.'

'Actually, Flatnose,' interrupts Rick, getting right into Finlay's face, 'I wasn't finished yet. Are you smart enough for a word game?'

He is met with a cold but confused glare.

Rick continues, all smiles.

'Rearrange the following words into a well-known phrase or saying. Yourself and the horse you rode in on. Go fuck.'

Finlay cracks him across the face with the barrel of his pistol.

'You were saying?' asks Finlay.

As Rick reels away, and Steve twitches impotently before the barrels of the guns, Cathy skips forward and hits Finlay a severe punch in the mouth.

Now he staggers backwards, screaming orders, and Steve and his small band are shepherded inside the hotel.

'Not her,' he indicates Cathy. 'I want her here.'

And he pulls a knife from his pocket.

44

The day seemed to disappear somehow, so by the time he leaves Fort William it is already late afternoon and the rain, apparently refreshed by its short break, is tumbling down with great enthusiasm.
Vidock's face is long and sour as he settles in his trailer, covering his head in a display of disinterest in all proceedings. They soon pass the Commando Memorial, and power on past Corriegour Lodge, which holds its own memories now.
At the top of Loch Lochy they swing briefly west to cross the Caledonian Canal before continuing northwards up the banks of Loch Oich.
As they approach the Well of the Seven Heads he slows his pace, looking across the water for the crazy guy who took a potshot on his downward journey.
He pulls up when he sees a small heap of clothes on the far shore, and determines that it is in fact a body.
He feels a strange sadness at the death of this harmless and probably lonely person that Finlay has found it necessary to eliminate for no reason.
They plough on through the still driving rain, cross the River Garry with another set of memories, and head towards the difficult part of the trip.
As the road climbs high above Loch Garry he is aware that on a clear day Ben Nevis can be seen almost twenty miles away towering over the surrounding countryside.
Today he can hardly see the side of the road.

When the A87 turns away from the loch there is a long steep climb, so Vidock clambers out for a gallop.

Before setting off he shakes himself thoroughly, ensuring that his already wet and weary companion shares in all his little pleasures.

However, due to the happy maxim that what goes up must also come down, they begin a long descent from high above Loch Loyne.

The second positive is that the rain, which has possibly been falling since he passed this way over a week before, has cleared away the last of the winter snow, although he knows there is worse to come.

Soon they hurtle across the River Moriston and through the junction with the A887 Inverness road, which brings them again to where, with Seanie and Grahamie, they met Fiona and Malky.

He hadn't thought, on his first trip up here back in October, that he'd become so familiar with the wretched road, which now had so many personal landmarks.

By the time they reach Loch Cluanie it's already dark and, with the heavy rainfall leaving deep puddles in the dips, and with some black ice remaining, the road is becoming too dangerous to continue.

They struggle along the loch side and spend the night, once again, in the Cluanie Inn, where his spirits are much lower than on his last stay here.

In the morning they are off again at first light, such as it is in the apparently unceasing downpour.

In the higher passes of Glen Shiel where the dog gambols happily, the man struggles up through patches of slushy snow and sees strange tyre treads too indistinct to tell him with any certainty what made them but, judging by the gap between them, he guesses that it's a trailer of sorts, presumably for Finlay's provisions.

There are also what look like motorbike tracks, so they've travelled much more quickly than he can.

They probably arrived in Plockton before he reached Fort William, so at least a day ago, and maybe longer.

He is seriously concerned about the welfare of the group he left behind, and thinks about the time spent in Troon rebuilding Susie's strength, and the delays on the road because of her.

But he's not a man for regrets, he acts as he thinks best, and doesn't hold himself responsible for events outwith his control.

That way lies madness.

He approaches Plockton carefully, and leaves the bike in a small estate of new houses a mile from town.

With Vidock in his usual point position, he advances warily, as yet unsure how to handle the conflict ahead.

He is aware that it could result in his death, but never considers abandoning the people who have depended on him.

He has only his knife, and grimly hopes that, should the need arise, Susie could actually fire the weapon he left with her.

Then, as they reach the railway bridge just before the high school, Vidock lifts his head, sniffs, and crouches.

45

Cathy finds her arms are pinned behind her by strong hands. The others have been hustled inside at gunpoint, so she is alone on the street, looking at Finlay as he advances with his long, slender-bladed knife.

'Doctor, a moment, please.'

A dark-haired woman she hadn't previously noticed approaches from the side.

She unwraps a scarf from around her face, and Cathy thinks immediately of the woman Sensei talked about during their first days here.

As Finlay turns his head she takes his arm and speaks with a smile.

'I don't think that's a great idea, Doctor. Just look at her, she's a handsome woman, looks strong and healthy, and young enough for at least one child. If you traumatise her now you risk losing that possibility. There's no rush, you have plenty of time to educate her afterwards.'

Finlay pauses, the violence sliding from his face.

He nods and smiles back.

'You're right, Sister Kirsty, as always. Your calmness is appreciated, I know I sometimes react without considering the implications.'

Cathy is amazed at his transformation.

Even his speech is different, quite formal, almost fake in its correctness.

'The same applies to the red-haired woman, Doctor. We

should return her son to her and ease the tensions all round. She too is good breeding stock.'

'Let me consider that overnight. I want to eat now, and think about tomorrow. Then I will make an example of someone, either the wretch from Fort William or the arrogant Sassenach who insulted me.'

His voice is rising again until Kirsty takes his arm and leads him to the low wall overlooking the loch.

She signals to Cathy's captor to take her into the hotel with the others.

'Relax,' she says. 'Tomorrow the rain will have stopped and it'll be beautiful here. Just breathe that air, okay. Keep doing deep breaths and I'll go make sure your dinner's being prepared properly.'

She pats his shoulder, kisses his cheek and heads towards the hotel, shaking her head.

46

I move quietly beside him and smell wood smoke.

Peering over the metal parapet, I see smoke drifting from the chimney of what was Plockton Railway Station, but which now contains self-catering accommodation for tourists.

When we first arrived here I considered taking advantage of its comforts for myself before deciding it was not as well placed strategically for defensive purposes as the Inn.

Others too expressed an interest, but were sensibly vetoed by Steve on security grounds.

I cross the bridge and move swiftly and silently down to Off The Rails, as it is now amusingly called.

Slipping onto the platform I peer through a window and see Malky sitting at a table eating porridge.

As I try to process this a man moves into view.

He is a tall rangy guy, with a bushy grey-black beard, wearing a traditional ghillie's outfit of heavy tweed trousers, jacket and waistcoat, stout hiking boots and what look like canvas gaiters.

The man Agnes described as having objected to Finlay's brutality in Fort William, I guess.

He says something to Malky, who looks up with a grin and answers.

Being somewhat confused, and acting on impulse, I bang on the door, with a shout 'You've to bring the boy!'

There's a brief pause.

'We're still at our breakfast!'

I gamble again.

'Aye, fine, I'll just tell him to wait, will I?'

I hear movement inside, then 'We're just coming, I'm just tying his hands. Two minutes, right?'

I hide round the corner of the building, so I'm behind them when they come out of the gate from the platform.

Malky is just in front, with a rope, which is looped loosely around his wrists behind his back, being held by the man who has a rifle in his other hand.

He is taller than I am by two or three inches, and I want him undamaged, so this is a quite tricky manoeuvre.

I move quickly behind him, throw my left arm around his neck and pull him backwards over my hip.

Off-balance but still on his feet, he sees the point of my knife almost touching his eye.

'No, Sensei!' shouts Malky, throwing the rope off. 'Don't hurt him, he's a friend!'

'Rifle down,' I say. 'Any other weapons?'

'Handgun in right hand pocket, knife in left hand.'

'Get them, Malky.'

As soon as he has them I turn abruptly, causing the man to fall heavily onto his back.

Malky throws his arms round me in a display of affection that surprises and touches me.

'I knew you'd come back and save us,' he laughs. 'I knew it all along! But don't hurt Alan, he's okay, he's looked after me.'

I lift the weapons, gesture to Alan to get up, then we go back inside.

Once I understand that Finlay has taken over Plockton without a shot being fired, I decide we might as well finish breakfast while Alan tells his story.

He speaks with a soft Highland brogue, his melodic phrasing suggesting that his mother tongue was probably the Gaelic.

47

My name is Hunter, Alan Hunter, which is quite appropriate, because I'm a ghillie, a hunting guide and a stalker, in the original sense of the word, by profession.
By inclination I'm a hill-walker and mountaineer, so I know my way around these parts pretty well.
I got involved with Finlay by accident.
Well, it wasn't what I wanted, I was coerced into joining him.
I had come across a young woman, just a lass really, who was living rough, actually barely living at all.
This was over near Boat of Garten, and she was all alone, so I helped her out, fed her, gave her supplements and suchlike.
So I got her a bit healthier, and she was a good wee soul, I liked her, Janey her name was, but my lifestyle wasn't for her and, to be honest, I didn't want the responsibility.
So I took her to Inverness, I knew there was a community there where she'd be better off, with a more stable life, maybe folk her own age.
Well, Inverness is a nightmare, this fucking crackpot dictator running it like his private world.
But I didn't cotton on till they'd taken Janey away to wash and feed and see what she needed.
Was for getting off then but this prick, Finlay he's called, no, Doctor Finlay, aye right, doctor my hairy Scotch arse, he kinda stopped me, asked my story.
So we're having a chat and a dram, y'know, civilised like, when he says he can use me.

I say thanks but no thanks, I'm a lone wolf kinda guy, I'm offski.

So he says that's a shame, Janey seems so nice.

So I say of course she is, what's the problem.

And he reckons she's just another mouth to feed so he needs something in return.

Me.

I've to work for him or she doesn't get fed.

Well I'm pretty pissed off as you might guess, tell him to go to hell, I'll just take her with me, but of course that's not an option now.

And there's guys with guns standing around, grinning.

So a day or two later he tells me we're off on a manhunt.

He says there's an evil murderer running about the West Highlands, so we're heading down to Fort William, see if he's there, and if not, just ask some questions.

When we got there I discovered just how fucking demented he is.

He battered a woman, had his thugs beat up a lad, then just shot the lad for not saying where this guy we're after is hiding.

I started to get ballistic at this point but he just said Janey's life was my responsibility, he couldn't guarantee her safety if I didn't follow orders.

Hell, I couldn't just abandon her, could I, even if I maybe should've.

At this point he gave me this mission.

Get on up to Plockton, stay out of sight, pick off a couple of them, but not the killer.

He described him to me.
I guess he meant you, am I right?
Aye well, you don't seem nearly as bad as that fuckhead.
Anyway, the lad here, Malky, great boy, isn't he?
{He sighs}
What I should have done, of course, is just walk on into Plockton and explain to the folk what was going on.
But the thing is, I'm not a fighting man, I was feart.
I can shoot an animal to eat, that's just survival, but I could never shoot a person.
And I didn't know what the reaction would be, didn't know about this mad murderer – you! – didn't want to get battered or tortured or killed.
So I thought I'd try to kinda warn them by shooting a window from across the bay there, and then seeing what happened.
I figured somebody'd come and investigate, probably the killer, so I set a trap, left my rifle and stuff out in the open and hid nearby with the handgun, though it's far from my favourite weapon.
I'm a stalker, right, I can hide, I can move quick and quiet, so I thought I'd get the drop on the bad guy and capture him and have a conversation.
Then of course Malky here turns up, bold as brass, the wee rascal, sneaking about like a bloody Apache or something, so I just stayed hid.
When he came back the second time I was surprised, I was expecting somebody with a gun, but I thought I'd catch him and find out what was happening down there.

I had to tie his hands, didn't like to, but had to.

I'm not a bad guy, I think he'll tell you that, we got on pretty well, I think.

So I took him down to Loch Lundie, just by Duirinish, there's a wee self-catering place there I'd sussed out on the way up, and we waited there till I got word from Finlay that they were here too.

At first he was furious I'd captured a kid, but I told him I hadn't seen you, so I'd fired a couple of long-range shots, wasn't sure who I'd hit, and then got a hostage, a bargaining chip.

When I asked where Janey was, he said she's gone back to Inverness with the other women.

So she'd be safe, he said!

I don't trust him as far as I can spit him, so I've been wondering all the while how to put things right, waiting for inspiration.

Aye, and courage, I'm ashamed to say.

But I've looked after the laddie here, just ask him yourself...

48

I start to formulate a plan which, as Helmuth von Moltke rightly said, never survives the first contact with the enemy. I tell Hunter and Malky to go to Portree, and tell Alex what's happening here.

'We'll ask him to come and help us,' says Malky, who is sitting on the floor, scratching Vidock's ears.

I shake my head.

'No point. If he wants to come, he will. If not, he won't. Asking him will make no difference. Just tell him I wanted him to be ready, tell him their numbers – about fifteen, you think, Alan? Maybe a couple less, now, that's good. Hopefully even fewer by the time they move on to Skye.'

'How will they go to Skye, Sensei, will you let them escape from here? You and Vidock will beat them, won't you?'

I laugh, and slap his shoulder.

'Just a precaution, Malky, in case things don't work out the way I intend.'

I catch Alan's eye, gesture with my head that he should say nothing to disillusion the boy.

He nods, understanding.

Something triggers a thought, and I ask about the rifleman at Loch Oich.

'Oh jeez, we were all traipsing down there, his lordship in his chariot… Aye, he has a chariot, gets towed along behind two bicycles. He had thought about motorcycles, but there weren't enough for everyone, so he just has two as outriders. You see, he didn't want to be undermanned in case of trouble, if he was out on his own with just a chosen few as protection.'

I listen in disbelief at the sheer arrogance of the man.

'Anyway, we're about the Well of the Seven Heads, aye, you'll know that, when there's a bang, and we see a guy across the loch, shaking his rifle. Well, I start to laugh, because it's raining and the light's pretty poor, and he's shooting at moving targets through trees, and at that distance. To be honest, I'm not even sure he fired at us, or just made a noise. Guy's maybe going out his head with loneliness.'

I nod, having had a similar thought.

'But Finlay, the fucking psychopath, he tells his riflemen, including me, to shoot the guy. I say no, I don't shoot people. And there's all these guns pointing at me. I tell him that with my old eyes I couldn't hit an elephant in that light at that distance.

So he speaks to the others, there's a couple who fancy themselves as marksmen, and they set up and let rip. And one of them gets lucky and the guy on the far side goes down. And then they're all jumping about doing the high five stuff! I get on my bike and pedal away. As if there's not been enough death in the past six months, eh?'

It seems Alan's bike is down in the village with the others, but I tell them to take mine, and Malky can have his own chariot, like the doctor and Vidock.

'Time to go,' I say.

I shake Alan's hand, and hold Malky by the shoulders, seeing the uncertainty in his eyes.

'Stay strong,' I say. 'Remember your mum and the others are counting on you.'

He nods, but I see his fear now, as he finally realises what I'm going up against.

I reach for Vidock's head.

'We'll be waiting here when you get back, okay?'

'Promise, Sensei?'

I nod.

'Promise.'

What I don't promise is that I'll still be alive.

49

And then we have the first contact with the enemy, and all my plans are in tatters.

I'm entirely to blame.

As we climb the gentle slope from the station to the bridge, I allow Malky to keep Vidock with him, rubbing his ears and chattering to him.

Two figures, a man and a boy, appear on the main road, see us, and stop.

I hold my hand up, not wanting to start the fight here, but the man lifts a rifle and fires.

I don't know where his shot goes, but I grab Alan's hunting rifle and fire back.

The first shot misses low to the right, so I reload and the second knocks him onto his back.

He doesn't get up again.

The boy grabs the weapon and runs.

Vidock has started forward, but I call him back.

'Go!' I tell Alan and Malky. 'Good luck.'

Alan tosses me a box of cartridges and I start to run.

By the time I reach the road he is almost a hundred yards away, running like a small deer.

I reckon it's half a mile to the Inn, the first place he might have friends, so I fire a warning shot, aimed to hit the road in front of him.

He jerks to a halt, swings round and fires back.

I stop.

There's nothing to be done, I can't shoot a boy, and I can't let him shoot Vidock.

I curse myself sideways and follow him down the road, trying to formulate a new plan.

I had hoped to get in among them before they knew I was here, maybe get directly to Finlay and finish this before it became a battle.

I jog down the road, Vidock tight at my heels, and as I pass the Primary School I see movement in front of the Inn and a couple of hugely optimistic shots are fired.

I see the two motorcycles parked outside, so I move forward, firing, reloading, firing at them, because I can't leave them operational to chase Alan and Malky.

I hit the rear tyre of each, and reckon that should disable them, so I dodge back into the school-yard, dive out of sight behind the building, and exit through a gate into a lane round the back.

I watch the road until I'm sure there is no pursuit, then consider my options.

But I have a terrible feeling that I know what the doctor's next move will be.

50

The prisoners file out of the back room where they are being held into the main hotel.
Steve, Hugh, Rick and Jack are in handcuffs.
From behind an array of weapons, the doctor addresses them.
'I need a volunteer,' he says, his smile wide. 'Someone who's not afraid to die would be my preference, but I'll settle for a snivelling coward.'
Steve steps forward, glaring daggers, but Rick jostles him aside.
'Don't be daft,' he grins. 'I'm the most expendable, and I don't much care one way or another. What's the plan, Flatface?'
Finlay bristles, but forces the smile to stay.
'Aha, the little Sassenach, it'll be a pleasure blowing your brains out.'
'Pity I can't do the same in return,' says Rick. 'But I'd never hit a target that small.'
'Get him outside,' snaps the doctor. 'The rest of you should listen carefully for a bang.'
'We've already heard gunshots,' smirks Steve. 'Have you got a bit of a problem out there?'
'Nothing that your little bald friend can't solve for me. Keep your ears open and be ready to welcome your friend back.'
He signals for them to be locked up again, and heads off whistling a bad version of Monty Python's 'Bright Side of Life'.
Inside they all talk at once, all asking pretty much the same

question in different ways.

'Hold up,' says Steve. 'I think I can explain what's going on. Sensei's back, and he's been seen. This lowlife is going to pull the old Shoot-a-Hostage routine.'

Again the questions are just a blur, and again they're all asking the same thing.

Steve shakes his head.

'He'll come in. He won't let Rick be shot in cold blood. It's the wrong decision, and he'll know it, but it's still what he'll do. Whoa, back off, don't shout at me! You asked what I thought and I've told you. Quieten down and think. We still need a plan to get out of here.'

In the silence they hear the sound of a megaphone being used, but none of them can make out the words.

A minute later they hear the megaphone again, followed by an eternity of nothingness.

Then they hear a single gunshot.

51

'Hello, Bossman! Hello, Sensei! I know you can hear me, so I'll keep this short and sweet. And simple enough for even your limited intelligence to grasp. You have five minutes to appear here in the Harbour Car Park, unarmed. Then I start shooting your friends, one by one, at five minute intervals. The obnoxious little Londoner is with me now, ready to die. Only you can save him. See you soon!'

The message is repeated sixty seconds later, with the appropriate time adjustment.

It is what I expected, and I can see only one possible alternative to surrender, and that depends on the doctor making a bad mistake.

He doesn't.

I tell Vidock to hide, and step out into view.

There are armed men covering all the approaches, I can't get near enough with the rifle to have a shot at him.

In addition, he is standing behind Rick, forcing his head back with a pistol under his chin, with men at either side of him.

I'd be happy to die if I thought I'd get him first, but it doesn't look possible, certainly not with a single-shot rifle as my only weapon.

A rifle that makes me wonder if Alan has a sense of humour, because I note with a wry grin that it's a Ruger American Hunter.

I just wish it was an AK-19.

52

'Okay,' says Steve, unhappily, 'I guess this is the plan. There are always two of them here when they let us out, one right at the door, opening it, the other at the far side of the room. And they always take the ladies out first. Cath?'

But Joni speaks first.

'Don't fret so much, Steve, we can handle it! We're all trained now, and we're not scared.'

'Yes, I know, but still. Are you sure you can distract him for long enough…'

Joni grins at him.

'Are you kidding me? He can barely keep his hands off me as it is!'

She shrugs off her heavy jacket, and pulls her Arran sweater over her head.

She starts to unbutton what she calls her lumberjack shirt, until they can see a black lacy bra.

'Whoa, okay!' says Steve, his hands making a calm down motion. 'I get it, he'll be distracted! Now get dressed, we don't want you to get pneumonia now!'

Joni laughs and thrusts her breasts at him.

'It's okay, I know you've got enough on your hands with Allie, you're safe from these!'

As she starts to cover herself, Cathy continues with the plan.

'I'll wrap my arms round his neck, Fiona attacks his legs, and Joni grabs the gun while he's off balance.'

'You only need to keep him occupied for a couple of seconds.

Now that we're out of the handcuffs, we'll have the element of surprise on our side. Hughie will tackle our guy, who's bound to take his eyes off us, Jack will jump him too, and I'll be across to help you in a nano-second. Rick and Seanie, our injured heroes, will back up where necessary.'

'When you say tackle, Steve, you do realise that I plan to just break his jaw, right?'

Steve grins back at Hugh.

'Whatever floats your boat, sir, I don't have any concerns about that! Last thing, and most important. Jules and Allie will be in that corner with Ronnie, the safest place, well out of the line of fire just in case a gun goes off accidentally.'

Jules snorts loudly.

'So we'll be safe while the rest of you go to war? I'm not so sure I'm okay with that. I mean, Allie and the wee one, okay, but I can fight too!'

'Behave yourself, woman,' says Hugh, gruffly. 'Your job's to keep the mother and baby safe, and leave the fighting to the rest of us.'

He looks round the group, the pride back in his eyes.

'We're soldiers, each and every one of us, and we're going to beat this bastard, okay!'

53

'Hello, my friend! Welcome! Good to see you again!'
Finlay is still cowered behind Rick, but playing the big man to his followers.
'Lose the rifle,' he shouts and, when I toss it aside, orders his men forward.
'Secure him now, you have your instructions. Bring him here.'
I feel my arms pulled roughly behind me, then my heart sinks as I feel a pair of rigid handcuffs going on.
These comprise a solid bar between the two bracelets, thus limiting movement more than the chain variety usually seen on US cop shows.
The doctor now pushes Rick into the hands of a gorilla at his side, freeing himself to approach me with a broad smile.
I note that Rick's face is cut and bruised, and have to control my anger at this abuse of a guy in his seventies.
I need to stay calm to find a way through this, although right now my only idea is to stall for time, assuming they'll get lax at some point.
Finlay stops a couple of steps away, no doubt remembering our last encounter.
'Hi there, ugly,' I grin, hoping to make him lose his temper and so make a mistake. 'You look like you got hit by a bus. Can you still breathe through that thing? And that looks like somebody else had a go too!'
I am amused by his lip, which is split and slightly swollen, and wonder who did it.

It doesn't look severe enough to have been Steve or Hughie, so I take a guess.

'You got yourself punched in the face by a wee lassie, did you?'

His smile disappears.

Angry is good – dangerous maybe, but good.

'Search him, and thoroughly!' he barks, gesturing to a different gorilla, and I wonder if these are the same two guys I chased off at gunpoint in Inverness.

Hell, I don't think I'll have many friends here!

Then I see Kevin, moving close to the doctor's right shoulder, with Kirsty not far behind him.

'Wotcha, Kev, still rocking that kilt, I see. Seems like rumours of your death were somewhat exaggerated, hmm? Either that or you have great powers of recovery.'

He reddens, mutters about the greater good, but Kirsty turns her head sharply towards the doctor, making me wonder.

'I'm glad to see you're feeling better,' I tell him. 'I wouldn't like to hang from a bridge for the murder of someone who's not really dead!'

And Kirsty is shaking her head.

'Hi, Rick, how're you doing?'

'You shouldn't have come, Sensei. I'm okay but this pathetic wee psycho is on the verge of a breakdown. He can only kill me once, but he's dying a bit more every minute of every day.'

'Shut up!' screams the doctor, and he smacks Rick across the face.

Rick flinches, then grins through bloodied teeth.

'See what I mean?'

I realise that he's discovered how to provoke Finlay, and I nod in acknowledgement.

The gorilla has eventually stumbled across my knife, sheathed in the small of my back.

'Look, doctor, I found this, he is still armed! What should I do with it?'

The good doctor scowls at him, then his face brightens.

'What would you like to do to this violent killer who threatened you at gunpoint when you were just carrying out your duty, following your lawful orders? What do you think would be fair, Corporal? After all, it is his knife, and he brought it here to hurt us.'

I have to admit that Finlay can talk well; he breaks his sentences with pauses and uses emphasis to influence his listener, guiding him carefully.

Corporal looks at the knife, looks at the doctor with a question on his face, gets a very positive nod in return, and reaches up to take hold of my ear.

'I could cut this off, doctor,' he says, with a plea in his voice. 'That would teach him to listen to you.'

I twist my head away and look him in the eye.

'I wouldn't, Corporal,' I say, making his rank sound like an insult. 'I have ways of inflicting pain on you that you couldn't begin to imagine.'

'Ha, don't listen to his empty threats,' says the doctor. 'He is never going to be in a position to hurt anyone ever again!'

I try to give Corporal the evil eye, but I suspect that Finlay might be right in this instance.

The big hand grabs my ear again, and the knife nicks my skin, drawing blood.

At least it's sharp, I think, so it should be quick and clean, he won't need to be hacking away for hours,

Then he screams in terror as ninety pounds of sharp-toothed hell lands on him, sending him sprawling on the tarmac.

That's not hiding, I think, as the knife goes flying and Vidock stands over him, his growl deep and atavistic, his bared teeth inches from the throat of the stunned man.

'Shoot him,' screams Finlay, 'Shoot him!'

But no one does, probably because they're not sure of missing Corporal.

'Sergeant!' Finlay is still roaring in panic. 'Get rid of that beast!'

Rick is hurled to the ground by his gorilla, who charges forward and gives Vidock a vicious kick near the top of his left leg.

He yelps, but retaliates by sinking his teeth into Corporal's face, the man shrieking and clawing at the dog's head to no avail.

Sergeant is poised ready to kick again, but I pull forward and deliver my own boot with fortuitous precision right between his legs, once again reducing the likelihood of imminent repopulation of the devastated land.

He drops to his knees and, as my captors considerately pull me back, he is in perfect position for my second kick which catches him violently under his chin.

The crunch is horrific as his jaw shatters and his head jerks backwards, snapping his neck.

There is consternation on all sides as I call Vidock to me, and he hobbles across with blood and skin dripping from his fangs.

Corporal is still howling in agony and clawing at the remnants of his face, where he seems to have lost an eye.

White-faced with fury and fear, the doctor pulls his own pistol and shoots the poor wretch in the head.

He turns to me, gun raised, as I try to get in front of Vidock, feeling that the grip on my

arms is less secure, probably because the two guys don't want to be too close when their mad boss starts shooting.

Maybe this is my chance.

54

Kirsty steps between the doctor and Sensei.
'Not now,' she says. 'You don't want to make it too easy for him, do you? Take your time, make him suffer for everything he's done.'
'Get out of my way, I'm going to kill that animal, it just ripped Corporal's face off! Did you see that, did you see what it did to him?'
He is almost hysterical now, and Sensei is tense, watching for any opportunity to strike.
'As for him, he killed Sergeant with his feet, while he was being held! They don't deserve to live, they are creatures from hell!'
Kirsty has both hands on his chest now, trying to calm him.
'Don't waste a bullet on the dog. Don't you see, doctor, that's his weakness, the only thing he cares about. You can use that to break him. Come on, you're the smart one, the great strategist, you can think of much better plans than I can. You always do, you just need to take a breath.'
Finlay is still trembling with rage and uncertainty, baffled at how this savage has twice turned the tables when he seemed beaten.
But Kirsty keeps talking, takes his arm and turns him away, and the moment has passed, for the doctor, the man and the dog.
Vidock is lying awkwardly, clearly in great pain, practically between Sensei's legs, but he shows his blood-stained fangs

and snarls menacingly at any approach.
Then, a few minutes later when Kirsty returns, he remains calm.
'Can I take the dog?'
'Where?'
'To your friends.'
Sensei nods, feeling he has little choice.
'Go,' he says to Vidock. 'Thanks for saving my ear, but you did disobey me! That was the worst bit of hiding I've ever seen.'
He rubs his knee against the big head.
'Go say hello to Cathy.'
Something flickers in Kirsty's eyes, but she bends and lifts the dog with surprising ease.
She tells the two men to hold their prisoner tight.
'When the doctor comes back you can beat this one to pulp.'
She starts to turn away, then pauses and looks deep into Sensei's eyes for the first time since Drumnadrochit.
Her lips twitch into a half-smile, and she almost nods before carrying Vidock away.
She pauses where Rick is still on the ground, struggling to rise with his hands tied behind him.
'Help him up!' she snaps at the nearest man.
'Come with me,' she says, heading towards the hotel.
Rick stumbles gratefully back to his friends.

55

It is mid-morning the following day and the rain is little more than a light drizzle when I am dragged out of the hotel and along Harbour Street to the car park which seems to be the default meeting place in the village.

Yesterday's beatings have left me with several loose teeth and at least two broken ribs.

I am badly bruised and aching all over as well as confused, wary and, with my hands cuffed behind my back and my feet tethered to allow only a shuffle, not overly confident that I can do what needs to be done.

Which is, quite simply, to kill the mad doctor.

I have requested a private meeting with him, without any of my friends.

I don't know why I'm doing this; I'm acting on trust following Kirsty's note late last night.

It was pushed under the door of the room where I am held apart from the others.

All it said was that I must ask for an early meeting, just the two of us.

I assume it is a trick, although I don't see what they have to gain by deceit when we are all prisoners.

They, apparently, are all packed together in the store room.

I think Vidock is with them, because when I managed eventually to force a whistle through my bleeding lips, I was rewarded by a muffled bark.

Despite her reaction when I confronted Kevin, and Agnes'

somewhat foggy description of what happened in Fort William, I not convinced that Kirsty's erratic behaviour means that her allegiance to Finlay has lessened significantly. Although her intervention yesterday could have been simply to save Vidock, rather than the reasons she gave.

As my two guards and I wait in the rain, I look out across the misty loch, wondering if this is when and where it all ends, and discovering that my main regret is that I can't kill this psychopath before I die.

I have no doubts that Alex and his people in Portree will defeat him, so at least Cathy and the other women should be okay, along with Malky and, I hope, Jack.

I can't see a future for Steve or the Frasers, or, painful to admit, for Vidock, so I feel pretty wretched about that too.

The doctor saunters down from the Inn, where he has taken over my quarters, accompanied by Kevin, now part of the inner clique, and two others.

He stops several yards away, too aware of the danger of getting too close to me, and pretends to study the view.

I assume that, for some reason, we are waiting for Kirsty, so I say nothing.

Eventually he speaks.

'Good morning. Probably your last, eh, Bossman, or Sensei, or whatever other names you have. Are you going to share that little nugget before you die, so we can put it on the pit we bury you in with your friends?'

'You can call me Death, because this futile mission is your Russian campaign, you won't survive it. And all because you

made a fool of yourself in front of a woman in Inverness.'
He starts to move towards me, then checks, thinking better of it, and simply glowers.

'Where is she? She asked me to let her attend this little farewell party! Ah, here she is now. Good morning, my dear. She told me she particularly wanted to hear you begging for your life. Shall we begin?'

But Kirsty ignores him and stops in front of me, looking up into my face.

'Sorry,' she says, almost silently, before stretching up and brushing her lips against mine, simultaneously pushing something into the pocket of my denims.

Then she makes a tiny gesture with her head towards the loch.
'Be ready,' she says, as quietly as before, and turns away.
'Good morning, doctor, I'm afraid I might have misled you slightly. I don't think our mysterious friend will be doing much in the way of pleading, it's not really his style, is it?'

Finlay's face reddens, and he starts to speak, but Kirsty talks over him.

'The truth of the matter is, doctor, that you have been misleading all of us from the beginning. You used drugs, lies, fear and mind manipulation techniques to keep us disoriented. You told me he' – she points over her shoulder at me - 'had murdered Kevin, but you said it was a different Kevin, and I actually believed you for a while.'

'Kirsty…' he barks, but she holds a hand up.

'Just shut up for once, will you? There are things that need to be said, and these morons' – she indicates the others – 'should know why they're dying.'

Again he tries to interrupt but she laughs at him.

'Afraid of what a wee Paki lassie might say, are you? Yes, I know that's what you call me when you talk to them, bitter because I never shared your bed, not even at my weakest.'

Finlay motions to Kevin, but Kirsty pulls a small handgun from her left-hand pocket and moves to the side so that she can see everyone in front of her.

'I don't have any plans to shoot you, doctor, I promise you that, but I will if anyone tries to stop me before I finish. Understood?'

I watch in amazement as this slender young woman dominates the group of armed men.

I have no idea what she has in mind, but I know from her warning that I have to react quickly when things kick off.

What that will achieve I can't tell but, judging from her words so far – 'these morons should know why they're dying' – there's about to be a bloodbath.

I guess she has backup of some sort, but to my knowledge there is only the dimwit guarding the prisoners and the youngster, who is nowhere to be seen.

And maybe the overnight guard, I'm not sure who he was. Seanie reckoned there were fifteen of them when they arrived at Fort William, but I'm now not sure if that included Kirsty. There are six here, plus two I've killed, one with his face ripped off by Vidock, then the guard, or maybe two, the lad and Alan.

I don't know how many went to Inverness with the women

from Fort William, but I'd bet on at least two.

So who and where is her backup?

The astonished doctor stares at the pistol in Kirsty's hand, then tells his men to relax.

'I'll take your word for that, Kirsty, so there's no need for anyone to get hurt here. We're all grown up, we can discuss our issues in a mature manner. Carry on, please.'

'Thank you. I was initially appalled at how our friend here assaulted you, but you're the only person who really knows how conditioned I was to accept your version of events. We were all already traumatised, so easy victims, I suppose. But as the winter progressed I saw your behaviour more clearly. I stopped taking your drugs long before you started to reduce them, just playing along and watching as my head cleared. Kevin!'

He had started to inch forward, now the doctor restrains him with a hand on an arm.

'She won't shoot me, I trust her word. Kirsty?'

'Thank you.'

Her politeness is more frightening than her gun, I think, and then I realise that I've seen behaviour like this before.

She's icy calm because she knows she's about to die.

'I tried to advise you against this stupid expedition. You didn't need to come down here, there were still lots of small places north and east of Inverness where we might have found survivors.'

She pauses, shaking her head.

'But then I understood it was all about him, not women, or

breeding stock, as you call them. He had humiliated you in front of your own people, and you remembered it every time you looked in a mirror.'

'I told you to set it straight, and you botched it!'

'I told you I wasn't a bloody doctor, but you insisted I do it, bleating "Women are better at these things than men." And you cried like a baby!'

Her mimicry is cruel, and his face goes tight with anger.

'No, your arrogance couldn't handle the fact that you met someone who beat you, even when you had home ground and a cast of thousands behind you and he was alone!'

'He had that bloody wolf, didn't he? A savage beast for a savage beast, they needed to be exterminated.'

'The thing is, doctor, that I had time to think. About things like why he'd come to Inverness in the first place.'

'And?'

'Well, he didn't come looking for trouble, he came looking for me. Because he'd been to Drumnadrochit, seen Dave's body, and wanted to be sure I was okay. He even included my friends in his concern.'

'So this beast wanted you for himself, what does that prove, that he's not a homosexual?'

'Oh shut up, your prejudices are showing. No, try thinking for once. Why is he here now?'

'Because I outsmarted him, made him walk into my trap!'

'No, you didn't trap him, he could just have walked away. He could've been on Skye by now, or halfway to Fort William, or just out there' – she waves the gun vaguely in a half-circle –

'in the great emptiness of the Highlands. But he's here.'
'Because he's stupid!'
'No, you fool, because he's human. And he's smart enough to understand that you're a butcher, who'd have killed any of his friends who weren't useful to you.'
'Kirsty, you know that's not true...'
'I know it *is* true! You went to Fort William, found the two laddies you'd sent after him, the boys you said he must have killed because they hadn't come back! But they didn't come back because they were scared of you, because you're a vindictive little tyrant. Whereas he had taken their weapons and then befriended them. Shut up, I'm not finished!'
She pauses, pushes her hair back off her face, which is dark with fury.
'And there you killed anyone who didn't tell you what you wanted to hear! Anyone who wasn't useful to you and your '*breeding*' program. And you let your *men*'
– she fills the word with contempt – 'rape the women there. But not here, oh no, because you wanted them all round about you all the time in case one man appeared, one real man, worth more than the whole lot of you put together.'
Red-faced with anger, the doctor searches for words, but Kirsty hasn't quite finished.
'He came in here, probably looking for a way to kill you, but prepared to sacrifice himself if necessary. He doesn't deserve to die. But you, you're a fucking monster and you do deserve to die. And we' – she waves her arm again, this time to include the others – 'all of us, we deserve to die as well for not

stopping you before it got too late.'

56

Sensei finds he's holding his breath, still trying to work out what she's going to do.
He can see no sign of any support for her, among the group here or anywhere else.
But she's quite unafraid, so it's clear she has a plan.
The doctor relaxes.
'Have you finished now,' he sneers. 'Are you now going to wipe us all out with that little gun you promised you wouldn't use?'
'No, Doctor, with this.'
And she pulls a small dark object from her right-hand pocket.
'This is a L109A1 HE Fragmentation Grenade. Do you remember that nice Mr "Seven-fingers" McCallum you asked to give us weapons and explosives training? He told me all about these things, and showed me how to use it. He said it would obliterate anyone within ten or twelve yards, and look how close and cosy we all are.'
There is a shuffling of feet as everyone suddenly understands the situation.
'Stand still! I'll shoot anyone who moves away.'
Finlay turns pale but motions to his men, who edge inches closer.
'Now, now, Kirsty, my love, you need to be careful with that sort of thing, it's not a toy, y'know. We don't want something like that going off by accident, do we?'
He steps towards her, hand extended.

'Oh, it's okay, Doctor Finlay, sir, it's not going to go off by accident.'

Her voice is heavy with sarcasm.

'No, when it goes off it'll be very intentional. You see, doctor, I removed the wee safety clip and the safety pin before I arrived here, so my hand is already quite tired holding the lever flat. In my pocket it was warm and tight, now, not so much. So, doctor, if you still want to hold me and kiss me like you always say, well then, now's your big chance.'

He stares blankly at her, his face drained of colour.

No one moves until he does.

He reaches as though to grab the grenade, and she shoots him low in the stomach, barely above the groin.

'I lied,' she says.

He stumbles onto his knees in front of her, eyes wide with pain and terror.

'Kirsty…'

She takes one step backwards and casually drops the grenade between them.

'Bang!' she says.

It is practically between his legs, in the middle of the tight circle of his men, when it explodes.

57

The blast causes the prisoners to leap towards the door.
Steve bangs it with both hands, shouting at the guard, but getting no response.
'Okay, Jack, lets have at this thing!'
Jack lifts his boot and crashes the heel against the lock.
Steve backs off and hurls himself shoulder first against the door.
Hugh does likewise with his considerable bulk and it shudders.
It is a fairly standard door, adequate for containment purposes with a guard outside, but not built to withstand the onslaught from three determined men.
Within minutes they are in Harbour Street, and see their guard staggering towards them with his hands over his mouth.
Behind him is a trail of vomit.
Cathy is first to pass him, running towards the car park.
Jack overtakes her in about three strides then stops dead.
He swivels away, his arms wide.
'No, no, no, don't go any further,' he screams futilely.
Vidock hobbles past him, lifts his head and howls, a long painful wail of pure anguish.
Gradually they all approach the carnage.
The ground is awash with blood, and littered with body parts.
Steve hears Allie arriving behind them, and signals to Joni to keep her away.
'Grenade,' he says.
They barely notice two of Finlay's group, the boy and their

overnight guard, backing up Innes Street towards the Inn, leaving pools of vomit in their wake.

Hugh tries to protect Jules from the scene but she shrugs him off.

They stand for a minute or two, before she voices the question they are all asking themselves.

'Which one is Sensei?'

Steve sinks to his haunches, his face in his hands, while Jack stumbles to the far side of the road and throws up against the building.

Cathy and Fiona turn to each other and embrace, both sobbing. Hugh eventually puts his arm around Jules' shoulder and tries to lead her away.

'No,' she says, 'We need to see what happened here, who is here, who is not accounted for. And we need to give Sensei a proper burial.'

Rick eventually speaks, pointing out the remnants of Finlay's coat.

'Looks like it blew right up his arse,' he says, not without some satisfaction.

'And these look like Kirsty's clothes,' he adds, 'but no one was more than what, ten or fifteen feet away?'

Jules is counting.

'Okay those two, then that's three and four, he's five, there's six and seven…'

'Does anyone recognise...'

But the shrapnel has destroyed bodies and obliterated faces.

The Fiona says 'Malky!'

Horrified heads turn towards her, mouths open.
'No, not here, on a boat, just arriving.'
Now the heads look west down the loch but, because of a house on a small out-jut, the pier is hidden from view.
'I need to...'
'It's okay, Fiona,' says Steve. 'Go see if he's there.'
Then Rick speaks, his voice sounding strange, broken.
'Steve...', he points over the wall.
They crowd across and see Sensei's bloody and twisted body, handcuffed and tied, lying face down on the seaweed-covered shingles.
As Fiona skips away, she shouts happily over her shoulder.
'I was wrong! He's alive!'
And she takes off along Harbour Street like Usain Bolt.

58

You were unconscious for about three weeks!
Well, maybe not, but it did seem almost that long until your eyes opened.
I was the only one who understood Fiona's words, realised she meant you, not Malky.
She'd always known he was okay.
So I jumped up on the wall and dropped down onto the beach.
Yes, Sensei, I put my hand on the parapet for balance like you showed me, I was well trained, I didn't forget, not even then!
When I knelt beside your body, I saw your leather jacket wasn't damaged, it was just caked in blood and bits of flesh.
So I grabbed your shoulder and turned you onto your back, not easy with your arms there.
I put an ear against your chest, thought I could hear a faint noise, and called to Steve.
He jumped up and over the wall, the three older folk ran along to the slipway, and by the time they got back Jack had joined us too.
'What is it, what's happening, is he alive? How can he be?'
They were all asking questions, and I didn't have any answers.
Your face and forehead were torn and bruised – well you know that now – and you were out cold.
We didn't realise about your shoulder until we tried to lift you, and then Jack threw up again.
I felt a bit green about the gills myself, but Jules and Hughie just handled it, and you, but carefully.

Well, that's pretty much when the cavalry arrived off the boat, and they helped carry you up here.

As you now know Alex's daughter Lexi is a vet, he brought her along just in case, so between us, me and her, sorry, she and I, managed to get your arm bone back into the socket.

Oh, and when we noticed the string hanging out of the pocket of your denims, we found the key to the handcuffs, and that confused us!

Ah, Kirsty, of course, it's all starting to make sense.

She brought Vidock to us, and a first-aid kit and splints, and a handcuff key.

That's how we were able to be ready for our escape the following morning.

We didn't have any ice for your shoulder, but there was no shortage of icy cold water, a whole bloody loch-full of the stuff!

After that we just treated you for concussion, kept you warm and hydrated, working in shifts.

Fiona was very involved, although I was confused that she seemed more interested in the vet than the patient.

And that was quickly reciprocated!

I guess Fiona is always full of surprises, hmm?

When they knew you were going to be okay, Steve and Alex set off to liberate Inverness, as they put it, with Alan Hunter and a couple more of Alex's guys.

As Alex told the story, there were a few would-be tough guys pretending they were still in control, but Steve just walked up to their leader and smacked him 'right in the coupon'!

That was the end of the fighting, the end of Finlay's rule of fear.

The folk there were good to go, quickly got themselves organised, and our lot came home.

Except Hunter, of course, he left when he was sure that Janey was safe and looked after.

You've heard the messages he sent to you, he really was very grateful for your trust in him.

Then Jack and a Skye guy went for Susie, and she's well, as you've seen.

The old dearie – Agnes? – wouldn't leave Fort William, she was born there and she was going to die there, end of discussion.

She said she'd wait for the others to come back, but she insisted that Susie go, and so she did, in tears, the two of them.

Now it seems that she is becoming good friends with Jack, they seem to be involved in a competition to see who eats the most...

Oh, did you know that Joni's been doing a bit of nursing too, and not just with Vidock?

God, she loves this dog!

But we all love you, don't we – she bends and scratches his ear and smiles as his tail thumps the floor – I always think you're the best of us.

Oh yes, Joni, she decided to take care of Seanie, as he'd been badly beaten pretty consistently from Fort William to here.

And he was devastated at Grahamie's death, blames himself, quite wrongly I think, it's probably just survivor's guilt.

But you know Joni, she could take any man's mind off his troubles!
Alex is ready to leave now, they'll all be going except for Lexi. She says she wants to stay a bit longer to oversee the recovery of her two patients.
She didn't mention Fiona to her dad, but I don't think she's fooling anybody!
Oh, and Alex asked me if I'd like to visit Portree.
I said I might, but there are things I need to do for myself first.
Here he is now, I'll talk to you later, okay?

59

'So Sensei, you're on the mend, I hear.'

'Your girl's been brilliant, Alex, and so have you and the rest of your guys. Everything all wrapped up while I lie about here like an invalid!'

'You got yourself pretty banged up, you're just lucky you landed on your head, or you might have been seriously hurt!'

'Yeah, if I'd jumped over I might have broken a leg, that would have been serious, so I just went head first.'

'So I guess you didn't know how much time you had?'

'No idea, just not a lot. The thing is, I couldn't tell when she released the lever, so when she shot him – ah, you didn't know that, of course. Yeah, he tried to grab it, and she shot his balls off! Anyway his guys all reacted, pointing their guns, no idea what to do, totally distracted, so I took a couple of hops – my feet were roped together – and just did a nosedive over the wall. It's not easy to be elegant with your hands cuffed behind you! I wasn't sure I could jump up on the wall, being a bit tied up and stiff and sore – yes, and old! – so I'd have had to sit and swing my legs round, and all that. Well, I kinda knew the damage those things could do at that sort of range, so I really didn't want to be hanging around when it popped.'

'True enough,' Alex laughs. 'And it might have hit something you've got need of! But you were covered in blood and body parts, yeah?'

Now Sensei laughs with him.

'Yeah, I figure that'd be Kevin, he'd be the one on Finlay's

right, nearest to the wall. Funny thing, he was the first guy I met in Inverness,way back when, and he seemed like an okay laddie. I guess it's true, power corrupts.'
'Well, apart from you an me, obviously. We're still pure and uncorrupted, are we not?'
'Very true, Alex, but did you ask your guys to come here, or did you just tell them?'
'Aye, I have to admit, I did just say you, you and you, get your gear, we're off to war! But I've got to be honest, I think it brightened them up a bit, it's been a long hard winter and not even the football on the telly!'
'I guess we all miss something…'
'Aye, we just try not to think about it, at least until we waken at 3 a.m., then there's not much choice, is there.'
'So true. I hear Steve handled himself well in Inverness?'
Alex laughs again.
'Brilliant! He walks up to these guys, all standing with their guns pointing at us, and he just picks the biggest one and bursts him in the mouth! When I said I admired his tactical nous, tongue-in-cheek, like, he just laughed and said sometimes you need to get your retaliation in first. He said he learnt that from the best. In Tyndrum, I think he said. Does that mean anything to you?'
Sensei smiles.
'I need to get some sleep now, buddy. Safe trip home.'
'Come visit, okay? You'll always be welcome.'

60

'Good to see you up and about again, Sensei, I thought for a while we'd lost you.'

'Nah, not me, Steve. I'll tell you, there's a French word I love, *indéchirable,* I saw it on a road map I bought on the motorway near Lyon one time. It means tear-proof, because the maps are that sort of plastic paper, you know what I mean, but I always kinda liked it and thought it applied to me.'

'Hmm, aye, I suppose, but you got a wee bit torn this time didn't you? What were you thinking when you gave yourself up?'

'I tell you, mon ami, I figured he'd shoot Rick, then 15 minutes later he'd shoot Hughie, then you, or maybe you then Hughie, then Jules, then Jack. Unless he swore allegiance to him, which I couldn't see happening. After that he'd start on the women, but he wouldn't kill them, of course. So I didn't have a choice. And it was my own stupid fault for getting distracted up at the bridge there, and getting spotted by a couple of hopeless idiots just delivering a message. And then not having the bottle to shoot the kid.'

'He was okay, actually, the lad, he went back to Inverness with the two other survivors of Finlay's regime. They weren't bad guys, just got themselves in a situation. And they've been warned, well warned!'

'That's good…'

'So how was your trip? I know you went to Cath's, she cried for days about that, but wouldn't let you see her like that, of course. And you found Susie near Troon, so you went home? But no luck?'

'I nearly killed a boy there, I think I might have a problem with my temper, I really can't tolerate arseholes any more!'

They both laugh.

'No, there was no one there, and hadn't been since... Well, y'know. So I've run out of ideas.'

'Anything else interesting? You meet anybody else on the road? Did you find out any more about what's happening in the world?'

'I bumped into a couple of wannabe hard men, and one really good guy who helped me bury Cathy's family. Oh aye, and a wee 'sojer' guarding the Erskine Bridge!'

'Against what? Was it being attacked?'

No, no. Against people crossing it!'

'What? Why?'

Sensei is still chuckling at the memory.

'That's what I asked him. Guess what he said.'

'Oh, I'll bet he was just following orders!'

'On the nose, man, right on the nose. And he knew nothing about what was happening inside Kentigern, hadn't been there himself. So...'

He shrugs.

'So after all that we're still none the wiser, eh? I really hope you'll stay here. Well, you'll need to for a while anyway, till you're both mobile again. Oh, Rick obviously told us about what happened with you and Vidock, how he ripped a guy's face off for touching you with a knife, and you booted another guy's head off! Maybe you both have temper issues!'

'Well, you've got to look after your friends, haven't you? And that's what we both did for each other.'

'That's what you've both done all along, for all of us. Stopping to pick you up was the best thing I've ever done. Get some rest now, okay.'

Steve stops at the door then, on impulse, straightens up and salutes before leaving.

61

'Tell me again about the guy who read the poem.'
I tell her again.
'Do you remember what he said?'
I don't have a singing voice like Mr Brownlie, so I recite the poem word for word, trying to convey the sense of the music.
'How can you remember all that?'
I smile awkwardly, thinking about my training, how my life depended on remembering every tiny seemingly insignificant detail.
And reluctant to admit, even to myself, how much I was moved at the time.
'Good memory, I guess.'
We're sitting on the shore wall, enjoying the evening sun.
It's one of those spring evenings where the light seems reluctant to leave, so we linger too, even as the warmth dissipates somewhat more rapidly.
But the birds are still busy, fluttering, scavenging, singing, and there's a feeling that spring is here at last.
Vidock is sprawled at our feet, and I rub his stomach with the toe of my boot.
'Do you think I'd like him,' she asks.
'I don't see why not, I did.'
'Do you think he'd come here?'
I turn my head and look directly into her eyes.
I see the sadness and the doubt there, and it hurts more than I thought possible.

All the lives we never live, I think to myself.

'If you ask him,' I say, 'He'd be a fool not to.'

Her eyes change slightly, understanding at last what she has to do.

After a while she speaks again.

'I know, it's my only fault.'

'What is?'

She smiles bravely.

'I'm not her.'

I look out across the loch, and say nothing.

'Will you take me there, so I can meet him, maybe ask him?'

'Yes.'

'Soon?'

'Whenever you like.'

There are tears in her eyes now, and regrets in my heart.

I think she's probably the best person I've ever met, and the woman I'd be happiest with in the long term.

But I know it's best for both of us.

And for lucky Mr Brownlie, if he's as smart as I think he is.

She stands, touches my shoulder, her cheeks damp.

'Thank you for everything. For saving my life, for saving all of us. But mostly for Karly's photos. And her artwork. I'll treasure it forever. And my memories of you.'

I nod, not trusting myself to speak.

'I know you'll do it, because you always keep your word, don't you?'

I avoid her eyes now, grunt and shrug.

'Have you ever broken a promise,' she asks, surprised at my

reaction.

'Not one I made to a person.'

What I don't say, of course, is that, to save the woman I loved, I broke the oath I swore when I joined the military.

And that I'd do it again without hesitation.

I guess we all have our own standards of honesty, the lines we will and won't cross.

She smiles at me, her eyes full of questions we both know she won't ask, then turns away towards the hotel in the centre of the village.

As I watch her go, thinking about how much I admire and adore her, and still not sure I'm doing the right thing, Vidock lifts his head abruptly, makes a strange whimpering sound, and struggles to his feet.

He shakes off my hand and ignores my voice.

His hip is still not quite right, maybe never will be, but he jolts forward and starts to move, a high-speed three-and-a-half-legged limp, as fast as he can, towards the road leading up past the Inn.

I understand belatedly, and then I'm on my feet too, hirpling after him, the rest of the world forgotten.

Fin

Other e-books by C. E. Ayr

Available on Amazon:
https://www.amazon.co.uk/C-E-Ayr/e/B07FNK9PRY/

The Second Request
Set in newly-independent Scotland, this short thriller covers a range of controversial topics including:
War, and how to avoid it
Peace, and how to ensure it
Education, the why and the how
And, of course, Myth and Magic.

Medville Matters
This collection of short stories covers a wide range of topics including love and murder, temptation and tragedy, mayhem and magic, often served with sharp, almost bitter humour. The reader should expect the unexpected; in Sound Bite Fiction nothing is ever quite what it seems.

Instants (French/English)
Twenty-five intriguing short stories from Medville Matters with accompanying French translations.
An excellent way to brush up your language skills.

About the Author

A Scot who has discovered Paradise in a small town he calls Medville on the Cote d'Azur, C. E. Ayr has spent a large part of his life in Scotland and a large part elsewhere.

Website: https://ceayr.com/
Email: ceayr99@gmail.com
https://www.goodreads.com/author/show/14050307.C_E_Ayr

His work also features in:
Scottish Book Trust – Scotland's Stories for Book Week Scotland 2022 (75,000 copies distributed free to schools, libraries, hospitals across Scotland)
Scottish Writers' Centre – Chapbook 3
Independence, Scottish political magazine (multiple issues)
Postbox Magazine, Red Squirrel Press (multiple issues)
Mighty Ant Anthology
Scottish Book Trust – Scotland's Stories – e-book:
https://www.scottishbooktrust.com/book-week-scotland/scotlands-stories

In collaboration with Jenne Gray, the Story Lady, his work is heard on:
Ayr Hospital Radio (regular slot)
Tsukure Community Radio, Ayr, Scotland (multiple broadcasts)

Writers Block Radio Hour on Super Sound Scotland Radio (multiple broadcasts)
The Mutual Audio Network in the USA (multiple broadcasts)
The Narada Radio Company Audio Drama in the USA

and, more entertainingly, in English and in French, on his YouTube Channel:
https://www.youtube.com/watch?v=jsELmvd7YSs&list=PL24dTvi6VNV0CTw-BZYLRgCQ3z-i97e7l

He is somewhat nomadic, fairly irresponsible and, according to his darling daughter, a bit random.
So, nobody's perfect.

Acknowledgements

The author wishes to thank the following people and businesses for their help during the writing of this story.

R. Macleod & Son of Tain, Scotland
https://rmacleod.co.uk/

Ameena Roy at RE/MAX Skye, Scotland
https://www.remax-skye.net/

Liam at Senjokai Karate Academy – Heathfield, Ayr, Scotland
https://www.facebook.com/SenjokaiScotland/

Glenmoriston Townhouse Hotel, Inverness, Scotland
https://www.glenmoristontownhouse.com/

Calum Mackenzie, Plockton, Scotland
https://www.calums-sealtrips.com/

And long-suffering beta readers Eunice, Helen, Lindsey, Margaret, Clark, Ken, Richard and Ron.

This is a novel, and any error of fact, geography or other detail is the fault of the author.

Printed in Great Britain
by Amazon